PIECES OF MODESTY

Peter O'Donnell

Souvenir Press

Contents

A Better Day to Die   1

The Giggle-Wrecker   32

I Had a Date with Lady Janet   72

A Perfect Night to Break Your Neck   110

Salamander Four   148

The Soo Girl Charity   185

THE REVEREND LEONARD JIMSON twisted his long fingers together and tried not to let his hatred encompass the dark-haired young woman who sat beside him. 'The curse of this world,' he said with passion, 'is violence. And you are an apostle and advocate of violence.'

'Never an apostle and rarely an advocate, Mr Jimson. I always try very hard to avoid it.' Modesty Blaise spoke absently. She was growing weary of this intense young missionary who sat with her in the small ancient bus as it jolted along the road which wound north to San Tremino.

'Please don't think my loathing and disgust are directed towards you personally. I assure you they are not,' Leonard Jimson said feverishly, his long bony face staring out through the fly-spattered window into the white glare of the sun. 'I am bound by my calling to love all mankind, and to hate only the evil of their ways. To hate the sin, not the sinner, you understand.'

'Yes,' said Modesty Blaise. It would be a good three hours before the bus threaded its way through the dry and lonely hills to emerge in San Tremino. Arguing with Jimson served only to stimulate his evangelical fervour. Better to hope that he might talk himself to a halt from lack of opposition. He had been at it for over an hour now, almost from the moment of leaving Orsita, and there was still no sign of flagging.

The trouble was that in the earlier and less censorious stages of his discourse she had been unwilling to shut him up with a direct snub, for she was under an obligation to him. And now it was too ate. He was carried away on the foaming flood-tide of his obsession.

It was last night that she and Willie Garvin had arrived by car at Orsita and put up at the one hotel the little town possessed. Their fellow guests were the Reverend Leonard Jimson, in charge of ten well-scrubbed but shabby girls in their middle teens, and the elderly walnut-faced driver of the even more elderly school bus.

Within the first half-hour at the hotel Willie Garvin, whose inquiring nature was matched by his gift for satisfying it, reported that the young priest with the fanatical blue eyes was named Jimson, that he worked for the South American Missionary Society which ran a school for orphaned girls in Saqueta, and that he was taking this small group of school-leavers to San Tremino, where the Society had arranged for the girls to go into service with several of the wealthier families there.

The normal route, the good main road, lay twenty miles to the west, but there the rebels under El Mico were making trouble again, and Jimson had decided to take his flock by the little-used road through the hills. Most traffic was looping far round to the east, but that put a full day on the journey. The mountain road was a sensible compromise.

It was the road Modesty and Willie had planned to take, but that was before Willie had returned on foot from the garage at eight o'clock this morning with a slightly dazed look and said: 'I laid an egg, Princess. I told 'em to service the car last night.'

'That's bad?'

'Bad enough. They ran it up on the ramp an' didn't worry about putting the handbrake on or lifting the stops. So it rolled off the end.'

Modesty winced. The car was a Mercedes. 'Right off?'

'No. Just the front wheels. Then it crunched down.'

She sighed. 'How long to fix it?'

'They reckon six or seven hours.'

'It's too long, Willie love. I want to be in San Tremino by noon or not long after.'

Garcia was dying in San Tremino. The cable from his daughter had been sent to Modesty in England, but she was in Buenos Aires with Willie Garvin at the time. Her houseboy, Weng, had re-transmitted the cable, and she had left with Willie scarcely an hour after its arrival.

Garcia, dying at sixty, held a very special place in Modesty's past. They had both been members of the Louche group, the smalltime gang in Tangier for which Modesty had spun a wheel in the casino when she was seventeen. When Louche died under the guns of a rival gang it was Modesty Blaise who took over the remnants of Louche's frightened men and held them together.

It had not been easy. Garcia alone had backed her, with words and fist and gun. With his help she had held them, fed courage into them, and remade the gang in a new mould. That had been the beginning of The Network, which in a few years became the most successful criminal organization outside America.

Now Garcia was dying in San Tremino, his home town, where he had retired a rich man when Modesty dissolved The Network. It would make him very happy to see her once again before he died, the cable had said.

The accident to the car in Orsita was maddening. She hated the thought of even a few hours delay. There was nothing to be had for hire. Most of the transport in the little town still consisted of donkey-drawn carts.

'I'll hitch a lift on that school bus, Willie,' she said. 'You follow on with the car when it's ready.'

'OK. You reckon 'is Reverence won't mind?'

'I'm not likely to corrupt his flock between here and San Tremino. Besides, it gives him the chance to play a

Good Samaritan.'

The Reverend Leonard Jimson had obliged. He had eyed her warily when she first approached him, and then with a strange startled glance when she introduced herself by name. She had been puzzled by his expression then, but was no longer puzzled. After ten minutes in the bus with him she knew the answer.

Of all the world's clerics she had fallen in with one who, astonishingly, knew her reputation in some detail. His first words when they were settled on the bus made that plain. 'We have a mutual acquaintance, Miss Blaise. You know Michael Delgado, I believe?'

'I used to know him.' She did not tell Jimson that Mike Delgado was dead; that in a valley in Afghanistan he had held her at gunpoint and mocked her because she was about to die; and that she had drawn and shot him dead in the blink of an eye as his own bullet tore through her arm. 'I haven't seen him for a couple of years now,' she said.

'Nor I for three years.' Jimson was grimly pleased about that. 'I had the misfortune to spend nearly two weeks in hospital with him in Rio, when he was hurt in a car accident. We were in adjoining beds. He is an evil man, Miss Blaise. A man of violence. And apart from his own exploits, he took pleasure in telling me a great deal about *you*—especially when he saw how deeply I was distressed by his tales.'

'He probably exaggerated. You made an ideal captive audience for him, and I've no doubt he'd extend himself to shock a man of your calling, Mr Jimson.'

'Oh, he enjoyed it immensely.' Jimson ground his palms together, jaw muscles twitching. 'But even allowing for exaggeration, I still find myself horrified that any woman should do the things you have done.'

There it had begun. From that point Jimson had developed his theme. It soon became clear that he was more than a pacifist. He was consumed by an obsessive conviction that violence was the root of all evil. He reviled every act of violence, criminal or otherwise, from warfare and gangsterdom down through mugging and what he called the vicious gladiatorial displays of boxing, to the domestic violence of smacking a child.

He rejected motive as irrelevant. Any act of violence, he claimed, whatever the motive, gave birth to concentric ripples of cause and effect, expanding to create further violence.

Half listening, Modesty wished that Willie were there. Willie Garvin's verse-by-verse knowledge of the Psalms with their many ringing martial phrases, a knowledge acquired long ago during a spell in a Calcutta jail with only a psalter to read, would have enabled him to enjoy a ding-dong battle with the Reverend Leonard Jimson.

There was little hope of Jimson running dry, she realized at last. His denunciation had already taken a personal trend, and he had plenty of material to work with.

'You have killed,' he said in a low voice, staring with lost eyes down the aisle of the little bus. The girls in his charge were chattering together in Spanish, taking no notice of him. Perhaps they spoke little English, or perhaps the theme was tediously familiar to them. 'You have killed,' he repeated, and shook his head as if dazed. 'That is an act beyond my imagination, an act so monstrous that it affronts human reason.'

Her boredom was turning to irritation. She said, 'The times it's happened, my reason wasn't affronted. I just took the only alternative to being killed myself.'

Jimson looked at her. 'It were better that you had died,' he said with grave sincerity.

'I see. Thank you.'

'I do not speak personally. Better that *I* should die than that I should kill.'

'Better for who?'

'For the world. For humanity. Humanity is far greater than the individual, Miss Blaise. Death comes to each one of us in time. You saved your life with violence—'

'By reacting to violence.'

'It is the *same thing*! Surely you see that? Reaction against violence is the food by which it grows. Had you submitted, had you not reacted, a root of violence would have withered unfed, a root from which untold acts of violence have since spread like suckers from some evil weed.'

Modesty said patiently, 'But I'd have withered too. And I'd rather stay alive. It may even be that by reacting I've withered a few nasty roots myself.'

Jimson closed his eyes for a moment as if in pain. 'You live by false and dangerous principles, Miss Blaise,' he said heavily. 'There is a day of reckoning for us all, and I think you will pay a terrible price for your principles when that day comes.'

'Then I'd better go on postponing it as long as I can.' She smiled to take the edge off her words, but he did not respond.

'There will be no laughter on that day,' he said.

She sat forward a little and plucked at the button-through shirt she wore outside her skirt, drawing cooler air to her body. She did not object to Jimson's obsession or his opinions, she had no quarrel with him, or with Flat-Earthers or with people who wanted to open Joanna Southcott's Box to solve the world's problems. But she was tired of Jimson's voice.

'You've talked a lot about evil, Mr Jimson,' she said reflectively. 'I wonder if you've ever seen the real thing. In close-up.'

'What do you imagine is the real thing?'

She hesitated fractionally, seeking fresh words to dress up a hackneyed thought, then was annoyed with herself for doing so. All realities were hackneyed, simply because they had been around for a long time.

'It's cruelty,' she said. 'It's the man who can only feel good when he's got his foot on somebody's neck. The man who feels like God when he's holding a gun. Who can only confirm his own existence by squeezing the marrow out of others. Cruelty comes in all sizes, and you find it in little packages all over. But when you see the real thing, in the jumbo king-size packet . . .' She shrugged and looked at him, eyeing his limp clerical collar. 'Well, then maybe you begin to think there's a Commandment missing. One that might even be more important than stealing or coveting your neighbour's ox.'

She stopped speaking, annoyed with herself again. It was not her habit to open her mind to strangers, particularly in this vein.

Jimson was staring at her wonderingly. He gave a helpless shake of his head, sighed, and then quite suddenly the intensity in his face vanished as he smiled at her with an engaging charm that astonished her. 'Oh dear,' he said. 'I'm afraid we fail completely to communicate.'

Her answering smile was friendly, inviting a truce. 'You're the one who's been trying to, Mr Jimson. We'd better stop wasting our time.'

'Perhaps so.' He sat back and relaxed. After a moment he said, 'I suppose you haven't heard any news of the test?'

'Test?'

'I'm sorry. I mean the Test Match against Australia. The last of the series started at the Oval on Thursday.'

'Oh, cricket!' Again he had surprised her. She searched her memory. 'England were 297 for six wickets at close of play yesterday.'

'You're a fan?' he said with pleasure.

'Only of village-green cricket, I'm afraid. But Willie Garvin likes the more sophisticated stuff. He managed to pick up an English news broadcast on the car radio last night. I take it you're a fan yourself?'

'I must confess it's my great passion,' Jimson said ruefully. I'm rather ashamed of it really. Fanatics can be terrible bores, whatever their obsession, don't you think?'

'I've suffered occasionally,' Modesty said gravely. 'Do you play cricket yourself, Mr Jimson?'

'I used to play regularly when I was up at Cambridge.' His voice was wistful.

'Were you chosen for your batting or bowling?'

'Oh, a little of each. I'd bat about number six and I wasn't too expensive as a change bowler. But I got in mainly on fielding, I think. I was really very useful in the covers.' He smiled shyly. Then, as if afraid of boring her, took out a worn pocket gospel, settled back in his seat and began to read.

She looked out of the window. They were passing along a broad valley. On each side the scrub-covered rock sloped up and away to a ridge, to vanish and appear again as a higher ridge beyond. The ground was seamed with thin twisting gulleys cut by a thousand rivulets in the wet season.

The road began to rise, turning sharply ahead. The driver changed down, slowed, then down again to take the bend.

Modesty saw the windscreen shatter and the shards of glass fly outwards before the sound of the shots registered. She was lunging down the aisle of the little bus even as her mind analyzed the happening. A very short burst, four shots from an automatic rifle, had been fired from the side and just behind the bus as it passed. One shot at least had hit the driver. He was slumping sideways.

The engine stalled. The bus was halfway round the bend. For a moment it stood still, then began to creep slowly back, the engine compression not quite holding it. Two of the girls were in the aisle, screaming, obstructing her. She shouldered them aside and reached for the handbrake, but even as she grasped it there came a slow crunching of metal as the rear of the bus ran off the road and hit the rising ground on the outer side of the bend. The bus stopped with hardly a jolt.

Above the screaming babble of the girls she could hear Jimson shouting in his far from perfect Spanish, trying to calm them. The driver lay huddled at her feet. Blood had welled from a hole in the back of his shirt, mingling with the dark sweat-stain. Ominously little blood. She eased him over gently, saw the exit hole in his chest, and knew that he was dead.

Lifting her head she looked out of the bus. Seven men, well spread out, were moving down the seamed slope towards the road. They wore trousers flared at the ankle and leather jerkins. Some were bare-headed, some wore shapeless felt or straw hats, two wore sombreros. The small-arms they carried were varied. Two of the men wore old-fashioned bandoliers, the rest ammunition pouches. A few carried stick-grenades hanging from their belts.

There came a shout, and a short burst of bullets flew high over the bus. Through the rear window Modesty saw five more men coming up the road from behind. She looked along the aisle. The girls had stopped screaming. They were either silent or whimpering now. Jimson was on his knees, hands clasped, eyes closed, his lips moving. She pushed her way towards him and shook him fiercely by the shoulder. He opened his eyes. There was anxiety in them, but no fear.

She said, 'Get the girls out. You go first with your hands up and waving a handkerchief. That last burst was a warning.'

He nodded, got quickly to his feet and moved towards the door, speaking calmly to the girls, telling them not to be afraid. Modesty collected her handbag and followed.

These would be El Mico's men, she thought. A small group which had penetrated deep into the hills. Dangerous men. Guerrillas, rebels, *bandoleros*—what you called them depended on which side you favoured. She did not know why they had shot up the bus. There did not have to be a reason, except that the bus was there.

The raw mid-morning sun beat down on her as she descended the step. Jimson was waving a handkerchief, standing in front of the girls as they huddled together outside the door. Modesty stayed behind the girls, using them as a screen. She opened her handbag and took out the little MAB 25 automatic, angry with herself for having left her suitcase for Willie to bring on. There were things in that case and in the car which she would have been glad to have now. Her handbag held only make-up, bare toilet necessities, the automatic and a miniature first-aid kit.

She opened the little first-aid tin and took out a roll of one-inch plaster. Putting her foot on the step of the bus, she pulled up her skirt and pressed one end of the plaster to her thigh. The MAB automatic was no more use than a pea-shooter at this moment, under the muzzles of a dozen guns. But if she could keep it hidden, strapped high up on the inside of her thigh, there might well be a chance to make good use of it later. How long her thigh would remain a safe hiding-place from El Mico's men was not an encouraging speculation.

No more than ten seconds had passed since she climbed from the bus. A voice was shouting again. The men were closer now. With the end of the plaster stuck firmly to her flesh, she reached for the gun which lay on the step beside her foot. A hand reached past her and snatched it up by the barrel. Her head snapped round. Jimson stepped back a pace, holding the gun out to one side as if it might contaminate him.

'No!' he said, staring fixedly at her face so that he should not glimpse her bare thigh. 'No, Miss Blaise!'

'Give it to me, you fool!' she said in a fierce whisper. 'It's the best chance we have.'

'No,' he repeated stubbornly, and shook his head. His arm swung. The automatic curved over the bonnet of the bus and disappeared in a patch of scrub twenty paces away.

Salt, black, blinding rage swept her. With an enormous effort she gathered control of herself, clearing her mind to adjust to the new situation, but her hand still shook slightly as she jerked the plaster from her leg and flung it aside.

That was useful, the shaking hand. She let fury rise up within her again, and pressed her fingers into the corners of her eyes. Tears began to run down her face. It was not hard to keep them coming as long as she focused on Jimson's lunacy.

She dragged her fingers through her hair, wiped a hand through the dust on the side of the bus and smeared her face. There came the clink of metal on metal, harsh male voices, the smell of leather and oil, sweat and guns. She let her shoulders droop, pressed her hands to her cheeks and began to sob. Like a chorus her wailing was taken up by the frightened girls as the guerrillas pushed brusquely among them.

The sun was high in the sky and they had trudged for two miles now along one of the winding tracks which cut into the hills.

The Reverend Leonard Jimson walked at the head of his flock as they moved between two groups of their captors at front and rear. He was singing a hymn with a marching rhythm, encouraging the girls to join him, but gaining only pathetic and spasmodic support.

The girls had stopped crying now, mainly from exhaustion. Modesty Blaise trailed behind them, stumbling, clumsy, fanning flies and mosquitoes from her face with a handful of long torquilla leaves. She felt almost satisfied that she had established herself as the most harmless member of a particularly harmless party.

Almost satisfied, but not quite. On the flank walked a man older than the rest of the guerrillas. Greying hair showed below the straw hat pushed back on his head. He had cold eyes set in a lean wary face, an experienced face. Every now and again he glanced at her thoughtfully. The AKM assault rifle he carried was held easily across his body, ready for immediate action.

Rodolfo was his name. She had heard the others use it. He was not in command of the group. The leader was Jacinto, a big swaggering young man in a sombrero. Modesty took the view that El Mico was not a good picker. Rodolfo should have been in charge. He was by far the smartest man here.

She had not used a word of Spanish. Twice she had called plaintively to Jimson, asking how much farther there was to go. After an exchange with the guerrillas Jimson had twice answered, 'Not very far, I think.'

She wondered what Jimson was feeling. He had not panicked, and seemed more concerned with quietening the girls' fears than with speculating on what might happen next. Listening to the guerrillas, Modesty gathered that they had been sent across country by El Mico as a strike force to cut the mountain road and deny it to all traffic for twenty-four hours while El Mico's main force carried out some major operation to the south. The twenty-four hours had now passed, and in that time there had been no traffic at all. Except, at last, the bus.

Shooting up the bus had been little more than a reaction to boredom, Modesty thought, though among themselves they were pretending that the attack had been either for some cunning military purpose or for loot. On both counts the results were disappointing.

True, they had found four hundred dollars in the handbag of the crying foreign woman, but the foreign priest and his miserable flock had almost nothing between them. A pity, after such a skilfully executed manoeuvre. It would not do to let the prisoners go, however. That would be for El Mico to decide when he arrived. Perhaps a ransom could be secured for the foreign woman?

One was a rebel and a fighter for freedom, of course, but the practice of holding for ransom had deep roots and it was as well not to discard all the old and profitable traditions of the *bandolero* too quickly . . .

Jimson stopped singing. One of the men ahead had spoken to him. He turned, pointed to the flank of a high ridge and said encouragingly, 'We're nearly there, girls. Don't be afraid. We're non-combatants and we have nothing to fear. I shall speak to El Mico when he arrives, and everything will be all right.'

Modesty Blaise gave a tearful, doubtful sniff. The doubt was not assumed. She dropped the remainder of the now sweat-soaked torquilla leaves in a bunch. At the start of the journey, when they had struck away from the road, she had let fall two or three of the broad leaves in the first hundred yards. Since then she had dropped one at each point where there might be doubt about the route they were taking.

Willie Garvin, even on this scrub-covered waste, would need no help in trailing a single man, much less a whole group. But the dusty, trampled leaves, where no leaves should be, would give him that much more speed and save him casting around where the trail split. Also, the last crumpled few, dropped together, would warn him that he was near the end of the trail and that it was time to move carefully.

The garage people had estimated seven hours to repair the car, but she knew Willie Garvin would never leave them to do it alone—not people who allowed a car to run off a ramp. He would probably take a hand in the work and would certainly supervise. His supervision would be very forceful. There would be no rest for the *garagistes* of Orsita until the work was done.

Modesty calculated time and distance. The best probability was that Willie Garvin would find the bus and the dead driver in about four hours from now. Allow another hour for him to follow the trail into the hills. So it would be five hours before he arrived on the scene. He would not arrive empty-handed. The Mercedes carried some useful items for emergencies.

But five hours was a long time, in which much could happen. El Mico's men had no reputation for civilized behaviour. Modesty thought it likely that if the bus had carried only men, they would have been used for target practice on the spot. These guerrillas were young and trigger-happy. The girls, and she herself, had other uses of course, though she fancied that she might be reserved for El Mico. Jimson's chances of survival were very small. His cloth would not save him; he was the wrong brand of priest, an interloper.

They had rounded the flank of the ridge now. After another quarter-mile the straggling column passed between two steep slopes of rock. Beyond lay a small valley hemmed by low peaks. Long ago the valley must have been used as grazing ground for a few goats, for on one side stood a dry-stone pen with a narrow gap in its roughly circular wall. At the far end of the valley a patch of struggling yellow grass suggested some small trickle of water along a gully there.

Not far from the pen was the guerrilla camp—three pack-mules hobbled near a scattering of bedrolls and bivouac tents.

And two more men. That made fourteen in all.

Rodolfo, his eyes resting on Modesty as they halted, said, 'Better to keep the prisoners out of the way, Jacinto. Away from the guns.'

Jacinto laughed and shrugged, pushing back his sombrero. 'These?' He gazed at the bedraggled group. 'You are an old woman, Rodolfo.'

'I wish to grow older still.'

Another shrug. 'Do what you please.'

'And you will post a guard for the camp?' Rodolfo pressed, glancing up at the slopes of the valley.

'Of course.' Jacinto snapped out the words irritably and turned away.

The brief exchange confirmed what Modesty already suspected, that Rodolfo was the only competent soldier among them. The rest were undisciplined *bandoleros* pretending to be rebels.

Rodolfo looked about him, then spoke to Jimson and pointed. To one side of the camp the ground rose for about ten feet in a natural ramp, then flattened again to form a small plateau set back in a half-circle of almost sheer rock.

'This way, girls,' said Jimson. 'That's splendid. We shall all be in the shade up there.'

The passing hours had no effect on Rodolfo. He was tireless in his quiet vigilance.

In the camp the guerrillas made a meal, ate, slept and gossiped. They sent a water-bottle to be passed round among the prisoners, and, for Rodolfo, a billycan of chopped meat and beans with thin cornmeal cakes. On a peak opposite the little plateau a man prowled, keeping watch on the approach to the valley. Twice a new man was sent up to relieve him.

But Rodolfo did not sleep, neither did he seem to want any relief. He sat near the edge of the ramp and to one side, his back to a rock, watching the prisoners, watching Modesty Blaise, the AKM resting across his knees.

Once she rose and began to wander about as if stretching her legs, drawing slowly nearer to him. He lifted the gun and spoke sharply. She pretended not to understand.

Jimson said anxiously, 'Miss Blaise, he's telling you to go back and sit down, otherwise he'll shoot you. I'm afraid he means it.' She looked scared and hurried back to where Jimson sat in the shade of the valley wall with the girls spread out around him, some of them dozing now.

As time passed their fears had dwindled with the subconscious belief that the longer nothing happened to them the less likely it was that anything would happen. Modesty hoped they were right, but with little confidence. The men were bored. They had eaten, they had slept for an hour or two, and now there was the rest of the day ahead with its long empty hours.

Her wristwatch had been taken. She glanced at the sun, knowing that her estimate of the time would be correct within ten minutes either way. Another hour and a half before Willie Garvin could be expected on the scene.

She thought bitterly of the MAB automatic for a moment. With that, she could have killed Rodolfo from where she sat and reached him in a dozen strides. His gun, the Russian AKM assault rifle firing a short 7.62-mm cartridge, was a good weapon. The average sub-machine-gun on single-shot would at best produce a twelve-to eighteen-inch group at a hundred yards. The AKM would group into six inches at that range. It carried a thirty-round magazine—and Rodolfo had at least two spare magazines in his pouches. She ran over the technical details in her head. Safety-catch mounted on the right-hand side of the receiver. Pushed fully up it was on safe. The middle position, marked by the Cyrillic letters AB, gave automatic fire. For semi-automatic you pushed the safety right down.

The edge of the ramp held a slight hummock, making dead ground on this side. Using that, and using as added cover the rock against which Rodolfo sat, she was reasonably sure that with the AKM she could have held off the whole band for a long time, perhaps even until their losses made them pull out. There would be plenty of losses. The camp was no more than forty yards away and the only cover was the dry-stone pen with its ten-foot diameter and its five-foot wall.

The first thirty seconds of firing would be tactically critical.

The purpose of it would be to stop as many men as possible reaching the pen, and to drive them back beyond grenade range. A grenade on this confined plateau would be very nasty. Using the AKM on fully automatic wasn't the answer. Too many wasted bullets. She would have to use semi-automatic, quick-fire single shots, choosing the right target for each shot and . . .

But the MAB lay in a patch of scrub two miles away, and Rodolfo had an instinct about her. He would never let her get within reach of him, in reach of the AKM.

Jacinto and another man came from the camp and up on to the higher level. Smirking, they surveyed the girls. For a moment Jacinto's eyes rested hotly on Modesty, then he shrugged regretfully and looked at the girls again.

So she was to be the first prize, kept for El Mico. Jacinto and his men would make do with second best. Modesty knew with heavy certainty which of the girls Jacinto would choose. Rosa, the plump one with a pretty face, who looked a year or two older than her age.

'Your name?' Jacinto said amiably, pointing.

The girl smiled nervously. 'Rosa.'

'A nice name. We have wine captured from a house we found on our way here, Rosa. Come and have a little drink with us.'

She looked frightened and glanced sideways at
Jimson. He stood up and said firmly, 'These girls do not
drink strong liquor. I must insist that they stay with me.
They are in my care, señor.'

The man standing beside Jacinto had a rifle slung on
one shoulder. He brought the butt up and round sharply,
hitting Jimson on the side of the jaw. The girls screamed.
Jimson teetered back, fell, then rolled over and got slowly
to his hands and knees. He stayed there, mouth wide open,
gulping in air and making wordless noises in his throat.

Modesty saw that Rodolfo's gun was lined up on her.
She did not move. Jacinto took Rosa by the wrist,
speaking smooth words, and began to walk away with
her. Her eyes were glazed, she did not resist. The other
man followed, grinning. 'Just a drink,' he said. 'It will
make you feel very good.'

Jimson was kneeling up now, eyes dazed, mouth still
wide, one hand pressed against a great lump high on his
jaw. He seemed to be trying to say something. Modesty
looked at Rodolfo, pointed to herself and then to Jimson.
Rodolfo hesitated then nodded, watching her carefully.
She got up, went to Jimson and said, 'Don't try to talk.
Your jaw's dislocated. Just keep still and bear up hard
with your head when I press down. Understand?'

He nodded, his face filmed with the sweat of pain.
She put her thumbs in his mouth, one on each side, resting
on the lower back teeth. 'Ready? Tense your neck and
press up . . . *now.*' She bore down hard, then sideways.
There was a click as the bone snapped back into place.
Jimson swayed on his knees, hands pressed to his cheeks.
She held him till he recovered.

'Thank you,' he panted. 'Thank you. I must fetch
Rosa . . .'

Her hands on his shoulders stopped him rising. She
said, 'There isn't anything you can do, Mr Jimson. They'll
kill you.'

'Then . . . they must do so,' he said hoarsely, and tried to push her hands away.

Rodolfo said calmly, 'Sit down.' They looked at him and he moved his gun slightly. Jerking his head towards the camp he said, 'They are fools. But I want no trouble. You sit down, sit still. Both.' His chin jerked towards a thin, plain girl huddled against the rock wall. 'Or I shoot that one. Not you. Her. And after her, another.'

Jimson shook his head slowly, stunned with horror. 'But . . .' he said helplessly. 'But—'

He sank back on his heels and put his head in his hands. Modesty sat down. Rodolfo relaxed.

Ten minutes later they heard Rosa laugh. A stupid, giggling laugh that mingled with the deeper voices of the men. Jimson shivered. Another five minutes later Rosa shrieked suddenly. Jimson jumped as if struck by a whip, the blood draining from his face. He said, 'Dear God, what are they doing to her?'

Modesty looked at him. 'What the hell do you think?' she said roughly.

His whole body was shaking. He stammered, 'Please! We—we must stop them!'

'Stop them?' she said, her eyes on Rodolfo. 'How, Mr Jimson? If we move, that man there will start shooting the girls.'

He pressed his hands over his ears to shut out the sound of Rosa's shrieking, then took them away again as if finding the silence even more intolerable. 'There must be something!' he cried desperately.

'There's nothing.' She lacked the charity to spare him, but there was neither satisfaction nor malice in her voice as she added bleakly, 'You threw away my gun. On principle. You're having to pay for your principles well ahead of the day of reckoning, Mr Jimson. So are the rest of us.'

He stared at her for long seconds and, strangely, her words seemed to calm him. His eyes became unfocused, gazing through her, and he said in a remote wondering voice, 'Yes . . . I am being tested.'

Rage seethed in her, but she held it down and said impassively, 'Rosa should be honoured.'

The screams of protest changed to wild sobbing for a while, then began anew. There were guffaws of male laughter, cries of encouragement and advice. Modesty blanked her mind to the sounds.

On the hill across the valley, three hundred yards away, she saw the sentry come prowling slowly into view, a big man wearing a sombrero, like Jacinto. His brother, perhaps. A bad sentry. They all were. Standing on top of a hill against the background of the sky was no way to keep watch.

A flash of light dazzled Modesty. She blinked, moved her head slightly, but the dazzle was repeated, flickering across her eyes. It came from the man on the hill, a reflection from some ornate belt-buckle perhaps . . .

Her heart thumped suddenly. She put up both hands and smoothed back her hair, twice. The dazzle stopped. The man in the sombrero put his right hand on his hip, dropped it to his side, put it on his hip again. Modesty kept her head down, watching from under her brows and feeling relief flow through her like a healing draught.

Willie Garvin.

The unfailing Willie Garvin, an hour earlier than she had dared to hope. One sentry disposed of. Willie was wearing the man's jerkin and sombrero. Not a reflection from a belt buckle but from the vanity mirror taken from behind the sun-visor of the Mercedes. Willie Garvin had a useful talent for looking ahead.

He stood with the sombrero tilted to shade his face, looking casually around, then brought one hand up slowly to his right ear. *What orders?*

She waited. He strolled away and passed below the skyline of the hill. Now he would be lying down, invisible in a fold of ground, watching her through binoculars. It took her over five minutes to send the message. The tick-tack code they used would have put it across in a quarter the time if she could have operated freely, but Rodolfo's eye was on her and she had to use the arm and body movements naturally, without emphasis, allowing long gaps between the signals.

At last she folded her arms. The sounds from Rosa were feeble with exhaustion now, just long shuddering sobs, barely audible at this distance. On the hill Willie Garvin stood up, put a hand to his left ear, and melted into the ground again. *Message understood.*

She turned her head to gaze absently at Rodolfo, and waited, glad that this was to be rifle work. With a hand-gun it was Willie Garvin's resigned boast that he could not hit a barn if he was standing inside it. His short-range weapon was the throwing-knife. With that he was deadly. With any good rifle he was also deadly.

He would have with him the two guns from under the back seat of the Mercedes. One was a CAR–15 carbine, ideal for close quarters. The other was an M14 National Match Rifle, with hooded aperture rear sight, selected barrel and glass-bedded action. It took a twenty-round staggered-row box magazine of 7.62-mm cartridges. With the selector-shaft and lock welded, it could not fire fully automatic. That was not its purpose. On semi-automatic, firing single shots, it was superbly accurate. That was its purpose.

She saw the great exit-wound appear in the side of Rodolfo's head a fraction of a second before the sound of the shot reached her. Even before he toppled sideways she was on her feet and moving fast.

As she snatched up the AKM she saw that it was cocked, with the safety in the middle position. She pushed it down for single-shot, took the three spare magazines from the blood-spattered pouches on Rodolfo's chest, then rolled his body forward to make an added barrier extending from the big rock on the edge of the ramp, leaving a small gap between his body and the rock for sighting.

Down flat in the firing position. Laminated wood stock cuddled into her shoulder. Behind her a rising babble of hysterical jabbering from the girls. At the rear of the little plateau they were safe as long as they did not stand up. She thought of calling to them to keep down, then shrugged the thought aside. Anybody who needed telling that would hardly be affected by a bullet through the brain.

Less than ten seconds since the shot. In the camp forty yards away the men were on their feet, staring towards the far hill. They had spread out a little and picked up their guns, puzzled rather than alarmed. A shot had been fired from somewhere up there, but they did not know where the bullet had gone. They did not know yet that Rodolfo was dead.

Rosa, stripped, was crouched on her hands and knees on a mattress of blankets. Hers was the only face turned towards the slope of the low ramp. Modesty raised her head and beckoned with a full-arm swing. Rosa got unsteadily to her feet, holding a blanket about her, and began to move forward. The men were talking, asking each other questions that nobody answered. Rosa was halfway to the ramp when one of them turned, saw her, and gave a shout.

Modesty sighted the AKM on Jacinto and lifted her voice, calling in Spanish. 'Jacinto! Tell your men to drop their guns. You're in crossfire.'

It was useless, as she had known it would be, and she sneered at herself for indulging in the kind of stupidity that costs lives. The wrong lives. Rosa's first, perhaps. Jacinto swung his sub-machine-gun up to the firing position. She dropped him with a shot through the chest, sighted on another man kneeling to aim, and fired again. One, two, three quick shots came from the hill, blending with the sound of her own firing.

Panic among the guerrillas. Three men were down, lying still; another crawling, dragging a useless leg. Rosa ran on, grey-faced, trailing the blanket behind her. Modesty held her fire to cover any man who might try to shoot at Rosa. The guerrillas raced for the dry-stone pen, ducking and swerving.

From the hill Willie Garvin fired steadily, not hurriedly, picking his shots. Six men down. Now the remaining guerrillas had reached cover, scrambling over the wall of the pen. Modesty knocked the last man off the wall as he clambered over.

Rosa was at the top of the ramp, eyes blind with terror. Modesty eased down behind Rodolfo's body and turned her head as the girl went past. Jimson was standing at the back of the plateau, a hand to his head as if dazed with bewilderment. The girls were huddled together, crouching or kneeling. With a wail of relief Rosa ran to them, and they received her among them with little cries of pity and comfort, not untinged by an element of awed fascination at the manner of her recent début into the ranks of the deflowered.

Modesty said in a low, fierce voice, 'Mr Jimson! We may get a grenade up here. Take the girls behind that huddle of rocks over on your right and make them lie down flat.'

Bullets spattered against the rock that gave her cover. She peered round the base of it, through the gap between the rock and Rodolfo's shoulders. From the hill came a long burst of automatic fire, spraying the pen. Willie had changed briefly to the CAR–15. It would do little harm, unless a lucky shot ricocheted inside the pen, but it served to keep heads down while Modesty studied the situation.

Six men lay scattered about the camp, dead or badly wounded. Willie had dealt with the sentry on the hill. Rodolfo was dead. And she had dropped another as he climbed into the pen. That left five, all under cover now. Even from the hill Willie would not be able to sight them over the five-foot wall. And there were one or two small gaps in that wall where stones had crumpled and fallen out. Good firing apertures for the defenders.

Bullets sprayed the ramp and she felt Rodolfo's body quiver as it was hit. From the hill, single shots again. Willie was back to the M14, trying for the apertures, trying for a ricochet in that confined space where five men crouched.

From the back of the plateau behind her came Jimson's voice, desperate and shaking. 'Miss Blaise! For God's sake stop this—this slaughter!'

She said viciously, 'Tell *them* that, for God's sake!' and she fired from one of the apertures, seeing dust spurt from it. But the angle was wrong, the bullet would have flattened against the inner surface of the hole.

'Miss Blaise, please—!' His voice was nearer. She turned her head and saw with hot anger that he was halfway across the open ground of the plateau, walking towards her. She said, 'Get *down,* you fool!'

Two quick shots from the hill. Her head snapped round just in time to see a man fall. He had stood up in the pen, and her stomach clenched as she saw why. The black globule of a grenade was soaring lazily through the air. Not a stick-grenade, but an egg-shaped fragmentation bomb. The man had made a good powerful throw in the instant of rising, too quick for Willie's snap-shot to prevent.

The grenade would pass ten feet above her head as she lay. No hope of jumping to catch it. She would be riddled by fire from the pen if she tried. What was the fuse timing? Anything from four to seven seconds. If the grenade exploded while still in the air she would be lucky to live. Very lucky. If it hit the ground first and the blast was reflected upwards, there was a chance for her if she hugged the ground. For her, but not for Jimson. Cheek to the ground, eyes watching the flight of the grenade passing overhead, she saw Jimson seemingly in exactly the same position as before. He could have moved only a single pace in the half-second since she had first shouted to him.

She cried *'Grenade!'* and in the same instant she saw him sight it as it curved down, falling towards his right. His pace changed. The whole manner of his gait changed, and suddenly he was moving with assured grace, forward and sideways, fast, not clumsily.

He caught the grenade one-handed at full stretch to his right and no more than eighteen inches from the ground. She saw his arm yield with the weight, absorb it, then bend and straighten as he threw, falling sideways and back to put the weight of his body behind the throw.

The grenade flashed by three feet above her head. It was the hard, low-trajectory throw of the cricketer, the first-class fielder making a return, with that characteristic whiplike flick of wrist and arm; the throw of a man able to hit the stumps sideways-on from thirty yards, six times out of ten.

There came a rattle of fire from the pen. Somebody there had glimpsed Jimson's moving figure above the line of the ramp. But he had already fallen and was hidden again. She had flinched instinctively as Jimson's throw sent the grenade skimming above her. Now she saw it hurtle on its way, spinning in the air, dipping towards the pen.

It had just cleared the wall when it exploded, six feet above the men crouched below.

There was an almost dreamlike quality about the silence that lay over the valley as the rending blast and its echoes faded. The silence was broken only by a single voice wailing thinly from within the pen, and the sound of Modesty's running feet. She had absorbed many surprises in her life, but few had been as swift and startling as this. Only long-nourished instinct surmounted the shock and sent her racing down the ramp before the echoes had died. In five seconds she was at the pen, gun ready, circling round to the slit opening at the back. Now was the time to finish things. There would never be a better time.

But there was nothing to finish. The feeble screaming stopped abruptly as she reached the opening in the dry-stone wall. Within was a sight as ugly as any she had seen, and her mouth grew dry even though she had braced herself against the expected nausea. The fragmentation of a grenade does not do pretty things to the human body.

She looked quickly towards the men scattered on the ground by the camp. Nobody was stirring. She lifted her gun and waved to Willie. A crunch of footsteps and Jimson was beside her. He looked into the pen, gasped, and turned away, retching. She did not look round at him but put down her gun and moved into the pen for the gruesome task of checking the torn bodies for any sign of life. A minute later Jimson said in a shivering voice, 'Are they . . . *all* dead?'

She lifted a man who lay face-down, then let him fall and straightened up. 'Yes. They're all dead. When you're only six feet from an exploding grenade you don't stand much chance. And the fragments must have ricocheted round this pen like a swarm of hornets.'

'Dear God,' he said shakily, and went down on his knees.

Willie Garvin was making his way down the slope of the hill. The girls appeared at the lip of the ramp. She called to them to stay where they were, picked up the AKM and walked across to the men who had fallen in the first moments of the battle, noting that the hobbled mules seemed to have escaped harm.

Three of the men were alive. One was unconscious. The other two were empty of aggression, their faces pallid with pain and fear. She gathered up all guns lying within reach, moved them to a safe spot, then made a quick examination. Two shoulder-wounds, one leg-wound, all serious. She knelt by the unconscious man and began to cut the blood-soaked shirt away from his shattered shoulder with his own knife.

Willie Garvin came trudging across the valley bottom, M14 slung, carbine swinging in his hand, a rucksack on his back. His gaze searched her keenly as he came up, looking for any sign of hurt.

She said, 'I'm all right, Willie love.'

He nodded, slipped off the rucksack, then surveyed the scene of battle with a look of disgust. 'A right shambles they made of it,' he said. 'I reckon the Salvation Army could've done better. Whoever was in charge of this lot ought to be bloody well shot.'

She looked up from her work to nod agreement. 'He was, Willie.'

There was a lot of blood down the front of the sentry's jerkin that Willie still wore. Dried blood, obviously not Willie's. No point in asking if the sentry on the hill was alive. Willie had probably had to take him at throwing-knife range, and had played for keeps. There had been too much at stake to risk any fancy work.

He had opened the rucksack and was taking out a big tin box, a well-stocked first-aid kit. She said, 'Let's have a field-dressing, then prop him up while I bandage him.'

Ten minutes later they had done what they could for the three men. Their wounds were plugged and bandaged, and they had been given a fifteen-milligram shot of morphia each. Modesty stood up and looked around. Jimson was still on his knees in prayer by the pen. The girls were sitting along the edge of the ramp, watching like birds perched on a branch.

She said, 'Have you got a cigarette?'

Willie took out a packet, gave her one and lit it for her, then surveyed the battlefield again with a frown of professional disapproval. 'They were better at rape,' he said. 'What about that girl? I saw four of them 'ave 'er before we started shooting.'

Modesty looked towards the ramp. Rosa, swathed in the blanket, was on her feet now, standing up straight, gazing at the scene with interest. Just as well it had been Rosa. She was a sturdy peasant type with nerves like sisal. In a little while she might even begin to relish the *cachet* of having been raped by guerrillas.

'She'll survive,' Modesty said. 'We'd better make a move, Willie. El Mico is supposed to be arriving sometime soon.'

Willie shook his head. 'El Mico's dead.'

'Dead?'

'I 'eard it on the car radio just before I found the bus. News flash. Triumphant music. The Army trapped El Mico's main forces in a pass down south. Pretty well wiped 'em out. They found El Mico's body after it was over.'

That made a big difference. With the road safe, they could afford now to be burdened by the wounded. She said, 'Do you think the bus is all right?'

'I 'ad a quick look. Just the exhaust crumpled and the wind-screen gone. I could drive that with the girls and the parson while you drive the Merc. We'll still be in San Tremino around sundown.'

'San Tremino?' It had been on her mind to return to Orsita.

'I was thinking of Garcia,' Willie said.

It was a moment before she remembered that she had been on her way to see Garcia because he was dying. That seemed a long time ago now.

'Orsita's much nearer,' she said. 'I mean for these three.' She looked at the wounded men. 'We can get them down to the bus on the mules. The quicker they get treatment the better.'

Willie said gently, 'They won't live long with the treatment they'll get if we take 'em in, Princess. What they do with rebels around these parts is hang 'em.'

'So they do.' She rubbed an eye with the back of her wrist; her hands were too dirty. 'I'm a bit slow today.'

'It's the weather.' Willie wiped his brow and looked at the sun. 'Too much humidity.'

She threw away her cigarette. Her mind felt sluggish, as if resentful of being set problems now that danger was past. Leave the men here and they would die; take them into a town for treatment and they would die.

Willie Garvin said, 'How did that grenade bit 'appen, Princess? I couldn't see from up there, but it was a fair old clincher.'

She moved her head to indicate Jimson, still kneeling near the pen. 'The parson did it. He used to play cricket for Cambridge. Nice clean catch-and-return in about one second dead.'

Willie whistled softly in astonishment, then grinned and said, 'El Mico could've used a few like 'im.'

'Hardly.' She smiled without humour. 'Until that grenade, Jimson bitched up everything all along the line. I'll tell you about it later.'

She walked across to the pen, Willie beside her. Jimson looked up as they halted, still kneeling with fingers locked in front of him. His eyes were pools of pain. He said in a low, shaking voice, 'You were right in one thing . . . I have never seen true evil before. Today I have seen it manifest. Today I have looked into hell.'

He got slowly to his feet. Modesty looked at the carnage in the pen and said tiredly, 'No. They weren't particularly evil, Mr Jimson. Just poor and primitive. And animal.'

He started at her, uncomprehending. 'I did not mean *them.*'

She looked at Willie, then back at Jimson, and lifted an eyebrow. 'Us, perhaps?'

Jimson shook his head, slowly, like a man in agony. 'Not you or your friend. *Myself,* Miss Blaise.'

Willie's face was blank. Modesty said patiently, 'You got rid of a grenade that would have killed us. It just happened to fall here when you threw it.'

Again he shook his head. 'No . . . I could have placed it anywhere,' he whispered despairingly, and bowed his head in his hands. 'I have the blood of five human beings on my head.'

'Better than 'aving yours on theirs,' Willie said cheerfully. 'What they did to the fat girl was just a start. There were only two ways it could end, and this was best.'

'No!' Jimson said feverishly. 'No, it can *never* be the best way. I have betrayed myself.'

Modesty gave a little shrug. Half her mind was busy with the pros and cons of decision. San Tremino or Orsita? Was Garcia still alive? How long would he last? Take the wounded guerrillas back to hang? Or leave them to die? It was all a muddle.

Strangely, despite the frustrations he had caused her, she found that she felt compassion for Jimson, even a liking for him. He was exasperatingly barmy, but that was not his fault. She respected his consistency and his courage. And perhaps somewhere in his hopelessly impractical obsession there was a grain of truth which might some day grow and flourish—in another time, another world.

But not now. And not here, in today's world.

She touched Willie's arm and turned away. 'Go and get the mules ready, Willie love. We'll load up the wounded.'

'OK. You're taking 'em in then?'

'Yes. The long way, to San Tremino. They might not last, but if the doctor in Orsita is anything like the garage mechanics we'll be doing them a favour. And if they hang . . .' She moved her shoulders. 'Tomorrow's always a better day to die.'

As Willie went to the mules she lifted an arm and beckoned the girls. Rosa would need treatment, too, and there was a hospital in San Tremino.

She hoped Garcia would last.

The sun was still hot, and her head ached. It had been a long, weary day. She walked across and began to help Willie Garvin unhobble the mules.

THE GIGGLE-WRECKER

~

THE Minister lightly underlined a few words on the report in front of him, then looked across his desk at Sir Gerald Tarrant and said, 'I'm advised that Professor Okubo is the best bacteriologist in the world. It's a vital aspect of defence today, and if he's available we want to have him. We must have him.'

Tarrant sighed inwardly. He held Waverly in good esteem and liked the man personally. But, perhaps like all politicians, Waverly sometimes allowed his judgement to be swayed by a particular enthusiasm; and as Minister of Defence, Waverly's great enthusiasm was scientific research in the military field.

'If you want Okubo badly, Minister,' Tarrant said, 'then I think you should talk to somebody else about it. My organization in East Berlin isn't geared for getting a defector out.'

Waverly began to fill his pipe. He was a stocky man with small, intelligent eyes set in a heavy face. 'I've persuaded the PM that this calls for a special effort,' he said.

Sixteen years ago Okubo had slipped away from American surveillance in Tokyo and reappeared in Moscow. It had long been known that he was a brilliant young scientist, but of suspect political views. Until his defection it was not known that he was a dedicated Communist. Now, at the age of forty, he had become disenchanted with Marx's brave new world, and had defected anew, but it was a messy and poorly planned defection. Tarrant did not like it at all.

He said, 'Even if we got him out, I don't think you could hold him for long. The Americans would offer him a million-pound laboratory set-up. Why should he stay with us and make do with a Bunsen burner and a bit of litmus paper?'

Waverly smiled. 'Come now. You know I've wrung enormous increases from the Treasury for scientific work. And we seem to be Okubo's personal choice. Just get him out and leave the rest to me.'

First news of Okubo's disappearance from Moscow had come direct to Waverly from the Embassy Intelligence there. Within forty-eight hours there had been rumours in foreign newspapers, followed by denials. It was then that Tarrant had been called in. He did not like being handed a job that was already begun and had been botched, though there was nobody to blame for this but Okubo himself.

The Minister said, 'You've done very well so far.'

'I haven't had the chance to do either well or badly yet,' Tarrant said courteously. 'You asked me to get a line on Okubo, and then he just turned up.'

'Yes.' Waverly looked down at the report again. 'This is very brief. How did he get from Moscow to Berlin?'

'By way of Prague. After the Russians walked in there our Prague Section managed to recruit one or two embittered Czech party members. One was a scientist who knew Okubo well. Apparently they hatched this clumsy escape plan between them. Okubo got to Prague under his own steam without any difficulty and went to ground there. Then his friend informed Prague Control, and they managed to get Okubo as far as East Berlin. I don't think it was the best thing to do, but from the report sent to me I fancy Okubo is an awkward customer who likes things done according to his own ideas. Anyway, Prague found themselves holding this very hot potato and I don't blame them for getting rid of Okubo as fast as they could. If he'd given us any warning of his intention to defect we could have handled things much more smoothly. Even now, given time and given his cooperation, I can get Okubo out, either by the Baltic coast or back through Czechoslovakia and over the border into Austria. But the man who's keeping Okubo under wraps at the moment reports that he won't cooperate.'

Waverly shrugged. 'It's understandable. When you're little more than a stone's throw from freedom, you don't want to start travelling the other way. Besides, we have to make allowances for scientific genius. You'll just have to accept the situation, and bring him out from East to West Berlin.'

Tarrant said bluntly. 'I'm sorry. I haven't the facilities.'

The Minister frowned. 'If he can be got from Moscow to Berlin, surely you can get him over the Wall? It's only another hundred yards or so.'

'A very particular hundred yards, Minister. Okubo is Japanese, and only four feet ten inches high. In an Aryan country he couldn't be more obvious if he carried a banner with his name on it. Getting him out would require a major operation. Worst of all, we're not the only ones who know he's in East Berlin. The KGB knows it, too.'

Waverly had been about to draw on his pipe. Now he paused. 'How do you know that?'

Tarrant hesitated. He hated giving needless information, even to a Minister of the Crown. Reluctantly he said, 'We've had a man in East German Security HQ for seven years now.'

'I see. I won't mention it at cocktail parties,' Waverly said with mild irony. He got up from his desk and walked to the window. 'If the Russians know Okubo is there, I imagine they're turning East Berlin upside down, and as you say, it can't be easy to hide a Japanese. The sooner he's out, the better.'

'The Russians aren't making a tooth-comb search,' Tarrant said. 'They know we have Okubo in a safe-house, and they're simply waiting for him to move. Then they'll net him. Starov's no fool.'

'Starov?'

'Major-General Starov. Head of Russian Security in East Berlin. He's very devious. A man I fear.'

Waverly returned to the desk. 'You said it would require a major operation to bring Okubo out. I see what you mean. But you'll just have to mount one.'

Tarrant kept a tight hold on the fear and anger he felt. 'We've spent fifteen years building up the network we have in East Berlin,' he said quietly. 'It takes time to recruit safely and to get people planted, but we have a very nice tight little network now. Agents have been spotted in carefully. They don't do anything. They're sleepers, and they've been placed there for one purpose only—so that we can activate them if and when the Berlin situation ever really catches fire. That's the real crunch, and they shouldn't be activated for anything else, however tempting. I suggest Okubo isn't worth it, Minister. It's like using *kamikaze* pilots to sink a row-boat.'

Waverly stared into space for a while, then said, 'Can you hire agents for the job? Money's no object for this.'

Tarrant sat up a little. 'No object to whom, Minister? The budget for all Secret Service departments was cut last year and again this year. We now have just over ten million pounds annually. I doubt if that would pay the CIA's telephone bill.'

Waverly shook his head. 'You're too old a hand to be disenchanted by Government parsimony. The Americans can afford it, and we can't. But you needn't touch your budget for this. I can secure money from the Special Fund.

Surely you can hire the necessary personnel? I understand there are more freelance agents in West Berlin than we have civil servants in Whitehall.'

'There are almost as many Intelligence groups as that,' Tarrant said dryly. 'Some agents have become so entangled in the situation that they find it hard to remember who they're working for. And since there's precious little liaison, they spend some of their time industriously liquidating each other's agents by mistake. The fact that many of the groups have been penetrated by Russian Intelligence complicates matters. Add in the freelances, the doubles and the triples, and you have a situation which must make the Russians laugh themselves to sleep at nights.'

Waverly smiled. It was a small and not very humorous smile. 'Then if you can trust nobody else, you'll have to use your own people.'

'I thought I'd covered that point, Minister.'

'No.' Waverly looked into Tarrant's eyes. 'No, not really. You said Okubo wasn't worth risking your network for. But what Okubo is worth is a Ministerial decision. My decision.'

There was a very long silence in the room. 'Of course,' Tarrant said at last, and got to his feet. 'I'll keep you fully informed, Minister.'

When Modesty Blaise came into the reception hall of the penthouse block she appeared to be accompanied by a small but very handsome walnut tallboy chest of Queen Anne's day, moving on human feet that protruded from beneath it.

Willie Garvin set the tallboy down and wiped his brow. He had sat with it resting across him in the back of Modesty's open Rolls while she drove the eighty-odd miles from the country house where the auction sale had been held.

She was looking apologetic now, as well as stunningly attractive in the powder-blue matching dress and jacket she wore. 'I'm sorry, Willie,' she said as he stretched his cramped muscles. 'I ought to have let them send it.'

'That's right,' Willie agreed amiably.

'But I kept remembering how that lovely little table was ruined last year.'

Willie nodded judicially. 'That's right, too.'

'So it was better to bring it with us, really.'

'That's right, Princess.'

She grinned suddenly, patted his arm and said, 'You ought to get mad at me sometimes for my own good.'

'Next time.' He looked past her and registered mild surprise. 'Look who's 'ere.'

A man had risen from an armchair in the reception hall and was moving towards them. He carried a bowler hat and a rolled umbrella. His name was Fraser, and he was Sir Gerald Tarrant's personal assistant.

Fraser was a small bespectacled man with a thin face and a timorous manner. The picture he chose to present most of the time was one of nervous humility. This was a role he had acted for so long that it was a part of him. Sometimes, within a tiny circle of close intimates, the role was dropped and the real Fraser appeared. This was another man, and a very hard personality indeed. Fraser had served as an agent in the field for fifteen years before returning to a desk job, and he had been one of the great agents.

Now he said with an anxious smile, 'I hope my visit isn't . . . I mean, I tried to telephone you, Miss Blaise, but — er . . . so I thought I'd come along and wait for you.'

'That's all right. I wanted to go over the policy with you before I signed,' Modesty said, and turned to the porter behind the reception desk. 'George, will you give Mr Garvin a hand to get this thing in the lift?'

A private lift served Modesty's penthouse. There was just room for the three of them and the tallboy. Going up in the lift, Fraser retained his servile manner, commenting fulsomely but knowledgeably on the tallboy.

Willie lifted it out and set it down in the tiled foyer. Modesty led the way into the big sitting-room, taking off her jacket, and said, 'Is something wrong, Jack?'

Fraser grimaced, threw the hat and umbrella on to a big couch and stared at them sourly. 'Tarrant's resigning,' he said, discarding his image. 'Bloody hell. The longer I live, the more I sympathize with Guy Fawkes, except that blowing up politicians is too good for them. Do you think I could have a drink?'

Modesty nodded to Willie, who moved to the bar and poured a double brandy. He knew Fraser's tastes.

'Why is he resigning?' Modesty asked.

'If I tell you that,' Fraser said, 'I shall be breaking the Official Secrets Act.' He sipped the brandy, sighed, and said, 'God, this is good. If anyone ever wants to ruin it with dry ginger, I hope you break their teeth.'

Modesty and Willie glanced at each other. Fraser was a badly worried man, and that was so unlikely as to be alarming.

'So let's drive a truck through the Official Secrets Act,' Fraser said with gloomy relish. 'There's some bloody Jap bacteriologist who's been working for the Russians for years. Professor Okubo. He's defected and he's in East Berlin now, being kept under wraps by our liaison man. Our masters want him. Waverly's told Tarrant to get him out—even though Starov *knows* he's in hiding there. We can't do it without activating the sleeper network. Tarrant's been told to go ahead and do just that.' Fraser shook his head. 'My sister's husband would have more sense, and I wouldn't match *him* against a smart dog, the thick bastard.'

Willie Garvin whistled softly. This was bad. He saw that Modesty was angry. Like him, she was thinking of the agents, the men and women who for years had lived the bleak, comfortless and restricted life of East Berliners, and who with luck might go on doing so for years more, simply so that they could be activated if ever a crisis got out of hand and the chips went down.

At very best the job was a sentence to long barren years of deprivation. At worst, a bad break would mean torture and death. God alone knew why they did it. But they did. And the very least acknowledgement they could be given was not to sell them down the river by needless exposure.

'If Tarrant resigns,' Fraser said brusquely, 'we lose the best man ever to hold the job. That's one thing. It's bad, but we seem to specialize in self-inflicted wounds, so it's nothing new. The second thing is this. If he resigns, they'll put in somebody who will agree to do what Tarrant won't. The new boy will activate the network to get this bloody Japanese measles expert out, and it's an odds-on chance that Starov will have the lot.' He looked down into his glass and said broodingly, 'I've been where they're sitting now. It's not funny.'

Modesty said, 'You're asking us to do something?'

Fraser gave her a lopsided, humourless smile. He looked suddenly tired. 'Not asking,' he said. 'I don't see what the hell you or anybody can do. I'm just telling you and hoping. Hoping you might think of *some* way to save those poor trusting buggers in East Berlin.'

Nobody spoke for a while. Fraser looked up and saw that Willie Garvin was leaning against the wall by the fireplace, looking at Modesty with an almost comically inquiring air, as if they were sharing some faintly amusing joke.

She got up and moved to the telephone, saying, 'Do you know where Sir Gerald is now?'

'At the office,' Fraser said, hardly daring to acknowledge the flare of hope that leapt within him. 'Composing his resignation, I imagine.'

She dialled the direct number, waited a few seconds, then said, 'It's Modesty. Do you think you could call here very soon, Sir Gerald? Something urgent has come up.' A pause. 'Thank you. In about twenty minutes, then.'

She put down the phone. Willie had moved and stood looking down at Fraser with a wicked grin. He said, 'Tarrant swore he'd never get the Princess tangled up in another caper. He's going to 'ave your guts for this, Fraser, my old mate.'

When Tarrant arrived, Willie Garvin was absent. The sight of Fraser, and his simple statement, 'I've told her,' left no need for further explanation. Even Tarrant's immense control was barely sufficient to contain his fury.

Fraser went into his humble and pathetic act, was blasted out of it, and sat in dour silence, his face a little pale, as Tarrant lashed him with a cold but blistering tongue.

Modesty allowed time for the first shock to be absorbed, then broke in briskly. 'He came to me because he's concerned about your sleeper network, Sir Gerald. Let's talk about that now.'

'No, my dear.' He turned to her. 'I wouldn't send one of my salaried agents into East Berlin for this job, much less you. Don't think me ungrateful. I even recognize Fraser's good intentions. But I won't allow you to attempt an impossible mission.'

'A few people who trust you are going to die if we don't do something.'

'I know.' There was a grey tinge to Tarrant's face. 'If I thought you stood a chance of getting Okubo out . . .' He shrugged. 'Perhaps I'd forget the promise I've made to myself, and ask your help. But there isn't a chance. The Berlin Wall is virtually impenetrable now. Oh, I know there have been plenty of escapes, but not recently. People used to escape over it, under it, and through it. But not any more.'

Absently he took the glass she handed him and muttered his thanks. 'It's different now,' he said. 'And it was never easy. You'd need three figures to count the tunnels dug during the years since the Wall was built, but only a dozen succeeded. Now there are detection devices to locate tunnels. People have crossed the Wall in every possible way. By breeches-buoy on a high cable. By battering through it with a steamroller. They've used locomotives on the railway and steamers on the canal. They've swum and they've run and they've climbed. Over two hundred have died. With each new idea, the East Germans have taken measures to prevent it being used again. And the West Berlin people have stopped being cooperative now. They don't like messy incidents at the Wall.'

He gave her a tired smile. 'I can't send you into that. There's not only the Wall itself. There are guards by the hundred, highly-trained guard-dogs, and anti-personnel mines. There's a wired-off thirty-yard death strip even before you can reach the Wall from the east. That's where most people die. There are infra-red cameras and trip wires and waterway patrols. And nobody gets smuggled through a checkpoint any more, certainly not Okubo.'

He emptied his glass and put it down. 'I know your ability and resources. Perhaps you could find a way out, given time. But you can't even get inside safely at short notice. You could never enter East Berlin as yourself, and a sound cover-identity would take months to establish.'

Modesty smiled at him. 'Don't be such an old misery. I have a friend with special facilities for entering East Berlin.'

Before Tarrant could answer there came the faint hum of the ascending lift. The doors in the foyer opened and a man stepped out. He was tall and wore a well-cut dark suit. His hair had once been fair but was now almost entirely grey, prematurely grey to judge by his face, which was rather round and bore a healthy tan. He wore horn-rimmed spectacles, and was beginning to thicken around the waist.

'Ah, there you are,' Modesty said as he moved forward and down the three steps which pierced the wrought-iron balustrade separating the foyer from the sitting-room. 'It's good of you to drop everything and come so quickly. Sir Gerald, I'd like you to meet Sven Jorgensen.'

The man shook hands and said in good English with a slight accent, 'A pleasure to meet you, Sir Gerald.'

Tarrant said, 'How do you do.' He was puzzled and a little distressed. Why the hell had Modesty brought in a foreign stranger, right in the middle of a top-secret discussion? He trusted her judgement completely, but—

Why on earth was Jorgensen prolonging the handshake, gazing at him in that odd way?

Jorgensen said in Willie Garvin's voice, 'You're not concentrating. Sir G.'

Tarrant heard Fraser rip off a delighted oath, and struggled hard not to show his own surprise. Yes, he could see it now, as if suddenly seeing the hidden face in a child's puzzle-picture. The disguise was not heavy. There was the superb and undetectable wig, and the pads which altered the shape of the face, but the rest of the transformation lay mainly in manner, posture and movement.

Tarrant said, 'Hallo, Willie. You're right. I wasn't concentrating.'

'We go in from Sweden by air,' Modesty said. 'Willie is Herr Jorgensen, who runs a small antique and rare-book business in Gothenberg. I'm his secretary. I can't show you what I'll look like just now because I have to dye my hair, but I'll be equally convincing.'

'I'm sure you will.' Tarrant shook his head slowly. 'But it still won't do, Modesty. Foreign businessmen or visitors are automatically suspect in East Germany, you know that. You'll be watched. Your rooms may be bugged, your passports intensely checked. You simply won't get away with it.'

'We have got away with it for the last five years,' Willie said in his rather stilted Jorgensen voice, and took out a packet of Swedish cigarettes. Tarrant looked at Modesty. She said, 'We've made a ten- or twelve-day trip to East Berlin from Sweden every year for the last five. The antique business in Gothenberg is quite genuine and belongs to us.'

Fraser said, 'But for Christ's sake, *why* do you do it?'

She gave a little shrug. 'We began it a year or two before we retired from crime. It seemed a useful provision, to see what went on behind the Curtain and to establish credible identities there. We kept it up because it seemed a pity to let the thing lapse. The East Berlin police have Herr Jorgensen and Fröken Osslund on record. We've been tailed and bugged and checked and politely questioned. They've given up tailing us now. We know that, because we always know if we're being tailed. They may still bug our rooms. We never bother to check, because even if the rooms were clean there might be three bugs in each when we got back from a trip. So when we talk in our rooms, we talk in character.'

'You make trips?' Tarrant said. 'Outside East Berlin?'

'Yes. We advertise in a few newspapers, and people with likely stuff to sell telephone us at the hotel. We go and see what they've got, and buy any reasonable antiques or books. Not just in Berlin, but in Potsdam, Dresden, Frankfurt and any number of small towns. We've kept our noses clean, we've done straight business, and we make immediate payment in kroner or dollars, then ship the stuff to Gothenberg. Nobody can suspect that we're anything other than what we seem.'

Fraser said in an awed voice, 'You actually go there once a year? You go and spend ten days or so in that God-awful country, just to maintain these identities?'

'It's a chore,' Modesty said, 'but it always seemed potentially useful. And now it's going to be. The only thing the security people there might suspect is that I'm Willie's bird and that he takes me on business trips so he can have a little fun at a safe distance from his own doorstep.' She grinned. 'They won't have heard any confirmation of that over the bugs.'

Willie lit a cigarette and moved to pour a drink. His walk and his mannerisms were still Jorgensen's. 'We can be there in thirty-six hours,' he said.

Tarrant rubbed his eyes with fingers and thumb, trying to collect his thoughts. 'You'd still have to find a way of getting Okubo *out*,' he said slowly.

A hand was laid on his arm and he heard Modesty's voice, warm and understanding. She would know that his part—the safe, waiting part—was always the most agonizing. 'Come on now,' she said. 'Don't worry so much. You know we've always come back before.'

'Just,' said Tarrant. 'Only just.' He opened his eyes to look at her. He was a widower and had lost his sons in the war. With sudden and painful perception he realized that this dark-haired girl, smiling at him now, had in some measure filled the long emptiness in him. For a moment he hated his job with weary passion, and hated himself for letting sentiment lay its soft fingers upon him. It was as if he were throwing his own flesh and blood to wolves when he said, 'Try to make coming back a little less marginal this time.'

She slipped her arm through his and moved towards the foyer. 'We'll be very careful. Come and see the tallboy I picked up at the Rothley Manor auction.'

It was a beautiful piece, with inlaid intarsia panels and in almost perfect condition. For a moment the sight and touch of it lifted Tarrant's depression by a degree. He saw that Modesty was completely absorbed and that her face was lit with pleasure.

She said, almost apologetically, 'Fifteen pounds.'

He could not believe it. 'My dear, you could get close to a thousand for it at Christie's any day. The dealers must have been blind.'

'There weren't any. If you go far enough out of London for a sale, you often find the dealers haven't bothered. But I didn't buy it to sell. I just want to enjoy it.'

The moment passed, and Tarrant felt aching anxiety descend on him again.

'For God's sake make sure you're able to,' he said.

The printing shop lay in a narrow street not far from Alexanderplatz. Toller was a fair, thickset man in his late forties. He said, 'Ah, yes. I don't know if the books have any great value, Herr Jorgensen, but when I read your advertisement I thought it worthwhile to telephone you. Come this way, please.'

Willie Garvin and Modesty Blaise followed him through the printing shop, where half a dozen men were working. Her hair was dark chestnut now, and body padding made her look thirty pounds heavier. Contact lenses gave her eyes a different colour, and a moulded hoop of plastic round the gum-line of her lower jaw had altered the shape of her face.

A small flat-bed machine was churning out propaganda pamphlets for the West. Bundles of these would be stuffed into papiermâché containers, loaded into modified mortars, and fired across at different points along the 850-mile frontier of minefields, watchtowers and barbed wire. The pamphlets bore pinpup pictures and enthusiastic accounts of the happy life led by one and all in the Democratic Republic.

In return, and because the prevailing wind was favourable, pamphlets from West Germany would come drifting across the frontier suspended from balloons with clockwork scatter-mechanism. It was all a heavy-handed exercise in pinprick irritation.

Toller closed the door of the print shop and opened another across the passage. They entered a small room, sparsely furnished, and when Toller closed the door all sound of machinery was muffled to a whisper.

'This room is safe,' Toller said softly. His manner was steady, but looking beneath the surface Modesty saw the underlying tension.

'You have him here?' she asked. They spoke in German.

Toller jerked his head back slightly, lifting his eyes towards the ceiling. 'Upstairs. It is three days since the courier brought instructions to me for making contact with you. Two days since I telephoned.'

'We had to maintain our routine,' Modesty said. 'Is communication with West Berlin difficult?'

'There is always some risk. Couriers must be foreign nationals and can operate only for a limited time. But as foreigners you can pass freely yourselves.'

'We won't do that. We've never gone to and fro before, and it would look suspicious if we started now. Zarov must be very much on his toes.'

Toller said, 'Very much. We use no radio. We have them, but for emergency only. The big emergency. Apart from that, communication with London Control must go through Local Control in West Berlin, by courier.'

London Control had moved to West Berlin. Tarrant himself was there now. But Modesty did not tell Toller that. A spy dislikes holding more information than is necessary for what he has to do. She said, 'I've arranged a new system of communication for this mission. I'll tell you about it after we've seen Okubo. We'll be taking him off your hands tonight.'

Toller said fervently, 'Thank God for that. He is very difficult. I have been more afraid in the last ten days than in the last ten years.'

Okubo was in a small upper room with a single shuttered window overlooking an enclosed yard. There was a bed, a chair set at a plain deal table, and a battered chest of drawers. A big china jug of water stood in a bowl on top of the chest. Okubo lay on the bed, smoking. He wore a rumpled dark-grey suit and was very short but well proportioned. His thick black hair was sleek, and he had a vestigial moustache of which the hairs could almost be counted. His eyes were unfriendly and arrogant.

He sat up and spoke in rather high-pitched, liquid English, with a marked American accent. 'Are these the people, Toller? I was beginning to wonder if they existed.'

'The situation is not easy for them,' Toller said. He sounded like a man who had said the same thing many times.

Okubo looked through Modesty, then stared at Willie without warmth. 'You will explain your plan.'

Modesty said, 'It's a simple one—'

'I did not address you,' Okubo broke in without looking at her.

Willie Garvin put his hands in his pockets, and Modesty saw his eyes behind the plain-glass spectacles go blank for a moment as he killed the instinctive flare of anger within him. Toller had not exaggerated in saying that Okubo was difficult. He was the best virus-man in the world, much sought after, and he knew it. Allied to his professional arrogance was the traditional male Japanese attitude towards the female. Okubo was not going to accept the idea of a woman running this operation.

She caught Willie's eye. He took over and said, speaking without his usual Cockney accent, 'We're using an opportunity that happens to be available. De Souta is in Berlin this week—'

'De Souta?'

'Special United Nations Representative for U Thant. He's having talks on both sides of the Wall at local level, trying to reduce tension.'

Okubo's mouth twisted in contempt. His reaction was justified. De Souta's efforts were futile. He no doubt knew this himself, but he was a dedicated man and had patiently suffered rebuffs in various parts of the world in the course of his peace-making attempts.

Willie said, 'He's staying at his own Embassy here, and there's a set pattern to the talks. West Berlin in the morning, East Berlin in the afternoon. Every day at 9 am he goes through the checkpoint in his car, with his own chauffeur. The guards know the car. They just make sure he's in it, then wave him through. It's the only car that isn't checked. Tomorrow, you'll be in the boot. It's a Daimler, so there'll be plenty of room.'

Okubo threw his cigarette end on the floor. It was Toller who trod it out. 'You must be a fool,' Okubo said. 'A United Nations representative would never involve himself.'

'He won't know,' Willie said. 'The car's kept in a lock-up garage near the Embassy. and we've hired a lock-up in the same block. We've made a dry run on this, and it works. We'll get you into the garage and into the boot by eight o'clock, so you'll only have an hour to wait. I drilled some air-holes last night, in the floor. The car stops at the Hilton. That's where De Souta talks to Mayor Klaus Schütz, to keep things informal. Wait five minutes after the car stops, then get out. I've fixed the lock so you can open the boot from inside. One of our men will be on the spot, waiting for you.'

Okubo lit another cigarette and stared at Willie coldly. 'It is a stupid plan,' he said. 'If your people want me, they should arrange a practical operation, meticulously organized, and covered by an experienced group—'

'Nobody's going to start a war to get you out,' Willie said. 'We're using an opportunity that's simple and that works.' He gave Okubo no time to reply but said to Toller, 'Can you bring him to that car park north of Rosenthaler Platz at midnight?'

Toller nodded.

'All right. We'll be there in a grey Skoda. I'll have the bonnet up and I'll be fiddling with the engine. Park alongside if you can. Have Okubo in overalls. He slides out and into the Skoda. Then you can forget him.'

Okubo's face was hard with anger. He said, 'I have told you—'

'I know you have,' Willie cut in. 'But don't. Don't tell us how to get you out of East Berlin, and we won't tell you how to breed foot-and-mouth bugs. All we want to know is if you're going to be in that car park at midnight.'

The hatred of pricked vanity flamed in Okubo's dark eyes. He looked away. After a long silence he said, 'Very well. You force me to agree.'

Toller's sigh of relief was audible. He opened the door, and followed Modesty and Willie out. In the room below, Willie exhaled and rubbed a hand across the back of his neck. He swore softly and said in English, 'We got a little beauty there. You signalled me to lean on 'im, Princess. I didn't make it too strong?'

'Just right. It worked. But he scares me.'

Toller nodded his head in grim agreement. 'It is a good plan. Very good. But Okubo has a great sense of his importance. I think he wishes for some big, dramatic affair.'

'Yes.' Modesty took a compact from her handbag and checked her appearance. Her face was too taut, and she worked the muscles to relax them. 'Dramatics are all right. But not when the man awarding the Oscars is Major-General Starov.'

In the afternoon they drove out to a village north of Halle, to see a farmer who had telephoned after reading one of their advertisements. He had, he said, over two dozen carved wooden fairground animals for sale, cockerels and horses and ostriches. The small antique business in Gothenberg was managed by a competent Swede who kept abreast of the whims of fashion and who had told Modesty that there was a ready market at up to eighty pounds apiece for these curiosities from the old fairground roundabouts.

At the farm they were shown round three big barns, almost filled with circus and fairground equipment. The owner of a tenting circus, a Hungarian, had disappeared with all the cash takings at the end of last summer, leaving the season's rent unpaid and the performers and handling staff short of a month's wages.

Some of the circus acts had taken their gear and departed. But others, perhaps recognizing that theirs was a dying profession, had simply abandoned their gear and dispersed. Since the Hungarian had chosen to decamp with the lady liontamer, the farmer had found himself with six mangy lions to feed until they were taken over by a zoo. He had a long and harrowing story to tell about this.

Willie, who in his early twenties had once worked for a spell in a circus, was fascinated by the evocative sights and smells of the tawdry equipment. There were mouldering tents, broken seating, sections of a dismantled roundabout and helter-skelter; rusting donkey engines and a miniature railway track; cages and cables, a huge cannon, a clowns' car with eccentric wheels, and a set of distorting mirrors with most of the silvering gone. But only the roundabout animals were of any real value. Beneath the dirt and peeling paint they were exceptionally good specimens, free from worm and dry-rot, beautifully carved, and with the wooden eyes which set them above the cheaper type with eyes of glass.

After some uncertain bargaining on the farmer's part, Willie agreed to buy the twenty best for eighteen hundred kroner or the dollar equivalent, and to pay all transport charges. Modesty made a note of the transaction in a little book. She was pleased with the afternoon's work. Doing genuine business was important in strengthening their cover.

They drove out past Leipzig to look at some clocks, and were back in Berlin by seven that evening. Willie drove the car into one of the hired lock-up garages, only three doors from the garage where the Daimler of the United Nations representative was kept.

As he switched off he said softly, 'I'll be glad when this one's over, Princess. That bug-fancier gets under my skin.'

Modesty felt the same. It was a neat and beautifully simple caper. Willie's idea. But like Willie, she felt that Okubo himself was the weak link, the dangerous element. And there was nothing they could do about that.

The pick-up at midnight went smoothly. Okubo was left to spend the night on the back seat of the Skoda in the garage. His manner was unchanged. He did not seem to be afraid, only resentful and ungracious, complaining of the inadequacy of the arrangements for his escape.

At eight in the morning, as Herr Jorgensen and his secretary, they left the hotel and took the Skoda out of the garage, with Okubo lying on the back seat. Willie immediately stalled it directly outside the door of the Daimler garage, and pretended to have difficulty in restarting. While he raised the bonnet and checked the leads, Modesty opened the door of the Daimler garage with the key Willie had made two days ago. Okubo slid out of the Skoda and into the darkness of the garage.

Surprisingly, he did not renew his complaints of the night before, but seemed subdued as he curled up in the big boot of the Daimler. She whispered, 'Don't worry.

We'll be watching you all the way.' He nodded, saying nothing, and she closed the boot. A minute later she was in the Skoda with Willie, heading for Toller's yard.

Now, an hour later, Okubo was less than half a mile from Checkpoint Charlie and freedom. The Daimler moved smoothly along the Friedrichstrasse and crossed the intersection of Unter den Linden. Willie Garvin, driving a dirty brown van, kept on its tail. He wore overalls which covered his Jorgensen suit, and a beret pulled down low. Immediately behind him, Modesty was driving the Skoda.

Ahead lay Leipziger Strade. Willie prepared to turn off. He could go no further without coming to the checkpoint.

It was then that shock hit him like a full-blooded jab under the heart. The Daimler was slowing, pulling into the kerb, moving a little bumpily. The nearside tyre was flat. He whispered, '*Jesus!*' The chauffeur would have to open the boot to release the spare wheel.

Willie Garvin became suddenly immensely calm. He put out his hand in a quick signal to Modesty, a wave-on followed by a chopping halt sign. As the Daimler stopped he pulled in behind it, leaving a space of no more than five feet between his front bumper and the rear of the Daimler. In the Skoda, Modesty came up alongside and stopped, covering the gap between the two vehicles.

She saw the flat tyre, saw the chauffeur alighting. Willie was already out of the van. He glanced at her without interest and she gave him a fractional nod. From long years of working dangerously together their minds were sensitively attuned. His glance had simply asked for her confirmation to go ahead with what they both knew was the only way to snatch Okubo from disaster.

Willie would meet the chauffeur at the rear of the Daimler and offer to help. When the chauffeur opened the boot, Willie would drop him with a body-jab at close quarters. And while Modesty, anxious and fluttering, tapped on the Daimler window to tell De Souta his chauffeur had apparently fainted, Willie would get Okubo out of the boot and into the van.

The whole move was electric with danger, but it would take only five seconds and there was no other option now. A car hooted and swung out past Modesty. She made an apologetic gesture, started the engine and stalled as soon as it fired. The chauffeur had spoken to his master and was moving round to the rear of the Daimler. With an air of hopeful cupidity Willie said in German, 'You want a hand with it?' The chauffeur looked slightly surprised. Then, grasping that goodwill was not the motive, he nodded indifferently and bent to open the boot. As he lifted the lid Modesty saw Willie's rigid hand poised to stab forward, his body hiding it from any passing pedestrian. Then he froze.

She could see into the boot, and it was empty. No Okubo. The chauffeur began to winch down the spare wheel from its resting place. Willie rubbed his chin and turned his head so that his gaze passed idly across her. Now what? She gave a little backward jerk of her head, then started the Skoda and moved off, turning down Leipziger Strade. Anger, relief and speculation all battled for a place in her mind.

An hour later Willie drove the van into Toller's yard. She was waiting for him in the big garage, and said, 'We're alone. It's safe to talk.'

He began to take off his overalls and said grimly, 'Where's the little bastard now?'

'Back where he started. Up in Toller's room.'

'You found 'im still in the lock-up garage?'

'Yes. He changed his mind at the last minute, he tells me, so he hid under a tarpaulin there when the chauffeur came to get the Daimler out.'

'Changed 'is mind? He wants to go back to Moscow?'

She shook her head. 'Changed his mind about accepting our plan for getting him out. I managed to smuggle him into the Skoda without anyone seeing, and I brought him back here. Toller was ripe to kill him when we turned up.'

Willie took off the beret and inserted the rubber pads in his cheeks. His movements were taut and precise. She knew that he was boiling with anger. Her own fury had had time to cool now. She said, 'It could have been worse, Willie love. I know that flat tyre was a million-to-one chance, but it happened. We might have scooped Okubo out of the boot and into the van safely, but we could only have brought him back here.'

Willie let out a long breath and nodded reluctant agreement. 'Did you tell Okubo what 'appened?'

She grimaced. 'No. He's bad enough without being given a chance to say I-told-you-so. I just tore him apart for fouling up the plan. But I'm female so he hardly listened. He just wants to know what the next move will be.'

'I wouldn't mind knowing that meself,' Willie said bleakly, and put on his plain-glass spectacles.

'I told him that we'd have to lay on a major operation, but that it would take a few days to organize.'

Willie stared. 'Activating Tarrant's lot?'

'Yes. That's what Okubo wants. A big show. I thought we might let him believe he'll get it.'

Willie relaxed, gazing at her curiously, trying to mesh with her thoughts. Then his eyebrows lifted and he gave a little nod of comprehension. 'Yes. You could be right, Princess.'

His anger had vanished now. They stood in silence for a while, their minds mutually preoccupied. At last Willie said, 'Tarrant should've got the message last night. It'll make 'im sweat when Okubo doesn't 'op out of that Daimler.'

'Yes.' She gave a wry shrug. 'He's used to sweating. We'll get another message to him tonight.'

'Same way?'

'The same way. I don't want to use couriers. I don't want to rely on anybody but us. And Toller. We'll use the pamphlet bomb again. Toller says they're firing nightly for the next two weeks at least.'

Willie grinned. The idea was Modesty's, and he thought it a knock-out. Toller printed the propaganda pamphlets and packed them in papiermâché 'bombs' which were fired over the border from crude mortars. He made a delivery of bombs nightly to gun sites along a four-mile stretch of the border south of Berlin.

It was easy to make a stronger bomb, a container which would not burst and scatter its contents. It would contain no pamphlets but would carry a homing device transmitting on a set frequency and activated by the shock of the discharge. Toller would deliver that bomb, with the usual issue, to a prearranged site. On the other side of the border, Tarrant had men on permanent listening watch, to get a cross-reference on the homing device in the fallen bomb. It would be located within minutes of landing, and it would contain whatever message Modesty wished to send.

Toller had been entranced by the idea. He hated using couriers, and the thought that the East German propaganda gunners would be acting as messengers gave him a pleasure that was rare in the unremittingly grey and dangerous life he lived.

Willie said, his grin fading, 'So all we've got to do is figure another way of getting Okubo out.'

'Just that small item.'

He sighed. 'There's only one good thing 'appened this morning,' he said gloomily. 'I got a dollar tip from that chauffeur for 'elping change the wheel.'

Throughout the rest of the day they made no conscious efforts to formulate a plan, but simply left their minds open to recognize any opportunity. This was their method, and this was how Willie had hit upon the first plan, several days ago, when he had seen the United Nations car pass by on its daily journey through Checkpoint Charlie.

When night came they were still without inspiration. Modesty lay in bed and reviewed the chances of using the same escape plan again, except that this time they would knock Okubo unconscious before putting him in the boot. But his cooperation would be needed until the last moment, and she knew they could not fool him for long enough to ensure that cooperation.

It was eleven o'clock. Within the next hour or two the East Germans would obligingly shoot her message to Tarrant over the border. It would be some relief to him to know that even though one attempt had failed, at least they had not been caught . . .

An association of ideas made her thoughts dart off at a tangent. She drew in a quick breath and sat up, her mind racing. The idea seemed hare-brained, but it might work. Yes . . . it just might. Willie would know, and he could make it work if it was in any way possible.

She got out of bed, pulled on a dressing-gown and went through the communicating door into his room. He woke at the faint sound of the door opening, sat up in bed and put on the bedside light. She beckoned him through to the bathroom and turned on the shower. It was possible the rooms were bugged, but unlikely that this included the bathroom. If so, then the sound of the shower would make the bug ineffective.

Willie sat beside her on the edge of the bath, his eyes eager, knowing she had an idea. She put her lips close to his ear and began to whisper. After the first ten seconds he suddenly hunched forward, a frantic expression on his face, then rammed the fingers of one hand into his mouth and closed his teeth on them, rocking back and forth in agonized struggle as he fought to subdue the gust of laughter that convulsed him, laughter so stupendous that if he had given vent to it the sound would have been heard through the walls.

She stared at him almost indignantly for a moment, then punched his arm gently in remonstrance. He shook his head in speechless apology, and doubled up again. Somehow he straightened, the breath rasping round the gag of his fingers. He looked at her, his face empurpled with strain, then nodded again and again, lifting his free hand to make a confirmatory circle with finger and thumb.

A new spasm gripped him, and suddenly she caught the infection. The same convulsive laughter welled up within her. Eyes closed, tears squeezing from under the lids, lips tightly compressed, she leaned against him and hugged her forearms across her stomach in the desperate struggle to keep silent.

Tarrant handed the sheet of paper to Berlin Control and fingered his moustache. Berlin Control read the message twice, a variety of expressions chasing one another over his face. At last he said simply, 'They must be joking.'

'That's the first impression one gets,' Tarrant agreed. 'But it's not tenable. So let's assume that this is just a typically unorthodox idea. We're going to comply with what they ask.'

It was two days since the earlier message had come through, giving no details but stating baldly that the first plan had failed and that another would be devised. Now this new message had come over the border. Berlin Control read it once again and said, 'It won't be easy to get this organized.'

Tarrant eyed him coldly. 'It's a bloody sight easier than what she and Willie have to organize, don't you think?'

'We only have thirty-six hours.'

'Then that will have to be long enough.' Tarrant frowned, trying to trap a fleeting thought of something he had seen or read in the last few days. He identified it and said, 'There's a man in the States called John Dall. A tycoon with all kinds of diverse interests. Get him on the phone for me.'

'I'll try. Tycoons usually have a screen of secretaries to shield them.'

'Give my name and say it concerns Modesty Blaise,' Tarrant said. 'You'll get through that screen as fast as if you were the President.'

It was an hour later, and 4 am in New York, when Tarrant picked up the phone and heard Dall's voice. 'Tarrant?'

'Yes. I'm sorry to disturb you at this hour—'

'Never mind. Have you got her into another peck of trouble?'

'I could have stopped her by putting her in a straitjacket, perhaps.'

He heard Dall give a sigh of resignation. Then, 'OK. I know what you mean. What can I do?'

'I believe you have a major interest in a film company which has a unit here at the moment, shooting scenes which include the Wall. They have, or can obtain, certain facilities she wants me to provide.'

There was a silence. Tarrant knew that Dall wanted to ask if Modesty was on the wrong side of the Wall, but would not do so on an open line. He said, 'Yes, she is, John.'

Dall said, 'Oh, my God. All right, the unit director is a guy called Joe Abrahams. I'll call him now. He'll make contact with you within the next couple of hours and he'll be under your orders for—how long do you want?'

'Thirty-six hours, please.'

'OK. Where does he contact you?'

Tarrant gave the address and number of a small travel agency. Dall said, 'I've got that. Will you have her ring me as soon as she's able to, please?'

'Of course. And thank you.' Tarrant put down the phone and looked at Berlin Control. 'I've seen them shooting scenes close to the Wall. They must have permission for it from the West Germans.'

'Yes. Are you going to ask the Gehlen Bureau for help? They have a lot of pull.'

'I don't think we need it now we have the film-location cover, and the fewer people involved the better.' Tarrant pointed to the message Berlin Control had picked up from the desk. 'Study that sketch map and the figures, then go and look at the site and see how best to set the scene.'

Okubo sat in the brown van with Modesty, in a lay-by on the Dresden road fifteen miles south of Berlin. It was just after half past eight, and night had fallen.

'There is to be a full conference?' Okubo said.

'Yes. Nobody likes the idea, but I persuaded them that we'd have to set up a major operation to get you out.'

'So I have said all along. What is the plan?'

'I don't know yet. It's to be settled tonight.'

'It must have my approval.'

'That's why you're here now and out of cover,' Modesty said dryly. 'It's dangerous for you and it's bad security for our people, but they've accepted the risk.'

An enormous furniture truck came rumbling along the road. It pulled into the lay-by behind them. The headlights were switched off, and Willie Garvin, dressed in overalls and a beret, climbed down from the cab of the truck and moved to the van. He nodded to Modesty. She said to Okubo, 'We move into the truck now.'

The little Japanese got out of the van and followed her round to the rear of the tall truck. A tarpaulin hung down from the back of the rectangular roof to join the tailboard. Willie lowered the tailboard and Okubo mounted it. He said, 'It is to be a mobile conference, then?'

'The Group Controller decided it was the safest way,' Modesty said, and followed Okubo as he ducked under the hanging tarpaulin.

There was nobody in the truck, but the vast bulk of some strange object filled it almost completely fore and aft, leaving a passageway on each side. Okubo stared in the darkness. The thing seemed to be an enormous cylinder, tapering slightly and angled up towards the rear of the truck. The cylinder was set on some kind of mounting or low carriage which seemed to be bolted to the floor.

It was a gun. A cannon. A caricature of a cannon. It was of metal and had once been brightly painted, but most of the paint had peeled off. The barrel was absurdly large. Large enough to take a man . . .

Watching, Modesty saw Okubo freeze with incredulity for a moment. Then he turned and sprang at her in the narrow gap between the side of the truck and the circus cannon. He jumped high, and one foot lashed out for her heart in a skilled karate kick. It was a reaction far quicker than she had anticipated, but instinct gave her a split-second warning of it.

She twisted, and his heel scraped her upper arm. She blocked the follow-up chop of his hand with an elbow driven paralysingly against his forearm; and then, as he landed, she was inside his guard and the kongo in her fist rapped home sharply under his ear. He fell like an empty sack.

Behind her, Willie Garvin said, 'Karate man, eh? And a lively little Professor all round. Caught on fast, but didn't fancy the idea much.'

'It's not a very dignified way of going over the Wall,' Modesty said, and took the hypodermic Willie handed her.

'It ought to be dramatic enough for him, but there's a certain loss of face about it. Did you test the cannon again today?'

'Three times on a set trajectory, with a sack of sand the same weight as Toller gave us for Okubo. There wasn't more than thirty inches variation on landing. If Tarrant fixes the net on the measurements we want, Okubo ought to land pretty well dead centre. And the size of net we asked for allows a margin of sixteen feet on width, and twice as much on length.'

Willie Garvin sounded very confident. The circus he had worked for long ago had boasted a Human Cannonball act, and one of Willie's jobs had been to check and test the cannon, and to load it with the compressed air which provided the fire-power.

Two days ago, undisguised and purporting to represent a Russian circus, Willie had visited the farm again and bought the cannon. He had spent a full day there, stripping down and adjusting the firing mechanism, scouring the inside of the barrel to mirror smoothness, getting the necessary compressed air cylinders, testing the cannon, and hiring the furniture truck.

The farmer had been mildly surprised, but this brusque circus man was a Russian, and one did not argue with one's allies and protectors.

There was a crash-helmet to protect Okubo's head, a stiff leather collar for his neck, and a small tarpaulin in which to wrap him up and so protect his limbs, since he would be unconscious while making the flight. The tarpaulin was oiled on the outside to give a smooth exit from the great barrel of the cannon. With the lightweight Okubo as projectile, the cannon's range was greater than usual. It had tested out well at just under ninety yards.

Modesty completed the injection of pentothal and straightened up. She said, 'All right, Willie. Let's get him loaded.'

Willie Garvin reached for the crash helmet and tarpaulin, and as he bent to the task his body shook with silent laughter.

Fifteen miles away, and on the other side of the Wall, Tarrant stood with Joe Abrahams in a side-street near Brunenstrade. Abrahams was a lean, eager man of great energy. At first resentful of interference by Dall from above, he had become ecstatic about the project as soon as Tarrant explained what was wanted. His only regret was that there was no film in the three cameras set up to cover the scene they were pretending to shoot.

Abrahams had conjured up a net, flown in from Bonn, after an urgent call to his property man there. It was forty yards long and fifteen wide. At this moment it lay carefully folded on top of three big trucks which stood facing the open ground between the end of the side-street and the Wall.

There was the usual apparent confusion that inevitably surrounds a film unit. Lights were being set up, powered by long cables run out from a generator. People sat around in canvas-backed chairs, drinking coffee served from a canteenvan. Others called instructions or made chalk marks on the ground for the actors to take up position when shooting began.

Abrahams ran his fingers through an untidy mop of hair and said, 'Your artillery friends had better be spot on ten-fifteen. When we run that net out, the guys in the watchtowers won't see it because we've fixed the lighting that way. But it'll only take maybe five minutes before the West German cops get around to making guesses and having us take it down.'

'My artillery friends are very reliable,' Tarrant said. 'Run the net out at twelve minutes past ten. I'm sure you can stall for seven or eight minutes from then. Once the fish is netted we'll whisk him away before anyone realizes what's happened. And don't worry about your crew. The East Germans won't fire into the West. Into the death-strip on their side, yes. But not over the Wall.'

One edge of the net was attached to the upper windows of the empty building against which the three trucks were tightly backed. On Abrahams' signal the drivers would move the trucks forward slowly, in line abreast, to a precisely measured line marked on the open ground just over thirty yards from the Wall, and the net would then be tautly spread.

Berlin Control looked at his watch for the twentieth time and said, 'Another eight minutes. I still think they're out of their minds.'

'I hope you double-checked the map and the measurements,' Tarrant said. 'Accuracy is going to be vital.'

'It bloody well is for Okubo,' Berlin Control said with feeling. 'I've triple-checked everything. But please don't ever send those two to get me over the Wall.'

Abrahams grinned wolfishly. 'They're creative people,' he said. 'I love 'em. Whoever they are, I love 'em.'

Modesty turned off Weinbergstrade into the network of side-streets. She was driving a different van now, a laundry van she had stolen from a car park only twenty minutes ago. She wore a plain head-scarf, and a loose sweater covered the upper half of the clothes she wore as Jorgensen's secretary.

Soon, in the headlights, she saw some way ahead of her the barbed-wire fence, eight feet high, which ran parallel to the Wall, leaving a thirty-yard gap in which guards and dogs patrolled — the death-strip. Behind her the lights of the lumbering furniture truck disappeared as it turned off.

She looked at her watch and drove on slowly. Okubo would be making a flight of eighty-eight yards, thirty-one on this side of the Wall and fifty-seven on the far side. According to Willie the risk to Okubo was very small, providing the net was in the right position at the right time. That part of the job was Tarrant's, and she wasted no anxiety on it.

Turning again, she drove down the road which paralleled the Wall, the most westerly road where traffic was allowed. At each intersection the street to her right was a cul-de-sac leading only to the wire fence and the Wall beyond. The buildings in these cul-de-sacs were empty and derelict.

The next intersection was the one she wanted. Ahead and beyond it she saw the furniture truck turn into the road and come towards her. She moved into the centre and stopped her engine. There was no room for the truck to pass. It halted. One or two people looked out from the window of a dingy café as Willie Garvin shouted to her in German.

She called back fluently, making her voice shrill, telling him she had stalled and her battery was flat. If he backed out of the way she could get started on the slight down-slope.

Grumbling, Willie Garvin put the big truck into reverse and backed slowly round the corner of the cul-de-sac. There was no laughter in him now. His eyes moved from side to side in total concentration as he centred the truck precisely . . . and kept backing.

Modesty let the laundry van roll forward a little. Now she could see obliquely along the side of the truck. When the back of it was within a yard of the barbed-wire fence she gave a short whistle. The truck stopped. She pushed back her sleeve and looked at the big stop-watch strapped to the inside of her forearm. It was ten-fourteen. Sixty seconds to wait. Her mouth became a little dry with tension.

The nearest observation platform was well over seventy yards away. Though the guards there could not see the truck now, they would have marked its passing along the road, and they were trained to suspicion. Their machine guns would be ready, covering the gap between wire and Wall, and they might well be calling the patrol guards by radio.

Distantly, from the far side of the Wall, a loud-hailer sounded harshly. An American voice. 'Right folks, settle down. We're all set to shoot. All set to shoot. Roll 'em. *Action!*'

She did not wonder what Tarrant had arranged, but thanked God for his wit in saving a dangerous minute of waiting. Her hand moved in a signal to Willie.

In the cab of the truck there were two ropes which ran through holes into the back. Willie picked up the rope with a wooden toggle on the end and pulled hard. There was some resistance for the first few feet, and then the rope went slack. The tarpaulin fell from the back of the truck, leaving the great barrel of the cannon clear for an unobstructed shot. It still could not be seen, except from directly behind the truck, and no patrolling guards had arrived in the death-strip yet. Only twenty seconds had passed since the truck started backing.

Willie picked up the second rope and jerked it. The truck vibrated slightly. In the sawdust ring of the circus there would have been a puff of smoke and a loud explosion, a fake effect. Now there was surprisingly little sound as compressed air exploded from the firing chamber, only a heavy and sonorous plop.

From the laundry van, Modesty picked up a momentary sight of the black, sausage-shaped object soaring up over the death-strip, over the Wall, still rising, then dipping down, rotating slowly, end over end. It was gone, and she doubted that any other eye on this side of the Wall had seen it.

She started the engine. Willie was out of the truck and moving towards her, not seeming to hurry but covering ground fast. She swung open the passenger door for him and let in the clutch as he settled beside her. The distant voice sounded on the loud-hailer. *'Cut! Okay folks — we'll print that one!'*

She turned a corner, heading away from the Wall, driving without obvious haste but keeping up a steady speed. Behind them a miniature searchlight beam stabbed along the Wall from the nearest watchtower, ranging back and forth uncertainly. An amplified voice began to call orders in German.

Five minutes later, when that section of the Wall was buzzing with activity and far behind them, they abandoned the laundry van in a poorly lit side-street off Prenzlauer Allee. Willie had stripped off his overalls and was in his Jorgensen guise. Modesty had taken off the head-scarf and sweater, and was his secretary again. They walked out into Prenzlauer Allee and turned towards the cinema car park where she had left the Skoda.

When they were in the car with the doors closed, Willie leaned back luxuriously in his seat, hands resting on the wheel, utterly content, smiling dreamily. 'Psalm Eighteen, Verse Ten,' he murmured. *'Yea, he did fly upon the wings of the wind.'* He picked up her hand and touched it to his cheek for a moment. It was his salute to her, his accolade.

She gave an aggrieved sigh. 'You don't love me for myself, Mr Jorgensen. Just for my nutty ideas.'

He shook his head. 'It worked. It was a cracker . . . a genuine twenty-two-carat masterpiece.' He chuckled exuberantly and his voice changed to a hoarse, strident whisper, a muted impression of a ring-master. 'Ladie-ees and Gentle-*men*! We now present to you! For the first time anywhere in the world! That Mighty Midget, that Brilliant, Breath-taking Bacteriologist ... *Professor Okubo — the Human Cannonball!*'

He choked and hunched forward. She had rarely seen him so delighted. She said, 'For God's sake forget it and think Jorgensen for the next twenty-four hours, Willie love. We'll be out by then.'

He nodded, controlling the rich and joyous emotion that bubbled within him. 'Out,' he said. 'That's what I want, Princess. I got to 'ave room to laugh.'

Three days later Tarrant sat in the Minister's Office once again. Waverly was in excellent humour. He said, 'Fraser reported that you'd got the man out safely, but he gave no details. Congratulations, Tarrant.'

'There were no important details to give at the time,' Tarrant said. 'And now I'm afraid you're going to be disappointed. The man wasn't Okubo.'

Waverly stared. 'I beg your pardon?'

'It wasn't Okubo. The first thing I did was to check identification. That took forty-eight hours, since we had to get hold of someone who knew Okubo personally.'

Waverly looked very shaken. 'And ... it wasn't him? I don't understand.'

'Okubo is still in Russia, and always was. The man who purported to defect was a Japanese agent called Yoshida, working for Major-General Starov. A put-up job. Starov banked on the fact that most Japanese look more or less alike to us, as we do to them, no doubt. He set up the whole thing to tempt us, hoping that we'd activate our sleeper network and expose it to Yoshida.'

'Oh, my God,' Waverly said softly.

'Yes. We'd have been wiped out there. Fortunately I didn't activate the network. I was able to make unofficial arrangements with two friends of mine who have some expertise in these matters.'

'Friends of yours?'

Tarrant allowed himself a small smile. 'I do have friends, Minister.'

'I didn't mean that. I meant—'

'I can't tell you who they are,' Tarrant cut in crisply. 'They aren't employed by us, and they weren't hired.'

Waverly gazed at him. 'I find this very baffling. People don't risk their necks for nothing.'

'It's unusual,' Tarrant agreed, and left the point. 'They came to suspect Okubo when their first escape-plan failed. He refused to go through with it at the last minute and kept pressing for a large-scale plan. If they had known for certain that he was an imposter, they would simply have killed him, because our liaison man who runs a safe-house there was already exposed. But there was no way to have Okubo identified, so they got him out.' Tarrant paused for Waverly to absorb the implications, then added, 'Fortunately he killed himself with a cyanide pill soon after we'd had him identified in West Berlin.'

Waverly realized that this last part might or might not be true. The man could not be held indefinitely, and as long as he was alive the safe-house and its agent were at risk. If Yoshida had not in fact killed himself, then Tarrant had seen to it. Waverly felt an inward chill, and for the first time realized with sharp clarity the awful and inexorable burdens of Tarrant's job.

He said, 'I must apologize to you. I made a serious error of judgement in the instructions I gave you.' Tarrant inclined his head in acknowledgement, and Waverly went on, 'How the devil did these two get the man out? He certainly wouldn't cooperate, and they could hardly do it *without* his cooperation.'

'They're very resourceful. They rendered him unconscious and shot him over the wall from a cannon.' Tarrant's face held no expression.

Waverly looked blank, then incredulous, then angry. Tarrant had been more than generous, but a Minister of the Crown could not be subjected to insolence. 'I asked you a serious question, Tarrant,' he said sharply.

'They shot him out of a cannon,' Tarrant repeated. 'Over the Berlin Wall. One of those Human Cannonball things they sometimes have in circuses. We caught him with a net.'

After twenty seconds Waverly said, 'Good God,' and began to laugh. Tarrant warmed to him, but prepared to exact the mild retribution he had planned. 'The performance wasn't entirely free, Minister,' he said. 'There are expenses. I shall want something from the Special Fund, as promised.'

Half an hour later, at a parking meter off Whitehall, Tarrant got into a Jensen and sat down beside Modesty Blaise. Once again he was intrigued by the fact that on her return from a situation of high danger she always looked younger, quite ridiculously young. He thought that perhaps this was how she had looked on the day Willie first saw her, when she was barely out of her teens.

She said, 'Willie sent his thanks for the lunch invitation but asked to be excused. He's gone away to forget his sorrows.'

'His sorrows?'

She smiled, almost giggled. 'He's very upset. This was the richest, funniest, most gorgeous caper he's ever known. But Yoshida ruined it. He killed the gag. Wrecked the giggle.'

'I don't quite follow.'

'Neither do I, quite. But then I'm not English and not a Cockney, so I don't always grasp the subtleties of Willie's weird sense of humour. I can only quote him.' Her voice sank to a deeper pitch and became gravelly, in imitation of Willie. 'Shooting a big-'eaded, bloody-minded little Jap bug-expert over the Wall, that's one thing, Princess. But Yoshida was just a Commie agent, and that takes all the bubbles out of it.' Her voice became normal. 'He's annoyed on my account. He takes the view that Yoshida ruined my punch-line.'

Tarrant reflected. 'Yes, I do see his point. Vaguely, perhaps, but I see it. Poor Willie.'

She was looking at him with an inquiring smile, and he remembered the little bunch of violets he was carrying. 'With my love,' he said, and presented them to her.

'Why, thank you. They're beautiful.'

'I could think of nothing else,' Tarrant said. 'The point is, they have a rarity value. They're not really from me, they'll be paid for out of the Special Fund. It's difficult to get money out of the Special Fund at any time, because the PM has to approve, but getting twenty thousand pounds would be easier than getting two shillings, which is what I've put in for. Waverly wanted to give me two shillings out of his pocket, but I wouldn't have it. I wish you could have seen his face.'

She laughed, and put her lips briefly to Tarrant's cheek. 'They're just what I've always wanted. I'll ask for a vase when we get to Claridge's. You hold them while I drive.' She started the Jensen and backed from the meter.

Tarrant said, 'How is Willie forgetting his sorrows?'

'With Mavis. He's flown to Jersey for a long weekend with her.'

'Mavis?'

'I haven't met her, but according to Willie she's a very tall showgirl with more and bigger curves than you'd think possible on any human being. Mentally as thick as two planks, but unfailingly cheerful and bursting with enthusiasm. He says it's like going to bed with four girls and a cylinder of laughing-gas. I think she's just the sort to take him out of himself.'

Tarrant sighed, baffled. You're a woman, and Willie is a part of you,' he said. 'Why on earth aren't you possessive about him?'

He saw humour touch her face. 'I suppose it's just the pattern,' she said patiently. With her eyes still on the road ahead she grinned suddenly. 'But if Mavis ever starts shooting people over the Berlin Wall with him, I might feel like bouncing some of those curves off her.'

Tarrant laughed. He felt very happy. It had started to rain, but for him the sun was shining today. 'I don't suppose it will ever come to that,' he said.

I HAD A DATE WITH LADY JANET

~

WE were pretty busy in The Treadmill that evening. At least it seemed that way to me, though Doris said it was about average, and she knows best. I'm an absentee landlord half the time.

Charlie had a night off, so I was helping Doris behind the bar. About ten o'clock I saw Lady Janet come in. She was wearing a lime-green trouser-suit, and it looked very nice against her short chestnut hair. She always wears slacks of some kind, because of her leg. She took her usual stool at the end of the bar, and I put out two glasses and opened a bottle of claret.

I had a date with Lady Janet that night. She's Lady Janet Gillam. You don't just call her Lady Gillam, because being the daughter of an earl she holds the title in her own right, not by marriage. So it's Lady Janet Gillam, with the first name thrown in.

She's Scottish, and she's my steady when I'm home at The Treadmill, which is a bit surprising seeing that I'm a roughneck Cockney. Still, we get on fine. She's thirty, and somewhere between good-looking and beautiful, with a nice figure and no spare fat. She works too hard for that.

By all accounts, especially her own, she was a swinging hellraiser as a debutante. Drove fast cars, flew Daddy's private plane, threw crazy parties, all that sort of thing. Then she married a Walter Mitty type called Gillam, who decided to be a rich farmer. He started off rich, and in two years he was a poor farmer. Then he went on the bottle, and crashed the car not far from The Treadmill one night. That was some years before I took it over. Janet was in the car with him. Gillam ended up dead, and she lost half a leg, which is why she always wears slacks.

But this is the thing. When she came out of hospital with a tin leg from the knee down, she didn't go home to Daddy Earl or ask him for help or money. The ex-swinging kid set her teeth into running that farm, and she turned it into a little goldmine. I like them with guts.

I don't think she even thought about men until two or three years ago, when I turned up on the scene, and even then we just said a polite 'Good evening' to each other for about a year before anything developed. She told me later she'd written herself off for men. She reckoned that with half a leg gone she wasn't the sort a man would want to take to bed unless he was a kink or after her money. She knows now I'm a million miles from both, but it took a little while before she could really believe that I liked the ninety per cent of her that was left much better than a hundred per cent of most girls.

Come right down to it, I admire her in a big way, so what difference does the leg make? You'd be pretty stupid if you only admired people who hadn't got hurt in a lousy accident.

What started us getting together was when I found out some small-time protection mob had moved out into the country a bit and started picking on easy-looking marks. Lady Janet was one of them, and when she stuck her heels in they began the kind of trouble that could have ruined the farm.

So I stuck my nose in. Went to see her and told her I'd sort it out. It seemed the neighbourly thing to do. She was pretty snooty at first, but I could see that underneath she was close to breaking. When she realized I meant it, she cried for about five seconds before she could get hold of herself. Then she was worried that I'd get hurt, and I had to explain that I wasn't really a beginner at sorting out trouble.

It wasn't much of a caper, really. I went and saw the top man, who wouldn't have rated seventh in most of the mobs I'd known. I didn't lower the boom on him right away. After the years I spent working for the Princess, I reckon to be better on technique than that. I just told him to lay off, or else.

So of course he sent his strong-arm boys in, to do me. There were three of them, and I put them in hospital, and then I went back to the boss-man and brought him to the farm, out cold in the boot of a car. He was fat and flabby. and I made him work like a slave, shovelling muck from dawn to dusk for a month, sleeping on straw in a locked out-house.

It nearly killed him, and it certainly changed him. A week after I let him go there was a lot of rain, and Janet got a letter from him saying please excuse the liberty, but her ladyship ought to keep an eye on the culvert at the south end of the valley bottom, because it got blocked easily and might cause flooding.

Anyway, during that month I had to stay on the farm to keep tabs on him. I started off in one of the cottages, but at the end of the week I moved into the farmhouse with Lady Janet, and we found we suited each other fine. There aren't any strings either way, and we both know there never will be. Now she's got over feeling bad about the leg, I hope one day she'll meet some nice bloke and marry again. I'll miss her a lot, so maybe I hope it won't happen too soon.

This night I'm talking about, I'd only been back from the States for three days and it was the first time I'd seen her since getting back. We'd fixed a date by phone, and when the pub closed we were going to drive up to town, see a late movie, then go on to a club. Nightclubs leave me cold, but they make quite a change for Janet these days, and now that trouser-suits are OK anywhere she can enjoy that sort of evening out.

We chatted a bit about the farm and what I'd been doing in the States, and then about ten minutes before closing-time Doris came up and said a gentleman at the other end of the bar was asking for me. I excused myself to Janet, and moved down the bar.

He was about thirty-eight, in a nice suit, no overcoat, with grey eyes and sandy hair going a bit thin. He had a long upper lip and a funny down-turned smile. I felt a sort of bristling at the back of my neck, because this one was dangerous. I gave him the nice cheery grin I save up for that kind, and said, 'What can I do for you?'

'I'd like a private word with you, Mr Garvin. My name's Fitch.' It was a very soft voice, a touch of Irish in it overlaid by something American. The American bit was intonation more than accent, the kind of thing you can pick up if you live over there a while. I registered the accent as one I might use sometime. I can do most voices, from BBC to Nashville, Tennessee, and I've often used them on capers, but for everyday I stick to Cockney because that's the natural me.

I said to Fitch, 'If it's private, we'd better 'ave a chat in the sitting-room.'

I told Doris to take care of closing-time, then let Fitch through the bar flap and led the way along the passage at the back. When I took over The Treadmill I had the living quarters fixed up very nicely. There's a kitchen, office and big sitting-room on the ground floor, and two bedroom suites with bathrooms and dressing-rooms upstairs. I needed the second suite for when the Princess stays with me sometimes.

I hadn't bothered to ask Fitch what it was all about, because I was damn sure he wasn't selling insurance or a new kind of bottle-opener. And I was right. When I closed the sitting-room door and turned round he had a gun in his hand, a .44 Magnum.

I stood where I was and said, 'You can get 'urt carrying one of those things.'

He said easily, 'Let's sit down. The gun's just in case you blow your top before I've finished spelling things out for you, Garvin.'

I chose an upright chair, because you can get moving from it quicker than from an armchair. Fitch did the same thing. He was confident, but not over-confident. And he wasn't feeling big just because he'd got a gun in his hand. Fitch was a pro, and the gun was his tool. I'd already tagged him as dangerous, and now I shoved the grading up a notch or two.

There are dangerous soft men and dangerous hard men. Fitch was hard. Take his gun away, and he wouldn't just fold. Break his arms and he'd keep coming at you with his teeth. I knew the type. They're rare, but Fitch was one of them.

He said in that soft voice with a bit of a lilt, 'I'm working for Rodelle. He sent me to pick you up.'

That was a laugh, so I laughed, and said, 'Rodelle sent you? Then you must be the first bloke to find a way back from hell.'

'Rodelle's not dead,' Fitch said. 'Only half dead, from the waist down. It was a long fall, I'm told.'

That made me think. There didn't seem any percentage for Fitch in lying about this, so suppose he was telling the truth? If Rodelle was alive, I wasn't pleased to hear it. I've known some nasty pieces of work, but they don't come any nastier than Rodelle. He was a Levantine, and he'd been in the flesh game, selling girls in South America, Saudi Arabia, and anywhere that he could get a good price.

Don't ever think that sort of thing went out with silent movies. It still goes on, and it's easier than you'd think. The experts who specialize in breaking in the girls before they're placed in red-lamp houses would have made Caligula throw up.

About three years before the Princess closed down The Network we tangled with Rodelle. He had a biggish mob, and they snatched a girl we used for smuggling diamonds. That's all the Princess needed. She'd hated Rodelle's guts for a long time. We got the girl back, and the Princess decided it was time for Rodelle to be put down. Call it murder if you like. I'd put it under Good Works.

I've heard Modesty called a ruthless killer. That's a load of old cobblers. She didn't just run the smartest organization since crime began, she ran the cleanest. Sometimes it seemed we spent more time breaking up dirty mobs than bringing in loot. And I remember we passed up a fifty-grand job once, because we couldn't figure a way to do it without a couple of fuzz getting hurt. Certainly she's signed a few people off, but it's always been the kind of bastard whose going leaves the world smelling a lot sweeter. Like Rodelle.

We went over to Istanbul to take care of him, just the Princess and me. She never sent any of the boys on that sort of thing. This caper turned out tough, and ended up as a minor pitched battle in a warehouse, against Rodelle and half a dozen others. I killed Rodelle myself. At least, I put a knife between his ribs from thirty paces, when he was firing down from a catwalk, and he fell fifty feet on to concrete, which seemed good enough.

Then we beat it back to Tangier. Rodelle's organization folded, and that was that. But now here was this Fitch, just the sort Rodelle would have working for him, telling me Rodelle was alive. And Fitch knew about the fall, too. He was just looking at me, waiting. His eyes were light grey and shallow, with no depth to them. I said, 'Yes, it was a long fall. If he's only 'alf dead, he was lucky.'

'He's been paralysed from the waist down ever since,' Fitch said. 'That's why he wants to see you, Garvin.' He smiled that down-turned smile. 'I don't think he's had much else on his mind in all that time.'

'He could've spent some of it thinking about a few thousand parcels of flesh he's sold,' I said. 'Where is he?'

Fitch shook his head. 'Later, Garvin. If I told you that now, it might make my job very difficult.'

I looked at the gun. 'You reckon I'm going to go along quietly just because you're 'olding that?'

'No.' He smiled a bit more. 'Because Rodelle has Modesty Blaise.'

That got me like a boot in the stomach. I gave him a grin. 'As easy as that?'

'It's always easy when they're not expecting it. We could have taken you the same way. But Rodelle wants you on the hoof, walking in with your eyes open.'

That figured. From what I knew of Rodelle, he'd never stick a knife in without twisting it. Fitch reached for the phone and pulled it towards him. He dialled a number, and right then I hated the Trunk Dialling System. He dialled more than seven digits, which meant it was a call outside London, but he didn't have to ask for any exchange, so I learned nothing.

He looked at his watch and said, 'They're expecting this call.' After a few seconds he said into the phone, 'I'm with him now. Put her on.' He laid the phone down on the table and pushed it across to me. I picked it up. She said, 'Willie?' It was her all right, nobody could fool me with an imitation of her voice.

I said, 'Where?' That's what I had to know. She came back quick. 'Don't know. *But don't go along with it, Willie*—' Then her voice was smothered. After a second or two a man's voice came on the phone, a voice with an accent. I didn't know it well enough to recognize, but I didn't have any doubts that it was Rodelle. I've never heard a voice so crawling with hate. He just said slowly, 'That was bad advice. Fitch will tell you what happens if you don't come, Garvin.' Then he cut the connexion.

As I put the phone down Fitch said, 'Rodelle has her. He's expecting us at a certain hour. If we don't arrive by then, he puts his experts to work on her.' He let it sink in, then stood up and slipped the gun into a shoulder holster. 'I guess that holds you better than a gun.'

They had it all weighed up just right. Anybody who knew the Princess and me could lay a million to one that I'd go along, even without an escort.

I stood up and said, 'I'll get me jacket.' I felt sick, and I reckon I looked it now. I was letting it show, to make Fitch feel easy. My jacket was on the back of another chair. I picked it up, tossed it in Fitch's face, and followed up. I gave him stiff fingers in the solar plexus and a chop under the ear as the jacket fell away from his head, then caught him as he went down. I chucked him over my shoulder and went out of the back door.

It was dark and quiet. There's a fair bit of ground between the pub and the river, with a brick path leading to what I call the gym, though it's more than that. It's a long brick building with no windows, or rather fake windows, and a special double door. There's a pistol range, a short archery range, a combat dojo, gym equipment, and showers. The whole building is soundproof. At the far end, separate, there's my workshop where I do a lot of fiddling around with electronics and micro-engineering.

I carried Fitch in and locked the outer door, then tied his hands behind him and took the gun away. I'd got to find out where the Princess was, and I knew the only way to do it was to break this bastard fast. Given time, I might have eased it out of him with scopolamine, but I didn't have any around and I didn't have time either.

Making someone talk has never been my line. And Fitch was tough, not just on the surface but deep down. If I thought about what Rodelle's experts would do to the Princess I suppose I could have got busy on Fitch without too much sweat, but even that was no good. I've been worked on myself, once with a hot iron, and you can ride the pain till it knocks you out. Fitch was the kind who'd do that. Or more likely still, he'd talk but lie—and there wasn't time to chase after false leads. I had to break him from the inside, so when he talked he gave the right answers.

I fetched a coil of rope, climbed one of the gym ropes and ran the end of the coil through a big pulley in a beam that ran across the gym. I dropped down, made a small bowline noose in the other end, and forced it over Fitch's head. Then I brought a chair from the workshop and stood it under the pulley.

Fitch was beginning to come round. While he was still half senseless I pulled on the rope and dragged him to his feet. After about ten seconds, when he could stand without his knees buckling, I heaved on the free end of the rope again. The chair was right beside him, and the only thing he could do was climb up on to it. He stood there swaying, head twisted, eyes sticking out, sweating cobs in case he overbalanced. I made the end of the rope fast round a wall-bar, keeping it taut, then went and stood in front of him, looking as vicious as I knew how.

'You stupid bloody fool,' I said, not loud, but cold and mean. 'You reckon I'm sucker enough to think it'd help Modesty Blaise if I let you take me in on a lead? I'm going to find Rodelle. In twenty minutes I'll 'ave contacts in London, Liverpool, Glasgow and Cardiff on the job. He's off 'is own turf, and they'll find 'im. It'll be too late

to 'elp, but not too late to kill the bastard. And you, Fitch
. . . you just stay 'ere and swing.'

I tipped the chair so he slipped off, then set it down
and went for the door at a run. There's a four-foot space
between the two doors, so I could look through the crack
of the inner door and see Fitch. There was no drop to
break his neck, and the noose wasn't a slip-knot, so he
wouldn't strangle right away. I could see him with his
head strained sideways, neck muscles standing out, body
swinging a bit, trying to get a foot on the chair I'd left
close alongside. I reckoned he'd make it, so I went quietly
out of the second door and ran up the path to the car park.

Doris had closed the pub and there was only one car left,
a Jaguar XJ6. It was locked, but that only stopped me for
about ten seconds. In the back I found a pair of handcuffs
bolted to the bodywork on a short bit of chain. They were
for keeping me quiet when we got near journey's end.

I walked back to the gym, opened the outer door and
went through the inner door at a run, heading for the
workshop at the far end. It was only when I was past
Fitch that I braked hard and turned to look at him, showing
a bit of surprise. He was standing on the chair, up on his
toes, leaning at an angle, his breath rasping like a saw
going through plywood. His face was reddish blue, the
flesh swollen. And his eyes weren't shallow now, there
was plenty of depth in them, and it was all fear.

I said, 'You must've stretched an inch or two, Fitch.'
Then I walked over and tilted him off the chair again. He
managed to croak, '*Listen—!*' But then the rope cut him
off. He hung there, swinging, his mouth working as if he
was trying to talk. I started to move away with the chair,
then stopped as if I'd had second thoughts. I said, as if I
was screwed up tight with hate, 'All right . . . you can
'ave it the slow way if that's what you fancy.' Then I put
the chair down close to his feet again.

I went through the door into the workshop and began putting a few things in a grip. I packed two or three knives, a Colt .32, which is one of the two guns the Princess likes best, some medical stuff, and an assortment of gadgets that I thought might come in useful. When I came out, Fitch was on the chair again, but he was shaking and wobbling, fighting for balance. It wouldn't last long. I walked past him and said, "Ave a good time.'

His voice sounded like a chronic bronchitis case whispering, but he managed to get it out. '*Garvin! Wait! They've got her in Glencroft Castle . . .*' His mouth kept moving but he'd run out of air. I walked back to him, slow, grabbed the back of the chair again and said, 'You lying sod.'

He heaved in a great whooping breath, his face all mottled. If you can scream in a whisper, that's how it came out when he said, '*God's truth! Glencroft Castle . . . Inverness!*'

I knew it was true. He hadn't even tried to bargain, because he didn't think I'd give him time. He'd just told me, and now he was looking at me with mad eyes, hoping for the best, begging for it. I said as if I couldn't believe it, 'You were supposed to take me to Inverness?' He tried to nod, nearly lost his balance, and croaked, '*All-night drive. Due tomorrow . . . noon.*'

So that was the deadline. It figured OK in terms of time and distance. And Fitch was in no shape to work out any nicely turned lies. I went to the wall-bar and united the rope. He fell off the chair and lay heaving and gasping. I opened the bag and took out a hypodermic. He didn't even try to move when I pushed his sleeve back and gave him a shot. Three grains of phenobarbitone. He'd be out for hours.

It hadn't been pretty, but he'd come out of it with a whole skin, and I reckoned he ought to be thankful for that.

I went to the phone in the workshop and rang Weng, Modesty's houseboy. He told me she was down at her cottage in Wiltshire. I told him different. It shook him a bit. I gave him a quick rundown on what was happening and told him to come down fast and take charge of Fitch.

Weng wouldn't make any mistakes. He had Modesty's keys to the gym. He'd truss Fitch up till only his nose was showing, then sit with a gun stuck under that for a week if need be.

When I rang off I picked up the bag, went out, and walked back to the pub. Lady Janet was in the sitting-room, looking through a magazine. As I came in she said in that soft burring voice, 'And what happened to your friend, then?' She looked up, saw my face, and stood up so quick you'd never have known she had a gammy leg. 'What happened to you, for God's sake?'

I was getting out Ordnance Survey maps and a guide-book. I said, 'Sorry Jan. The date's off. I got big trouble.'

Castle Glencroft was in the guide-book. It was described as a fortified house and only rated three lines, so I knew it wasn't very big, probably one of those old mansions with a castellated roof.

Lady Janet said, 'Is it Her Highness?'

That's how she always spoke of Modesty. Before they knew each other there used to be a bit of acid in it, but they've met quite a few times when the Princess has been staying with me, and I think they got on pretty well. Janet still spoke of 'Her Highness', but it was just a sort of joke now, with no needle in it.

I said, 'She's been grabbed, Jan. An old grudge and a bad one. They're the kind of men you've never even met in nightmares, and they've got her at a place called Glencroft Castle. At noon tomorrow they'll start taking her apart.'

That must have raised a lot of questions, but Janet didn't ask any. As I went to the phone she limped across and put a hand on my arm and said in a quiet voice, 'She's good at looking after herself, surely.'

I didn't need telling that. She'd look after herself all right if she could see them coming, but this was different. I told Janet so while I was looking up Dave Craythorpe's number. Dave has a Beagle Pup that he keeps at White Waltham, not very far from The Treadmill. He's done quite a few flying jobs for us. I was praying that he was at home, and available, or if not, that I could borrow his Beagle to fly myself up to Glasgow.

The phone kept ringing. Janet said, 'Who are you trying to get, Willie? And why?'

I told her. She put her hand on the phone-cradle and cut me off. 'There's Daddy's Beechcraft Baron at Heathrow,' she said. 'He came down on Tuesday and he's still in town. I'll fly you up to Glasgow myself, Willie.'

Jesus! Good old Daddy Earl. I didn't ask if he'd let her borrow the plane because I had an idea she wasn't going to bother about permission. Nobody at Heathrow would stop her, not when she gave them that look with ten generations of earls behind it. And the Beechcraft could do 225 mph against the Beagle's 120.

I put my arms round her and kissed her as if I meant it, which I did. She smelt fresh and cool, and she was good to kiss. Then I rang a Glasgow number and this time I got through right away. Wee Jock Miller said, 'Aye?' and I told him I wanted a good car waiting at Glasgow Airport from 2 am onwards. He just said 'Aye, Willie,' and we rang off. Jock had a Network pension because a bullet wound had cost him the sight of one eye, and he ran a garage in Glasgow now. He'd never talked much, but if he said, 'Aye,' then you could stop worrying.

Janet said, 'I was inside Castle Glencroft once when I was a wee thing. It's no more than a big house, Willie, north of Loch Shiel and nothing for miles around.' I told her I knew there was a phone laid on, so I reckoned the place was still habitable. I was moving about the room opening drawers, repacking the bag, taking a few things out, putting a few in. Janet didn't blink as she saw the gear. She'd picked up quite a bit about Modesty and me, and I suppose she'd guessed quite a bit more.

'The family lived there till a few years ago,' she said. 'Then they moved out. I don't know if they sold Glencroft, but likely enough they couldn't. Maybe whoever's there now rented it for a while.'

That sounded about right. I zipped up the bag. While Janet was getting the car out I went upstairs and changed into black denims. There were twin sheaths stitched inside the breast of the denim windcheater, and I slipped a knife into each sheath.

I felt cooler now, and I didn't go mad driving to Heathrow. Fitch was supposed to bring me in by noon. If we didn't arrive then, Rodelle would start work on the Princess. But now, with any luck we'd be in Glasgow by two-thirty and I'd reach Glencroft Castle by four-thirty. That meant I'd have a few hours of darkness and all morning to clean things up.

At Heathrow we were lucky getting clearance for a quick take-off. Janet brought the Baron round on course, set the controls on auto-pilot and asked for a cigarette. She couldn't tell me much about Glencroft Castle, except that it was ringed by a high wall and built in a sort of E-shape with the middle stroke missing. One wing had been condemned years ago, and the family had lived in the other wing.

We didn't talk very much during the flight. I suppose Janet felt there wasn't much that could be said, and I was busy with a few mental tricks that stop you burning up all your juice with adrenalin fatigue. All I remember is that after a long time she said a bit uncertainly, as if she wasn't sure how I'd react,

'Willie . . . you think an awful lot of her, don't you?'

Well, I don't often try to explain this, because it can't be done, but I reckoned Janet was entitled to an answer. It's a long story, and I could only give her the bones of it, which don't mean much really. Most of my life I was a mean, stupid, twisted bum, who hated everything and everyone, and who was always in trouble. Then the Princess came along. She was only twenty then, but she'd been running The Network for two years and was already big-time. She picked me out of the gutter, or out of jail to be exact, gave me a job to do, and trusted me. It was like being melted down and remoulded. I came out of it . . . well, different.

Different? Try imagining something that's always lived in pitch dark, groping around at the bottom of the sea, and then suddenly it finds it can live in the open, in the air and sun. It was like that. Or like if suddenly you found you could take off and fly like a bird. It was that different.

When I'd finished blundering around with words, trying to explain all this to Janet, she sat thinking for a bit and then said slowly, 'I have an idea of what you mean, Willie. You're the only man I know who's . . . exhilarated all the time.' She looked at me. 'I see what she's meant to you. Maybe finding you has meant quite a lot to her, too.' She smiled then, a nice easy smile, and reached out to rest her knuckles against my cheek. 'All right. She's your Princess and you're her faithful courtier. There's plenty left, and I'll settle for that.'

We landed at two-thirty. Jock Miller had two cars waiting in the car park. I chose the E-type Jag and put my bag in. When I introduced Lady Janet to him, Wee Jock's scarred and wicked little face went dull red with pleasure. I wouldn't say he's a snob, but he'd certainly swing a claymore for the aristocracy, providing they were Scottish. I told him Rodelle had got the Princess, and his eyes went ugly. He looked up at me from his five foot nothing and said, 'I'll borrow a razor an' come wi' ye Wullie.'

I said, 'You bloody well won't, Jock. It's got to be done sneaky, and one's sneakier than two. So you look after Lady Janet and get 'er fixed up at an hotel. I'll call you as soon as I can.'

I kissed Janet goodbye, and she hung on to me tight for just a second. Then I got in the car and drove off. In the mirror I could see the two of them looking after me until I turned out of sight.

The winter snows had gone and the roads were clear. I made good time up past Loch Lomond, and didn't lose a lot on the road through the Grampians. Then there was Rannoch Moor and the long curve round to Fort William before I took the minor road running north. Half an hour later I turned down a track leading to Glencroft Castle. It was nearly a mile away, but I drove with no lights. After about half a mile I pulled off the track into a little rocky lay-by, got the bag out, and went ahead on foot.

It wasn't four yet, and up north here I knew it wouldn't be dawn till well after eight. I was feeling nice and easy inside now. I'd got there, I'd got time in hand, and I'd got the initiative, which was the most important thing of all. As far as Rodelle knew, I was in a car with Fitch and had probably only just cleared the Midlands at this moment.

Glencroft was a miniature castle, as Janet had said, and there was a crenellated wall right round it, about thirty feet high. As the castle itself only had three floors, the wall was way out of proportion. But God knows why anyone had built the place there anyway. It didn't defend anything, except whoever was inside it. Still, with the clans always feuding, that had probably been the point.

I took a look all round the wall. There was one big main gate with spikes on top. It was newer than the castle, not more than a century old, of very solid timber, and locked or barred on the inside. The barbed wire reinforcing the spikes was newer still, not even rusty yet. The wall arched over the top of the gate, and the small gap was filled with these spikes and barbed wire. On the eastern side there was a small door set in the wall, again very solid, and barred on the inside.

I decided to go over the top, so I sorted out the stuff in the bag, put a selection of it in a small pack, and strapped this on my back. Then I took a length of knotted nylon rope with a grapnel at the end. The tines of the grapnel were sheathed in rubber, except for the tips. It hardly made any noise when I tossed it up and got it hooked over one of the crenels.

It was an easy walk up the wall. I was trying to think what they call the bits that stick up between the crenels. About four feet from the top I remembered they're called merlons. And at just about the same time I felt the rope give. The mortar holding the big stone that the grapnel was hooked on must have been weak and crumbly, because I could see this stone, about eighteen inches long and a foot thick, leaning over as it tilted out from the top of the wall.

Then we both fell. I'm not laying it on when I say I can take a twenty-five-foot fall on to turf without worrying too much. Falling is something I can do quite well, which isn't much to boast about. The smart bloke is the one who doesn't fall.

This fall had problems, though. I didn't want to land on my back, because I was wearing the pack with a lot of hardware in it. Another thing I didn't want was to have a hundredweight block of stone land on top of me, so I was fending this off as I went down — or rather trying to push myself aside from underneath it.

That was the last thing I remember for a bit. When I opened my eyes I felt cold as a deep-freeze except for my left shoulder, which was on fire. The block of stone lay a yard away, and it hadn't hit me. I hadn't landed on my back, either, because that didn't hurt. What I'd done was to dislocate my left shoulder. When I sat up and touched it, I could feel the lump where the bone was out of the socket.

Charming.

After a bit I stood up and leaned against the wall with my good shoulder, wondering. In some places my name carries quite a reputation, and I was wondering why. My own opinion of Garvin just then was that with a lot of help he might just about make the grade as a village idiot.

There was nothing I could do about the shoulder, not on my own, so I spent a little while wrapping the pain up in black velvet and shutting it away where it couldn't reach me. It's a mental trick, and it's one of about a million things I owe to the Princess. You don't learn it in an hour or a day. There's an old chap called Sivaji in the Thar desert north of Jodhpur who says he's a hundred and twenty-seven. I think he's a liar. He's a hundred and fifty if he's a day. The Princess sent me to him years back, and I spent two of the weirdest months of my life learning a lot of useful things.

After a while, when the pain was a long way off, I moved along the wall a few yards and tossed the grapnel up again. This time I put my weight on it for about five minutes before I started to climb. It's not all that funny, climbing with one hand and two feet, but it must be possible because I managed it. Then I dropped the rope inside the wall and climbed down.

Two minutes later I was at a window of the west wing, where a light was showing. The curtains weren't drawn and I could look straight into the room. A big fire was blazing in the old fireplace, and there were five men. Four sat at a table playing cards, with full ashtrays and half-full glasses. The fifth was Rodelle. He sat in wheelchair with a rug over his knees, a big brandy-glass in one hand, looking into the fire. I remembered him as a big man with a hard brown face. He was still big, but his face was yellow and the flesh had gone from it now, leaving it shrunken and taut. It was as if some acid had been eating away for years inside his skull. And I suppose it had.

The other four were just the kind I expected, variations of Fitch. That sort cost money, but they're worth it to a man like Rodelle. I wasn't surprised that they were up and playing cards at this hour. Rodelle was always a night owl.

Immediately inside the window was a big grille with close-set bars. This wasn't new, so I guessed it was part of the fittings, and that these grilles were fitted inside all the ground-floor windows to prevent theft when the place was empty. I checked another half-dozen windows, and they were all the same. I thought it likely the upper windows would be free of grilles, but decided to have another look in the lighted room before I started climbing again.

When I got back to it I saw that one of the men had brought some plates and a big dish of thick sandwiches. Rodelle hadn't moved and wasn't eating, but the rest were. Then the door opened and a new man came in, herding the Princess ahead of him with a gun.

I felt my stomach jump like a trout. Her hands were behind her, and she wore the sweater and cord slacks she often wears for riding when she's down at Benildon. Her hair was a bit tousled and there was a bruise on her face, but she was all right. She walked in, cool as a model on a catwalk, and even in those old riding clothes she looked like something out of *Vogue*. Really, she's not all that big, about five foot six, but somehow she seemed a head taller than anyone in the room.

I got that funny little ache in the throat for a second, same as I always get when I see her again after a little while. The new man shoved her towards a chair by the table. When she turned round to sit down I saw that her wrists were tied with wire. Barbed wire. I could see dried blood on her hands and on the sleeves of her sweater.

I swallowed a big bubble of hate, and chalked that one up on the slate to be settled later. They put a plate with a door-step sandwich in front of her, and the new man said something. Rodelle moved for the first time, turning to watch. It was just the sort of thing he'd enjoy, watching her get her face down to gnaw at the sandwich like a dog. But it didn't bother me, because I knew it wouldn't bother the Princess. Food's energy, and that's a lot more important than pride when you're on a caper.

She bent and bit at the sandwich. It struck me that this was a good time for me to try the upstairs windows. If I could get inside and then down, I could see where she was taken when she finished eating. Now that I knew she wasn't under heavy sedation, I wanted to get her free of that barbed wire before starting a rumble.

It didn't improve my opinion of that genius Garvin to realize that one thing I hadn't got in the pack was a pair of pliers for wire cutting, so it was going to take a bit more than a trice to get her free.

Five minutes later I'd got the rope and grapnel from the outer wall and was standing under a window about twenty yards from the lighted room. On the second try I managed to get the grapnel hooked on the sill. I tested it well, then started up. Now and again the pain in the shoulder kept breaking through, and the arm itself was useless. But somehow I made the climb. Then I saw the bars of a grille inside the window. This didn't seem to be my night. I sat on the sill and felt cold, and suddenly I was sick. Next second a light went on in the room, and I got off the sill so fast I nearly fell. I hung by one hand, groping for the rope with my feet, and realized that I must have picked the room where the Princess was kept, and that the guard had just brought her back to it.

I eased myself up until I could look over the sill. The new man was just going out, and before he closed the door I saw the makeshift drop-bar fixed on the outside of it. The Princess was sitting on an iron bedstead with no mattress. There was nothing else in the room, except a wooden chair. I'll never know how I got up on the still again one-handed, but after about a hundred years I found myself sitting there.

The Princess had moved and was half squatting on the floor against the foot of the bed. She eased herself over as if she was doing a sideways roll. I realized she'd managed to wedge the plier-twisted ends of the wire into a crack of the bedstead, and was trying to untwist them. It wasn't surprising I'd seen blood on her hands if she'd been doing that for long.

I tapped on the window with a finger nail. Her head turned, then she got up and came towards me. Her face was almost against the bars as she stared out, trying to see me. Then she lit up suddenly with a smile. This one was a very special smile she's got, and you don't see it often, but I reckon it's what the Helen of Troy girl must have had when she got a thousand ships launched. It's a smile where her eyes dance and sparkle and laugh, warm as sunshine.

Then it was gone, with just the ghost of it left as she lifted an eyebrow at me. I got a glass-cutter out of my windcheater pocket, scribed a quadrant in a lower corner of the glass, and tapped it loose. She bent down to the hole, and I whispered, 'The grille?'

She whispered back, 'Hinged one side, padlock the other. Have you got a probe, Willie love?'

I'd got half a dozen probes. I spread them in my hand and reached through the hole and the bars. She turned round so she could get her hands to the probes, and took the one she wanted, then brought the chair, set it to one side of the window, climbed on it, and turned her back again to work on the padlock.

After about two minutes she climbed down from the chair and gave me a nod. I reached through the hole in the glass and pushed the grille. It swung inwards. She moved the chair, stood on it again, and managed to unfasten the casement catch. Ten seconds later I was inside.

Now that she could see me in the light she stared again, and this time she wasn't smiling. I suppose I'd lost a bit of colour and was hunched up on one side, because she whispered, 'You look like parchment—what have you done to your shoulder, Willie?' I started to tell her, but didn't get very far. It must have been the reaction from finding her OK that made me lose my grip on the pain, but suddenly the whole shoulder seemed to turn into raw acid. Everything went grey and whoozy, and I only just got to the bed before I passed out.

It was no more than a minute or two, I think, but when I came round I was lying on the bed on my back, with the pack off. The Princess's hands were still bound, but they were in front of her now. She'd managed to wriggle her bottom and legs through her arms; try it with barbed wire round your wrist sometime. She was at the door, listening. I could see her slacks were badly torn, and there was blood on her thighs now as well as new blood on her wrists.

She saw I'd come round, and whispered, 'He'll be back soon. They never leave me for more than ten minutes.' She moved quickly to the bed. 'Got to get that shoulder back in place first, Willie. Take another little nap for a few seconds.' Her hands went round my throat, not tightly, and I felt a little scratch on my chest from one of the barbs. Then her thumbs began pressing steadily on the two carotid arteries.

I didn't feel myself going, I just went. That's the way with a sleeper hold. I knew what she was going to do, and I was glad to be out of it for the next half-minute or so.

She was going to lie head to toe with me on the bed, put a foot in my left armpit, grip my wrist, and give a mighty heave to click the bone snugly back into the socket. And that's what she did. When I came round again, even after just that little time, it was like waking up in a new world. If you've ever had a joint put back in place, you'll know what I mean. The shoulder ached and was sore, but all the fire and pain from the stretched tendons had gone, and I could move it without too much trouble.

She was sitting on the edge of the bed, looking down at me, sort of half smiling but concerned at the same time. I'm eight years older than she is, but sometimes she makes me feel like a kid with a grazed knee who comes running to have it kissed better. I gave her a big grin, and it was a real one. Next second she was on her feet and moving towards the door fast. I must have been a bit dopey still, because I hadn't heard anything.

The door opened and the man came in, the man who'd brought her up here maybe ten minutes ago. He wore no jacket and there was a gun in his shoulder holster. I reached for a knife under the open windcheater. Besides falling well, that's another thing I can usually manage—drawing a knife and throwing it without a lot of time-wasting. Say about three-tenths of a second.

This time you wouldn't have needed a stop-watch, you could have timed me with a calendar. That left it to the Princess, her hands still bound with that bloody wire.

What happened next shows just how fast she thinks. She took off and went sailing at him feet first, but not in a dropkick because of the noise when he fell in the passage.

He was still moving forward, only just registering the situation, when her feet went one on either side of his neck and her whole body twisted so that she was face down in mid-air, his neck locked between her crossed shins, her feet turned in and hooked behind his neck. She held it as she hit the floor with her palms, getting some horrible punctures from the barbs, and in the same instant she ducked her head and went into a high-powered forward roll. The man at the end of her legs was whipped over the top of her as she rolled. He went flying head-first through the air, parallel to the bed, like a fishing-line flies after the rod when you make a cast.

He travelled about four feet while she held the grip, and another five feet after that. His head went straight into the solid wall just beside me with a quiet, nasty noise. My only contribution was that as I knew what was coming, I managed to swing both legs round, spread wide under his body, to break the fall after he hit the wall. At least it helped to make sure there was hardly any noise.

I heaved him off my legs and sat on the edge of the bed looking down at his head. It was unnaturally flat on top, like an egg hit with a spoon, and a trickle of blood was running through his hair. As the Princess came to her feet I said, 'If there's a vacancy for a ghost in the castle, this bloke's just qualified.'

'It was meant,' she said, then sat down beside me and held out her hands. When I looked at them I didn't blame her for meaning it. I got busy on the ends of the wire. They were twisted solidly together and I used the notch of the glass-cutter to work on them, slowly getting them untwisted.

It took a few minutes, and we talked in whispers. They'd picked her up in the stables at Benildon. She'd walked in and found three guns looking at her. They'd brought her up north in a car, drugged. She'd been here thirty-six hours now.

The wire came off at last. I got the little medical kit from the pack, put Usol on her wrists and bandaged them up. She stripped off her torn slacks and lay face down on the bed while I doctored the punctures and gashes in her thighs. I told her my side of things, and how I'd got up here so fast. We weren't wasting time. There was some work to be done soon, I needed to be in fair shape for it, and this little break while I patched her up was working wonders. With the shoulder in place and her free, I felt better every minute.

When I'd finished the first-aid bit she pulled on the slacks and said, 'Think of something pretty special I can do for your Lady Janet sometime, Willie.'

I told her I'd try, then said, 'What was Rodelle going to do?'

'It was you he wanted to get at,' she said in a kind of tired voice. 'The knife just missed killing him that night in Istanbul, but the fall crippled him. I think he's been eaten up by hate ever since. He's been planning this and relishing it.' We were sorting out the things in the pack, and she was buckling on the belt with the Colt 32, slipping the kongo into her pocket. I checked the knives in their sheaths under my windcheater. It was automatic. All I was thinking of was Rodelle, and wondering exactly what 'it' was that he'd been relishing.

'He wanted you to walk in here under your own steam,' she said. 'There are big cellars under the castle. He was going to put you in shackles, then have his experts get busy on me in front of you. He wasn't going to kill you. Being dead doesn't hurt much. He was going to hurt you for life, the best way he knew.'

I felt cold again. It wasn't the same sick cold, it was a deadly sort of cold.

She said, 'You were going to watch while his men did this and that to me. And at the end of it all they were going to use a whip till I was dead.'

I wiped the sweat from my face and stood up. I don't much fancy killing a man in a wheelchair, but I was going to kill Rodelle without any second thoughts at all. 'Let's get it over with, Princess,' I said.

Just for a minute I thought of Janet, and how she'd come back fighting after that lousy accident. Rodelle hadn't come back fighting, just hating. It had made him even less human than he'd been before, and I'd never have believed that was possible.

We went out of the room and along a broad passage to the head of the stairs. There wasn't any planning to do. We were just going to go into the room and get busy. Five men, including Rodelle. With that Colt the Princess could take three of them in about a second. I couldn't use my left arm comfortably yet, but even with one arm I could take the other two men with knives in about the same time.

The hall and stairway were poorly lit and I could see the crack of brighter light under the door where Rodelle and the others were. We'd got about halfway down the stairs when something went wrong, though we'll never know exactly how it happened. Maybe they heard a noise, maybe somebody had taken a walk outside and found the rope hanging from the window. Whatever it was, they knew the game had changed.

Suddenly the light in the hall went out. So did the light showing under the door. I think they shorted the circuit and blew the fuse. Next second the door was open and somebody was firing a sub-machine-gun at us.

Not exactly at us, he was firing blind, but near enough. We went back up those stairs like a couple of hares in overdrive. Down below I could hear Rodelle's voice shouting. It was shrill, more like screaming than shouting. Then torches came on, shining up the long curve of the stairs, but we were at the top by then.

House fighting in the dark is a dodgy business. It gives the edge to the side with the most firepower, and Rodelle's lot had that all right. The Princess hung over the balustrade at the top, trying to sight a torch to fire at, but we could only see the beams of light, not the torches. There came another burst of firing and we hopped back a bit smartly. The beams of light moved, and shone up from the foot of the stairs.

It was a nice piece of work. The torch-men were keeping out of the line of fire until we'd been driven back, or knocked off, by a spray-from the smg. As soon as we moved back, the torch-men advanced while the gunner moved forward in the dark. So we had no target.

I started wishing I'd primed the two grenades I carried in the pack, but until now there hadn't been much likelihood that we'd need them, and this wasn't the moment to start fumbling around. The gunner was moving up the stairs throwing a quick burst at intervals.

The princess touched me on the arm, and we ran. She said, 'Down and up behind them, if we can find the way.' It made sense. A slow retreat from a slow advance wasn't going to help us. Our best move was to go like the clappers while they edged forward, so we could get down by another staircase and then along the ground floor and up behind them. I still say it was the right move, even though it worked out so badly I might have thought of it myself.

There had to be another staircase, of course, and there was. But if I could find out the name of the mad Scot who built the small staircase at the end of west wing so that it by-passed the ground floor and went straight down to the cellars, I'd go and jump on his grave.

We went down. And down. I'd got my own torch out now, because there were no lights anywhere. From the sound of firing, the advance wasn't as slow as we might have hoped.

Then we went through a doorway, with broken hinges and no door, into a long damp cellar with arches of mildewed stone, inches of sodden dust, and all kind of debris, the sort of stuff you can't imagine was ever bought, or used, but which seems to be specially manufactured to fill cellars.

We slowed down a little and weaved between the stone piers, looking for one of the other doors that must lead up to the ground floor.

No door. We'd already turned the corner into the stretch of cellar that lay under the connecting hall, and soon we reached the next and last corner, where the other end of the hall joined the east wing. Still no door. We moved on, under the east wing. I stopped and shone the torch round slowly. Dampstained walls. Crumbling stone piers swelling to vaulted sections of ceiling. Dust. Cobwebs. Junk. No door. No trapdoor.

The Princess said through her teeth, 'Who built this bloody place?' It's not often she swears, but she was hopping mad now. I always want to laugh when she's like that. She doesn't lose her temper over someone like Rodelle setting his experts to work on her. It's always little things, female sort of peeves, that make her blow her top, like why the clown who built Glencroft Castle hadn't put a door there for us to get out of three hundred years later. Mind you, he wasn't my favourite builder either.

Quite suddenly there came a burst of firing that sounded much nearer, and I realized that Rodelle's men had reached the cellar door we'd come in by. The only door. They were still round two corners from us, but they wouldn't be long arriving now. I put the torch on the ground and began to prime the two grenades. I was by a stone pier, and the Princess was on one knee beside me. She'd gone dead calm again now. She pushed back a bit of hair that had fallen over one eye and just knelt there, the Colt in her hand, watching the right-angle turn of the wall where Rodelle's men would have to show up eventually.

In a funny sort of way I felt quite happy, like I always do when we're in a spot together. I've tried to figure why, but I can't. I certainly don't have any death-wish, just the opposite. Maybe it's because deep down I reckon that if the Princess is there we'll come out of it. That makes more sense than you'd think, because, Modesty's the great survivor, right from ever since she can remember. She's got a will to survive that's as hard as the Koh-i-noor diamond, and just as big.

Even now I was backing her to outshoot Rodelle's gunmen, if it came to that. But it didn't come to that. I had plenty of time to prime the grenades, because nothing at all happened for a while. It was only later that we found out why, and then it was hard to believe.

All we knew at the time was that they left us alone along enough for me to prime the two grenades. A lot longer, really, because it's not a big job. As soon as it was done the Princess gave me a nod. I wormed my way up to the angle of the wall while she covered me, then I edged half an eye round the corner.

All I could see was blackness, so I signalled and she came up beside me, bringing the torch but switched off now. For five minutes we just waited. Then we saw some light at the far end, by the other corner. Rodelle's men were moving forward slowly, dodging from pier to pier.

I felt Modesty snake away, and knew what she was going to do. It was about a minute later that her torch beam flashed out, lighting up the centre stretch of the cellar. There came a racket of firing, but I knew she was well away from the torch by then and taking cover behind the angle of the wall.

Not one bullet hit the torch, where she'd propped it on some crate or sixteenth-century headsman's block she'd found. But it wouldn't have mattered anyway, because in the first two seconds I'd seen all I wanted to - three men half hidden behind piers about twenty paces away, and a fourth darting between piers, a little nearer.

I pulled the pin from the grenade, counted three, tossed it so it fell a bit beyond where they were hidden, then ducked back. It made a nice impressive bang, and the shrapnel seemed to keep flying around for about ten seconds, ringing against the walls and the piers and screaming off in ricochets. What happened next was more impressive still.

The castle fell down. I must be one of the few men who ever knocked down a castle with a Mills bomb. Not exactly the whole castle, or the outer walls, but at least half the interior ground floor and quite a bit above that. It began slowly, with a weird sort of creaking as the echoes of the grenade faded.

That was when I remembered that we were under the wing that wasn't in use, the wing Janet had told me was condemned as unsafe. After the creaking there came a long rending crash as some big beam broke and fell, probably making about a million woodworms homeless. From then on it was like a house of cards collapsing as one bit of the cellar ceiling after another came down.

The dust was like a sand storm, and if the damp hadn't kept it down to some extent we'd probably have choked to death. I wasn't feeling happy any more, I was scared rigid. As soon as the first crash came I jumped up and went running from the corner, yelling 'Princess!' Don't ask me how I saw her, maybe it was because she'd run and grabbed the torch, which was another bit of fast thinking, but when I saw her she was lying huddled at the base of a wall pier, her arms wrapped round her head. I took one great dive and landed on top of her.

Afterwards I discovered that she wasn't hurt, at least not until I made that pancake landing which knocked all the breath out of her. I could hear her panting in my ear and I could feel her heart beating, which was a relief. I spread myself out over her as much as I could, and listened to the splintering of beams and the crunch of great stones as the castle came tumbling down. It went on slowly, in a kind of continuous process, for about two minutes. Then at last everything became quiet, and we were still alive.

From underneath me the Princess said, a bit muffled and gasping, 'I . . . don't want to disturb you, Willie love . . . but the torch is digging into my ribs.'

I rolled off her, and about five pounds of dust fell off my back. 'You're getting soft,' I said. 'It's like that story about the princess and the pea. She could feel it through twenty matresses.'

I heard her grunt and give a little laugh as she sat up. She groped around, found me, put her hand on my face for a moment, and said, 'Thanks anyway, Willie.' A moment later the torch clicked on.

We looked around. Whoever had condemned this east wing had only been half right. He should have double-condemned the whole hall between the two wings. Not a great deal had fallen close to us, but where the centre section joined the wing there was nothing but a great pile of stones and rubble with broken beams and joists sticking out of it.

The roof had certainly fallen in on Rodelle's men, which was a good thing. Not such a good thing was the fact that we were entombed. The Princes switched off the torch and we waited for our eyes to get used to the dark. After about five minutes she touched me and said, 'There, Willie.' I felt along her arm to find where she was pointing. Then I looked and saw it, a tiny crack of light, moonlight or starlight, coming in through a pile of debris that sloped up against the angle of the wall.

It took me an hour to make anything of that gap, and we spent most of it working on chunks of stone that Cheops could have used for building his pyramid. We had to handle them gently, edging them an inch at a time and then waiting to see what happened to the rest of the great heap before making another move.

Having a half-useless shoulder didn't help, but luckily I'm quite strong, and weight for weight I reckon the Princess is even stronger. I don't know where she packs it, because she certainly doesn't bulge with muscle.

At last we dragged clear a joist that was holding a pile of small rubble, and when the dust settled we could see our way out, a narrowing hole that wove up through the wreckage to the ground floor level. The light we could see seemed to be coming in through an uncurtained window there. The Princess looked at this horrible shaky tunnel for a while in the light of the torch, then she said, 'It's never going to get any better, so let's go.' We didn't argue about who was going to risk it first. At five stone lighter it made more sense for her to give it a try. She was just starting to crawl up the first bit of the slope when a voice from somewhere said, 'Please . . .'

It wasn't loud, but it was quite clear, and the echo in that cellar made the word hover in the air so creepily that my hair bristled. We froze. Then the Princess backed down and pointed. I swung the torch and we moved forward to where a great mass of wreckage had spilled forward at the point where the centre section joined the wing.

That's when we found that Rodelle was with us, and it explained the delay earlier. They'd spent time carrying him down those stairs at the far end in his wheel-chair, and when they advanced he must have trundled himself along the far wall of the centre section, the south wall. The only reason I can work out is that he wanted to see the end of it all. He'd missed out on his main idea, and he knew he'd never round us up alive, so he didn't want to miss seeing us killed. I suppose when the grenade went off he must have been forward of it, and covered by a pier.

At first when we saw him I thought he'd fallen through from the floor above, but he was pinned under a beam and he must have been below when the cellar roof fell in. The wheelchair had saved him. It was on its side, with him still in it, half buried under small rubble and with this beam lying across it. The chair was partly crushed, but it held the beam just enough to stop it squashing him. He looked a mess, but so did we all.

There it was, then. An hour before, we'd been out to kill him. Now we were looking at that beam and figuring how to get him free. Don't ask me why it works that way, it just does. He looked into the light with flat dead eyes from a face black with dust and said, 'Please,' again.

The Princess said, 'If you can crawl under that beam and ease it up a fraction, Willie . . .' So I did. It really creased me. I felt I was lifting the whole castle. She managed to get him by the shoulders and drag him out, his useless legs trailing. I lowered the beam the couple of inches I'd lifted it, then crawled out backwards. A second later there was a great crunch as tons of stuff settled down on the place where I'd just been.

I said, 'Christ!' and that was all the breath I could spare for a while. The Princess knelt holding the torch on Rodelle, and holding the Colt on him too. Nobody said anything. When I could move, I checked him. His shoulder holster was empty and there was no gun in his pockets.

The Princess put her Colt away and we looked at this crazy little tunnel again. I still had a coil of rope in the pack, but we couldn't just climb out and then drag him up. I didn't mind him taking the last and nastiest chance, but this tunnel through the wreckage wasn't a smooth slope up, it ran through a pile of tangled joists and blocks of stone, all very dodgily balanced.

Try to drag a crippled man up through that, and he'd get snagged every few feet. Increase the pull, and the whole lot would come down on him. I waited for the Princess to say what I knew she was going to say, and I felt my stomach shrinking to the size of a golf ball.

She said in a fed-up voice, sort of irritably, 'Oh, let's get on with it. You first, Willie. I'll go up with him and ease him over the snags.'

I'd have liked to argue, but it was no good. I'm that much stronger, and it had to be me hauling on the rope. I heaved Rodelle to the foot of the slope on his back, tied a bowline noose round under his armpits, then took the other end of the rope and went up that long, shaky hole. It was a petrifying trip. I could feel everything shuddering, including me. But nothing gave way, and I came out at last through a gap where floorboards were missing, on to a bit of solid flooring in the room above. Then I took up the slack of the rope very gently.

From below, the Princess called, 'Right, Willie.' I heaved very slowly, about an inch a second. After about half a minute she called, 'Stop.' Then I heard a scrambling and the rattle of little stones falling from way down the hole. It seemed to go on for hours, and I was scared spitless. I had to remember to breathe. She called, 'Right,' and I started the slow-motion heaving again. That's the way it sent on, start-stop-wait, as she eased him up that death-trap with creakings and groanings and little whispering falls of rubble that took years off my life.

At last I saw her head. She was on her back, with most of Rodelle's trunk on her legs. She had to be that way, to get him over the snags. Even then she didn't hurry, which made sense, but I had to dredge up all the control I could find to stop myself heaving like mad.

From start to finish it took ten minutes. Then she scrambled clear and I gave a last heave that dragged Rodelle out and on to the solid floor—I mean solid compared to the rest.

She said, 'I didn't like that much,' and wiped her filthy face with the sleeve of her filthy sweater. I was so relieved, and so sort of proud of her, I wanted to hug her till my muscles cracked. I got out a probe and unfastened the padlock on the grille over the window, then went and picked up Rodelle. Two minutes later we were outside, and we didn't stop moving until we'd crossed the space between the castle and the outer wall, I suppose you'd call it the bailey in a real castle.

I put Rodelle down, propped against the wall near the big gate, and started to draw the bars. The Princess said, 'Give me a few minutes, Willie,' and sat down cross-legged, hands resting on her knees, upright but relaxed. She started to breathe very slowly, eyes open but not seeing anything. I knew she was starting one of Sivaji's processes to ease the knots out of her nerves, and after all she'd been through I didn't wonder. If we'd been alone, without Rodelle, she'd have turned to me and had a little weep for a minute or so, and that would have unwound her completely. But she'll never do that unless we're alone.

I drew the bars, lit a cigarette and walked a few paces back towards the castle. From the outside it didn't look too bad, because the outer walls had held. There was a full bright moon, low down, and everything showed up clearly. It was six-thirty, still a long way short of sunrise.

Suddenly my ears prickled, and that's a sure sign of trouble. I swung round, and saw it like a tableau. Rodelle had a little gun in his hand, an automatic. He was sitting propped against the wall and he had the fist holding the gun resting on his left forearm at eye-level, taking very careful aim at the Princess, only six paces away, her back half turned to him.

Somehow I'd missed the gun when I'd checked him, and now he was going to kill her. Not me. Her. Because that was the thing that would crucify me.

I'm fast with a knife, but I've never drawn and thrown one as fast as I did then. It was only twenty paces, and I can split a matchbox sideways at that range, but I couldn't risk anything fancy.

I couldn't see his chest, because of the forearm covering it, but I could just see his throat over the top of the forearm. The first knife grazed his gun-hand and went straight into his neck. His hands jerked up with a shock, and a single shot whistled high towards the castle. I heard it break a widow just as the second knife thumped into his heart below the breastbone.

He fell over sideways with hardly any sound. I saw the Princess turn her head slowly to look, and I went across to Rodelle. The right leg of his trousers was rucked up almost to the knee, and there were two broad strips of plaster still half clinging to the side of his leg at about mid-calf.

The Princess was standing beside me now, her eyes a bit funny from her having been jerked back to normal just as she was starting to slow everything down. I pointed and said, 'The gun was stuck to 'is leg. Sorry, Princess.'

She said, 'You think I wouldn't have missed it?'

I didn't argue. I picked up Rodelle and we walked back to the Castle and climbed in through the same window. At the top of that hole the Princess had dragged him up, I pulled the knives out of his chest and throat. Being very dead, he hardly bled at all. I shoved him head first down the hole. He slid about six feet down, then jammed.

The wreckage creaked and groaned as I jumped about. But now we wanted it to collapse, it wouldn't. I got out the other grenade, pulled the pin, and tossed it down so that it bounced on Rodelle and then went rolling on below.

We didn't wait. We went out of that window like greyhounds out of a trap, and kept running. Five seconds later we heard the bang, then a lot of crashing and grinding. When it stopped, we walked back and looked through the window. The whole floor had fallen in. Rodelle was entombed with the rest of his friends, and I thought it likely they'd stay there a very long while, if not for ever. Nobody in their senses would want to start rebuilding Glencroft Castle.

We walked away, and out of the gate. A big old mounting block stood just to one side of it. The Princess said, 'Willie . . .' and turned to me. I put my arms round her, sat down on the mounting block with her on my lap, and held her close. She didn't make any noise when she cried. I could just feel her shaking a bit, and the tears making my neck wet. It's not often she does it after a caper, but this one had been a real nerve-twister, especially her part of it.

Now I felt the opposite of what I'd felt when she fixed my shoulder. It makes me feel about ten feet tall when she turns to me like that. I talked nonsense and made a bit of a joke now and again until she felt all quiet and relaxed in my arms. Then she sat up, borrowed my handkerchief, blew her nose, and grinned at me through the streaky mask of dirt on her face.

I said, 'Weng's sitting in the gym at The Treadmill with a cannon stuck in Fitch's ear.'

We got up and walked half a mile up the track to where I'd left the car. There were two cars now. Lady Janet Gillam was there, carrying a sporting rifle, and so was Wee Jock Miller.

Jock said, 'She was going to come an' ask for ye at sunrise. I could'nae stop her. If she wasn't out in ten minutes, I was to go an' bring the fuzz.' Well, in Bonnie Scotland the police would have come looking for Lady Janet Gillam fast enough, but I wouldn't like to bet they'd have found her alive.

The Princess said, 'Hallo, Janet. Thanks for all the help.' There was a lot more in her voice than just the words.

Janet gave her a smile, nice one, then looked at us both and said, 'Jock has showers at the garage. We'd best be moving.

The Princess said, 'I'll go with Jock,' and got in the E-type with him, leaving the Rover for Janet and me.

Janet said, 'Are you hurt under all that muck, Willie?' But her voice started shaking and she only just got it out. Then I saw some tears on her face. I was going to cuddle her up and tell her everything was all right, but I was coated in filth, so I stopped.

Janet said, her voice all up and down, 'Never mind the dirt, what the hell do you think she went on ahead for? We're not all made of teak and she could see I was going to cry, so hold me a wee while, Willie.'

So I did, which was the second time in about ten minutes. But I didn't tell Lady Janet that.

A PERFECT NIGHT TO BREAK YOUR NECK

~

'WE won't argue about this,' Stephen Collier said firmly, whisking the bill away before Willie Garvin could pick it up. 'If I have any trouble I shall invite you and that female bruiser to step outside with me and put your fists up.' He stared menacingly at Modesty Blaise.

His Canadian wife, Dinah, small and shapely with honey-coloured hair, said, 'That'll fix 'em, Tiger. How do they look?' Dinah had been blind since childhood.

'White-faced,' said Collier, counting notes on to a plate, 'Modesty's cringing and Willie's moistening dry lips.'

It was four days since the Colliers had come out from England to spend a few weeks with Modesty Blaise and Willie Garvin at the villa Modesty had rented on Cap d'Antibes. Tonight they had spent dining and dancing at the Boule d'Or, which lay a mile or two inland on the road to Biot. It was well past midnight now, and most of the guests had gone.

Modesty put down her glass and said, 'Don't be silly, Steve. You're on that idiotic travel allowance. This will make an awful hole in it.'

'But this isn't our travel allowance, darling,' Collier said as the waiter picked up the plate. 'When we left London my unscrupulous wife carried a little wad of currency secreted on her person in a manner she refused to disclose even to me, her master. Possibly it was in the soles of those Army surplus boots she favours for casual wear.'

'He said if they caught me he was going to swear he'd never seen me before in his life,' said Dinah. 'He's a cowardly bum, that's what.'

'Prudent, my pet, a prudent bum,' Collier amended. His eye caught two men as they moved across the restaurant to a door which led to the lounge bar. 'Hallo, there's the mad playboy.'

Caspar came bounding towards them. He was dark and wiry, with short cropped hair, a young but wrinkled face and darting brown eyes. He had appeared on the Mediterranean playgrounds of the rich quite recently, and had quickly become an accepted character. Caspar was at home in several languages, but since he spoke them all with a foreign accent nobody knew what his native tongue was. His conversation was confusing, being peppered with irrelevant exclamations and with foreign phrases often literally translated.

His companion, McReedy, made a strange contrast. A compact man, he looked no older than forty but was completely bald. His eyes were pale grey, set in a square humourless face. His whole manner made him the most unlikely companion for a playboy. He hung back a little now, halting and giving a stiff nod of greeting as Caspar rushed up to the table. Collier watched, intrigued. He had been introduced to the two men between boat and quayside, but that was all.

'Modesty, my old!' Caspar snatched up her hand and kissed it. 'I am possessed by a brilliant idea. Let us get married *tout de suite*, old bean. *Heiut! Oggi!* As captain of the *Delphine*, I will perform the ceremony. Tovarich Garvin shall be best man. God save the Queen! The *inglese* Collier can give you away, and his beautiful squaw lady shall be bridesmaid. Sacred bruises! We will honeymoon on the yacht. What say you, Contessa?'

'I don't quite know how to tell you this, Caspar,' Modesty said, 'but no'.

Caspar yelled with laughter. McReedy said to him stolidly, 'Matron of honour. Mrs Collier can't be bridesmaid. A married lady can only be matron of honour.'

Caspar rolled up his eyes. 'You have reason, brave,' he said soothingly. 'So we make another suggestion. Excelsior!' He turned to Modesty again. 'Come to my party tomorrow night. All of you. Best bibs and tuckers, by jingo. Everybody will be there. I wish to have a very scintillating affair.'

Willie Garvin grinned. 'Is it going to be like that party you 'ad on the Costa Smeralda?' he said.

Caspar beat his brow with the heel of his hand. 'The robbers! Ah, not that again! Sons of a bitch. But no. *Donner* and *blitzen* will not strike twice in the same place. Wear your gold sock-suspenders without fear, Willie, old fruit. God bless America !'

Modesty said, 'We'll let you know. A million thanks for the invitation, and *vive l'Empereur.*'

Caspar was convulsed. He released her hand and said, 'The good McReedy and I are having a drink in the bar. Join us when you are finished here, *bellissima.*' He turned away. McReedy said, 'You'll want to know the venue of the party, Miss Blaise. It's the Coromandel. Caspar has taken the terrace lounge overlooking the sea.' He inclined his head, then turned and followed Caspar.

'The venue . . .' Collier echoed wonderingly. 'What a magnificently stodgy word. How on earth does he make the same scene as Caspar?'

Modesty shrugged, 'Maybe Caspar employs him as a kind of stabilizer.'

'What happened at this party on the Costa Smeralda?' Dinah asked.

'A hold-up.' It was Willie who answered. 'The same mob have done three this year. They chose Caspar's party for this one. Usual ritzy bunch. Gilded youth, middle-aged ravers, ageing jet-set. Suddenly there's 'alf a dozen blokes wearing hoods. And with guns. They take a collection. Walk off with a tray-load of cash, gold accessories and jewellery worth nearly a hundred and fifty thousand quid. Disappear out to sea in a couple of fast boats.'

'And nobody stopped them?' Dinah said.

'One of Caspar's crew from the yacht was acting as bouncer to keep out gate-crashers. He tried, soon as the mob showed. Got shot in the leg. It made everyone else think twice.'

'It wouldn't have made me think twice,' Collier said reflectively. 'Or rather it would only have confirmed my first thought. The price of a whole skin is above rubies. My skin, that is. Our family crest is two white feathers, couchant, on a field of bilious yellow. Our motto, *Don't shoot, I'm coming out with my hands up*.' He glanced at Modesty. 'If we go to this junket, you'll have to take on the job of describing the dresses and their inhabitants for Dinah. I lack the vocabulary.'

Modesty smiled and said, 'All right. Willie?'

'I'm all for it, Princess.' He looked hopeful. 'I might find meself a bit of talent there. It's quite a while since I went trapping for mink.'

'It's three weeks,' said Modesty. 'What about that Italian sardine-canner's daughter?'

Willie shook his head. 'Squirrel, maybe. Not mink. But you couldn't fault 'er for effort.'

Collier laughed and said, 'Lechery most blatant.' He glanced round the restaurant. 'I notice the band has gone home, we're the only customers left, and the head waiter looks as if he's going to put his pyjamas on any minute. Shall we take the hint?'

Modesty nodded. 'Willie and I will go and tell Caspar we'll be along to his party. You and Dinah go on ahead to the car, then we'll have an excuse to get away from Caspar. Otherwise he'll keep us till the bar closes.'

'OK.' Collier got up. 'We'll see you in a few minutes.'

They had no coats, for the night was warm. A long dark drive ran down the side of the Boule d'Or to a car park area at the back. Collier strolled contentedly, holding his wife's arm. Then, for a moment, his contentment faltered as the grey problems at the back of his mind stirred restlessly. He wondered, with a sense of emptiness, how long it might be before Dinah would be able to enjoy herself again in the way she was enjoying herself now. They both knew that these few weeks were a last fling. The years ahead held little promise, except of pallid monotony. Perhaps he had been a fool to do what he had done . . .

He was suddenly angry with himself, realizing that he had come close to self-pity, and afraid that Dinah might sense his mood. He squeezed her arm gently and said, 'Happy, sweetheart?'

She nodded. 'It's good being with Modesty and Willie. I guess it's because we always feel right deep down at home with them.'

Collier said slowly, 'When you go through a pretty fair imitation of hell with people, and you're damn sure you're all going to die, I suppose personalities get stripped down to the bone. And then, if somehow you come through it and find you're still alive . . . well, you discover you've forged bonds that are a bit special.' He gave a little laugh to dispel any weightiness in his words. 'Like an Old Comrades Association.'

'Something like that,' Dinah said soberly. 'Anyway, it gives just a little clue about what Modesty and Willie feel for each other—' She broke off abruptly, for he had stopped short and she could feel that his whole body had gone rigid.

He said in a quiet, despairing voice, 'Oh, God. I've got to stop them. Get Modesty, quick! Don't argue !'

He was turning her to face the way she should go, and before she could speak he gave her a little push and said frantically, 'Go on!' Then she was running, arms outstretched ahead of her. Her lips were pursed, making a series of almost noiseless whistles which her hypersensitive ears could pick up as the sound was reflected back from any object in her path. In her mind was her own strange audio-tactile impressions of the route she must take to reach the entrance of the restaurant. She ran fast, without stumbling, holding down the fear that surged within her.

There were only two cars left in the car park. One was Modesty's. Collier had seen the man go down near the other car, on the edge of the pool of light from the single lamp fixed to the old stone wall. He thought it was McReedy, for he had glimpsed the smooth bald head as the blow was struck.

There were two attackers. The smaller man stood back, watching. The other, a big man, had kicked hard and deliberately at the limp body as Collier sent Dinah on her way. Now he kicked again, viciously.

Collier ran forward. His mouth was dry, his heart pounding. Fighting hand to hand against another man was something he had known only once in his life, for a few brief seconds. And this might be worse than hand to hand. His quick imagination cringed away from the mental image of a knife slicing into his flesh, of a bullet hammering into bone.

He covered the last few yards fast. The man standing back saw him first and uttered a quick warning word. Collier swung a foot, aiming for the groin of the bigger man, who was shaping to kick again. There was blood on the victim's heavy square face. McReedy's face.

Collier's kick landed glancingly. He heard a gasp, as much of anger as of pain, and then his own impetus carried him to close quarters. The man had not gone down, but was bent over a little, coming up, his head a good target.

A Modesty Blaise dictum from some idle conversation in the past sounded in Collier's mind. *Never use your fist on anyone's head, Steve, it's bone against bone. That's strictly for television . . .*

He lunged, striking with the heel of his hand to the side of the jaw, and was astonished at the result. The man reeled dizzily away and fell to his hands and knees. Collier moved to place himself between the unconscious McReedy and his assailants, suddenly feeling at a loss.

The smaller man was moving forward, crouching a little. The blade of a knife gleamed in the lamplight. Collier's stomach contracted and the sweat of renewed fear broke out on his body. The knife . . . the sharp steel sliding through muscle and gut . . . through the soft organs . . .

A Willie Garvin comment: *Villains 'ave it dead easy most of the time, but if you make it look dodgy for 'em they're not so keen . . .*

Collier's hand darted under his jacket. When he brought it out, something thin and steely projected from his fist. He held it low, angled upwards, his thumb on the sharp steel. At the same moment, feeling slightly idiotic in some part of his mind that remained aloof and observed the scene, he bent his knees in a crouch and extended his bent left arm forward a little, palm down, hand flat and rigid. It was a very reasonable imitation of a knife-fighter's posture.

His right hand weaved back and forth menacingly, never still. He found that without willing it his lips had drawn back from his teeth in a snarling grimace.

The knife man stopped short. Then, after long seconds, he began to inch forward again, very warily. Beyond him, the other man was coming slowly to his feet. Collier felt the onset of despair. His meagre resources were just about used up. So far he had held his own by surprise and bluff. But surprise was over now, and his bluff was about to be called.

His legs twitched, trying to run. But McReedy lay helpless and vulnerable. Collier held his unwilling body rigidly in its menacing pose, held the aching snarl. He could only play it out to the end now.

A whisper of sound from behind him. Sudden new alarm in the face of the knife man. Modesty's voice said, 'All right, Steve. Back off now, darling.'

They came past him, one on each side, almost soundlessly, Willie in crêpe soles, Modesty barefoot, free of her flimsy evening shoes, clearing McReedy's body with a raking stride, her short skirt riding up high on the long beautiful legs.

She went straight for the knife man. Collier let out a shuddering breath and watched limply, without anxiety. He had seen too much to doubt the outcome. The blade drove forward. He saw her body curve sweetly as her hips swung sideways in a lovely flowing movement, outside the thrusting arm, so that the knife passed four inches wide of her ribs. Collier heard himself snigger foolishly. Then her right hand shot forward with the impetus of her body behind it, and the heel of her hand smashed up under the man's chin in a jolt that rammed his head back and sideways with such force that it seemed his feet must be lifted clear of the ground.

He fell bonelessly. Modesty was already turning away. She knelt over McReedy and began to examine him gently. Collier shifted his gaze. Willie Garvin was holding the bigger man against the high stone wall with one hand, with the other he was rummaging unhurriedly under the man's jacket. He produced a gun. Its owner showed neither interest nor resistance. Willie let go of him. He slipped limply down against the wall, fell over sideways and lay still. Collier realized that he must have missed some significant part of the engagement.

Modesty straightened up and moved towards him, looking at him strangely. 'For God's sake, since when did you start carrying a blade, Steve?'

Collier looked down at his clenched hand. It still held the silver pencil. He had gripped it in this fist by the extreme end, keeping his hand moving to prevent a clear view of it.

'Held him off for a bit,' he said in a voice which did not sound like his own. He showed her the pencil. 'It was all I could think of.'

She went on staring at him. 'For a man with your family crest, it wasn't bad. Go and tell Dinah you're all right. She'll be worried sick about you.'

'I've been bloody well worried sick about myself,' Collier said with feeling, and heard Willie's deep-throated chuckle as he turned away. He was halfway across the car park when Dinah appeared from the end of the drive, running. Caspar held her arm. Two of the restaurant staff hurried behind them. Dinah was calling, her voice a little high-pitched with anxiety. 'Steve! Modesty, is he all right?'

'Unscathed,' Collier said, and took her in his arms as she ran to the sound of his voice. Then, to Caspar, 'A couple of thugs were putting the boot in on your friend McReedy. Modesty doesn't seem too worried about him, but you'd better lend a hand.'

Caspar swore and ran on, the two waiters following him. Dinah said, holding Collier tightly, her cheek on his chest, 'I didn't know what was happening. I only knew it was something horrible. When you stopped and spoke . . . I could smell the fear.'

'A lesser nose than yours could have done that, my sweet,' Collier said ruefully. He was neither surprised nor offended. He knew that Dinah lived in a world of smells and sounds and touch. She could identify by scent as readily as a dog, and could even sense strong emotion. Tonight she had scented his fear.

She said, 'Those thugs. Did you have to—to fight them?'

He laughed, suddenly feeling on top of the world. 'By the time I've worked this story up, there'll have been nothing like it since Stalingrad. But between our-selves, there wasn't much physical contact. I held them off with a pencil.'

'A pencil?'

He explained briefly. 'To be honest, I don't think they were top quality thugs, darling. It was strictly Amateur Night out there until Modesty and Willie came along.'

'They're OK?'

Collier laughed again. Before he could answer, Modesty and Willie came walking away from the lamplight and joined them. Modesty held the shoes she had kicked off. She said, 'McReedy's coming round already. I've told Caspar to take over. We'll be on our way. If we get involved with French policemen taking statements, we'll grow old here.'

They moved to where their car was parked. As Collier opened the rear door for Dinah he realized that Modesty and Willie were looking at him, smiling, and with something in their expressions that made him feel suddenly embarrassed. 'Look,' he said hastily, 'for God's sake don't make a thing of this. The only reason I didn't run was because my blasted legs wouldn't move.'

'They were kicking him and you ran towards them,' Dinah said. 'I think you're a living doll.'

'Just get in,' said Collier. 'And nobody goes to bed tonight until I've re-enacted the whole scene for you, move by move. Wait till Modesty and Willie see my snarl and my knife-fighter's crouch. It'll turn their hair white. You'd better have some smelling salts ready for them, darling.'

Modesty Blaise was wrestling with a caught zipper at the back of her dress when Willie knocked and entered at her call. He freed the zipper, then went and sat on the bed, looking absently out of the open window at the dark sea.

'Steve was in form when we got back,' Modesty said. 'That fight scene was a classic, even for him.'

'Yes. More like 'is old self.' Willie pondered for a moment. 'That's the first time since they got 'ere. I know he's been doing his funny bits like always, but you could see it was an effort.'

Modesty took off her dress, went into the bathroom, and came out a few moments later wrapped to the chin in a long jade-green dressing-gown. Willie gave her a cigarette and she sat down beside him. 'I know he's been a little quiet,' she said, 'but I didn't like to ask why'.

'I've dug it out of Dinah a bit at a time, playing it crafty so she wouldn't realize.' Willie inhaled moodily on his cigarette. 'It's money.'

'Money?' She turned her head to stare at him. 'Steve was never loaded, but he has a good steady income from those mathematical text-books he writes. Enough so he can run around all over the place on his psychic investigation hobby.'

'Not now,' Willie said. 'Soon as they were married he set out to see if there was any way Dinah could get 'er sight back. She didn't want 'im to, she's been through it all before, but Steve wouldn't listen. Took 'er to doctors in Sweden, Germany, the States, South Africa . . . all over.

Some genius in the States 'ad Dinah in a private nursing 'ome for six weeks and charged two thousand quid for saying there was nothing could be done.'

Modesty got up and moved to the window. 'We know how he feels about Dinah,' she said. 'If he had it all to do again, I guess he'd do the same thing. Is he really broke, Willie?'

'I know there's a big bank loan. He's got to assign all future royalties in the bank's favour, to clear it. The 'ouse in Surrey, that's got to go.' He shrugged. 'Dinah's got no money of 'er own, so it looks like Steve takes some teaching job and chucks up everything else while he spends the next few years trying to get back to square one. Trouble is, Dinah feels she's to blame for it all.'

'He'll have to give up his real work, and she knows what that means to him,' Modesty said. In the field of psychic investigation Collier was among the world's top experts, but it was an activity that paid no money. She flicked her cigarette out of the window and said with quiet anger, 'Goddam it to hell. Why is it you can help your friends, people you love, with anything but money?' She came back to the bed and sat down, frowning. 'We could make them a present of ten or fifteen thousand and never miss it. But . . .'

'That's right. But.' Willie shook his head. 'We've only got to suggest it and you'll never see 'em for dust.' He paused, and when he spoke again his voice sounded tired. 'It's not a disaster, I s'pose. There's lots worse off, and all that. But it's going to 'urt bad. I feel lousy about it, Princess. I mean, you can see what's going to 'appen.'

Modesty nodded. She could see it clearly enough. If your friends fell on hard times, if they could not afford even a token return of hospitality, then they ducked out, quietly cut themselves off. You lost them.

She was silent for a full minute. Then—'I was thinking about something else when you knocked, Willie. How do you figure that McReedy business tonight?'

The change of subject did not surprise him. He knew she had compartments in her mind, and that the Steve-Dinah problem was now simmering in one of them. He said, 'Just one of those things, I reckon. Caspar and McReedy dropped in for a drink. McReedy went out to the car for some of those fancy fags Caspar smokes, and the muscle jumped 'im.'

'But they didn't rob him. They were working him over. Why?'

Willie rubbed his chin. 'We don't know enough to make guesses, Princess. Want me to look into it?'

'No.' She spoke rather quickly and got up from the bed. 'It's not important. I was just curious.'

He looked at her sharply but could read nothing in her face. Yet, when he wished her goodnight and went to his room, for no valid reason some of the heaviness had lifted from his spirits.

At noon the next day, Collier sat in the stern of a big powerboat and looked along the hundred and twenty feet of tow-rope which angled up over the sea. At the far end, the great blue-and-white sail of the kite shimmered in the sun.

Willie Garvin, a brown figure in faded blue trunks, hung from the trapeze bar beneath the sail, thirty feet above the quiet, sun-dappled water, a slalom ski on his feet. The smaller figure of Dinah rode on his back. Collier could see her face over Willie's shoulder. She was catching her breath, laughing with exhilaration as they flew at a steady thirty-five mph. Half an hour earlier he had watched Modesty and then Willie as they performed tricks with the kite—toe hangs and knee hangs, 360-degree turns, and dramatic free layouts in which the kiter hung horizontally below the bar without touching it, suspended only by the harness.

Willie was doing no tricks now, only an occasional gentle slalom from side to side, for to carry a passenger was no easy task, even a lightweight like Dinah, and this was her first time up.

His hand hovering over the tow-rope release gear, Collier saw her wrap her legs more tightly round Willie and then lift one hand to wave. He almost waved back. Dinah made so light of her blindness that it was easy to forget.

Modesty sat at the wheel of the boat, her head turned, watching the kite carefully. Collier lifted his voice above the surprisingly quiet growl of the twin 35-hp engines. 'She's loving it,' he said. 'She must be out of her little pink mind.' Modesty smiled. 'You'd love it, too. It's like champagne.'

'I'll settle for a bottle of Bollinger, thanks.'

The kite swept down wide on the port quarter. Willie's ski was almost touching the sea when he moved his weight along the bar. At the same moment Modesty opened the throttle wider. The kite zoomed up and across, soaring sixty feet in two seconds. Willie slalomed to starboard.

She eased back the throttle and said, 'That's something you won't get out of a bottle. And don't worry, Steve. She's Dresden china as far as Willie's concerned.'

Collier nodded. 'I know. I'm not worried about Dinah, I'm worried about me.' He looked at the release gear. 'If the kite goes wild I have to wait till it's almost down before I hit the release. If I do it too soon they'll cop a few bruises hitting the sea. But it's nothing to what I'll cop. You'll all be on to me, baying like dogs, quoting instructions, debating my sanity.' He rubbed the inside of one thigh broodingly. 'I remember how it was two days ago, when you tried to get me up on skis from a wet start.'

A small explosion of laughter escaped Modesty. 'But we told you a dozen times to hold the bar in *front* of your knees, not with the rope between them.'

'That's my point. You told me about a million things a dozen times. Only a computer could have absorbed them all. I forgot just one. Next minute I was lying flat on my back with lacerated thighs, floating in my own gore.'

'It was only a graze !' That was true, but when the returning boat reached Collier he had demanded an immediate heart transplant.

Again Willie viraged with the kite, the lightweight terylene of the sail curving tautly in the wind.

Watching intently, Collier said, 'You know, it baffles me. I wouldn't have said that you and Willie were notably cautious, but for this kiting you wear crash helmets and inch-thick safety jackets of expanded neoprene. And you check all your gear as if you were making a moon-shot.'

'Willie made the framework collapsible, and we don't want it to collapse in the air. We don't want to get hurt, either. What on earth makes you think we're reckless?'

Collier shot a quick, wondering glance at her, knowing she was quite serious. She wore a very dark blue swimsuit that matched her eyes, and her black hair was bound in a short club at her neck. Her body was very brown. From where Collier sat he could see only one faint scar, on her right arm and a few inches below the shoulder, but in days gone by he had counted others. Not long ago he had witnessed the sword-thrust that had made the wound in her arm, and the memory of that long savage duel under a desert sun could still bring sweat to his brow.

'My sweet,' he said helplessly, 'by no wish of my own I've been involved in two very rough capers with you. Dinah in one of them. I've seen you take risks beside which going over Niagara in a paper bag would seem attractive. So I can't rate you very high for caution.'

'You don't understand, Steve,' she said absently, her eyes sweeping the empty sea ahead. 'I save up my luck for when I need it. You've never seen me take a serious risk except to save my neck.'

Without reflection Collier could think of four occasions. Her own neck had not been at stake, but if she had not taken appalling chances, other people would have died. Collier himself for one, Dinah for another. But it was pointless to argue. The simple fact was that if you had Modesty Blaise for a friend, then your neck was counted as her own. 'It's too hot to argue,' he said lazily, and glanced towards the land. 'Hazard approaching. That's Caspar's boat, isn't it?'

A red and blue speedboat was hurtling out towards them, hydroplaning over the glassy water. Modesty glanced quickly towards it, then up at the kite. 'I'll bring them down,' she said. 'Can't watch the kite with Caspar screaming around.'

She waved a hand to Willie and throttled down, keeping the boat into the wind as she had done throughout the run. The headwind gave more lift for Dinah's extra weight, and with Willie carrying her as passenger it was important to take no chance of catching a crosswind on the turn.

The kite descended steadily. Willie's ski touched the surface. He skimmed along smoothly for a few seconds, Dinah still clinging to his back, and then, as Modesty closed the throttle, the two of them sank down into the water. The kite settled, supported by the two cylindrical floats on the fore and aft members of the dural NS 4 framework. The sail slanted up like an awning above the heads of Willie and Dinah. The polypropylene tow-rope floated on the surface.

Collier hauled in and reached down to help Dinah aboard. Willie began to dismantle the framework of the kite. Breathless, her face alight, Dinah said, 'Boy! Did you see me, Steve? It's out of this world!'

Caspar made a spectacular turning halt, then eased the speedboat gently alongside. His smile and his eyes were as bright as ever, but there was a hint of strain under the surface, as if the shock of last night had left its mark.

'Long live Chairman Mao!' he cried. 'I bring word from the good McReedy, my little cabbages. He is suffused with gratitude to you all, and will shortly render same personally in toto and with flowers, by God—'

'Did the police find out why those two worked him over?' Modesty broke in.

Caspar gave a crow of pained laughter. 'Ah, sacred thunder! Will you be very angry if I tell you they escaped, Modesty, my small?'

'*Escaped*?'

'In my own car, *madre de Dios*! And by my own fault. It was while we waited for the police to come. I had their gun which you gave me, but I dropped it.'

Collier said, 'Jesus, man! Are you joking?'

'No joke, my old. I was trying to spin it on my finger, as one sees on the movies. When it fell, the bigger one was very quick.' He screwed up his face, wincing. 'The police were not pleased. *A la Bastille!* I thought they would arrest me.'

Modesty said, 'You could always plead insanity, Caspar.'

He gave a yelp of laughter. 'Who would believe me? But to confirm. You will come and scintillate at my party tonight, *nicht wahr*?'

'It's still on?'

'Certainly! *Le monde doré* will be there. Come and out-glitter them, *cara mia*. I insist.'

'All right. Now shove off with that fire-cracker while we sort ourselves out, will you?'

Caspar flourished a hand, edged the speedboat clear, shouted 'Till soon!' and went roaring away.

'Spinning it on his finger,' Collier said blankly. 'I'll bet McReedy was charmed. If the thug who grabbed the gun had put a bullet through Caspar's head I doubt if we'd notice any difference.'

That evening Collier brought his wife into the sitting-room and said, 'I've told her that her lipstick's on straight and that all hooks and zippers are done up, but she wants a second opinion.'

Dinah was wearing a short black dress. It was not expensive but it looked very good on her. She said, 'He means well, but he's not very bright. He let me go out with a price tag on the other week.'

Modesty looked Dinah over carefully. 'You're fine,' she said. 'But that dress needs a bit of jewellery for this kind of party. Have you got anything with you?'

'We travelled light,' said Collier. 'At home she has a magnificent diamond brooch I bought for her in Algiers from a one-legged mendicant. He swore the rocks were genuine. If he lied, I've been swindled out of three pounds ten.'

'She can borrow something,' Modesty said, and moved to the door. For a moment her hand touched her throat and she lifted an eyebrow at Willie. He gave a quick nod of approval. When she came down from her bedroom she carried a pearl necklace. 'Here. If Caspar wants glitter he'll get it. Better than glitter. There'll be plenty of sparklers about, but this will knock them cold.'

'God, no!' Collier said hastily. 'Not those!'

'What is it?' Dinah felt the pearls and looked startled. She knew them, knew their history, had been a part of their history. She knew that the necklace was insured for over thirty thousand pounds, and was unique. It was a present to Modesty from Willie Garvin. There were thirty-seven pearls, ranging from a hundred grains down to twenty-five grains, and they came from all the major pearl beds of the world. Willie had not bought them, he had dived for them, spending five or six weeks on the task each year for seven years, unknown to Modesty.

To find the selection of matched and graded pearls he wanted, he had lifted more than fifty thousand shells.

'I can't!' Dinah said. 'My God, I didn't know you kept them around, Modesty. They ought to be in a bank!'

'I didn't give 'em for that,' Willie said amiably. 'They're for pleasure, not shutting away. Now turn around so the Princess can put 'em on for you.'

By midnight Caspar's party was in full swing. At one end of the long terrace room a five-piece band thumped out beat music. Caspar was darting about, uttering yelps of laughter and chattering feverishly to his guests. Willie was dancing with Dinah.

'I shall ask you to dance,' Collier said, refilling Modesty's glass and his own with champagne, 'as soon as I've managed to analyze what's expected of me. I'm out of touch, of course. I don't know if this is the frug or watusi or whatever. But no two dancers seem to agree on its execution. The lady there with the blue hair is alternately sagging at the knees and throwing her arms in the air, while the heavy gentleman with the gleaming jowls seems to be riding an invisible horse. Which method do you favour?'

Before Modesty could reply there came a sudden untimely crash of the cymbals, very loud. The music faltered and faded. The chattering voices rose sharply, then dwindled to a hush.

A man stood on the low platform occupied by the band. He wore an ankle-length plastic mack, and the whole of his head was covered by a hood. There were no eye-holes. The fabric could presumably be seen through from within, though it was opaque from without. He held a sawn-off shotgun.

Another hooded man stood by the door from the landing stage, a third by the door leading through to the hotel. Both carried sawn-off shotguns. Collier saw the dancers fall back as three more men, similarly hooded, moved briskly down the length of the floor. These three carried service revolvers.

They split up, one moving to each side and the third continuing to the end of the room. There was silence. The man by the band spoke in French, slowly and with an accent. 'Listen carefully, please. I shall say this only once. In a few moments one of the waiters will be passing round with a tray. You will place your valuables upon it. If you resist or refuse, you will be hurt. That is all.'

He signalled to the band. After a moment or two of hesitation they began to play. His free hand beat the air impatiently, commanding them to play louder. The noise rose.

Caspar stood holding his hands to his head, eyes closed, lips moving. Suddenly he ran at one of the hooded men. The report of the revolver was almost lost in the noise from the band. Caspar stopped short, wincing. He clapped a hand to his arm and went down on his knees, a startled look at his face. The band blared. Nobody moved.

A white-faced waiter was beckoned forward and a tray was thrust in his hands. Collier saw Willie and Dinah standing close together halfway down the room. Willie was looking towards Modesty. Collier turned his gaze to her. Her face was impassive, her eyes on Willie. She shook her head, and began to unpin the emerald brooch she wore.

Collier looked towards Dinah again and saw that her face was milk white, her hands pressed against her chest high up near her throat. It was then he remembered that she was wearing Modesty's pearls, and he felt the blood drain from his own face with shock.

The waiter was in front of Dinah now. Willie Garvin gently drew her hands away, unfastened the necklace and dropped it on the tray. Collier felt sick with despair. Some time later he put his own slim wallet on the tray, and saw Modesty's emerald brooch join the glittering pile of jewellery and gold there.

The withdrawal was as efficient as the rest of the operation. Two men with shotguns remained by the terrace door while the others moved out on to the long landing stage. There came the roar of an engine. The two men turned and disappeared. As the band stopped playing and a bedlam of voices rose, there came the sound of a powerful boat racing away into the darkness.

Casper still knelt in the middle of the floor, head bowed, blood creeping between the fingers of the hand clamped on his arm. Modesty was beside him now.

'Again . . .' he said dazedly. 'Oh God, it has happened *again*!'

'Let's see to your arm, Caspar.'

'My arm? It's nothing . . . a gouge in the flesh.' He looked at her with blank eyes and got unsteadily to his feet. 'There is a goddam doctor here I invited . . .' He suddenly wrenched away, his face twisting with rage. 'The manager—where is the bastard? Where is he?' His voice rose. 'Where are the useless goddam police?'

He lurched through the milling, babbling crowd. Modesty turned to find Willie at her side, Collier with an arm round his shivering wife. 'Might as well get out of 'ere, Princess,' Willie said.

She nodded. 'We can make our statements in the morning. Let's go.'

Willie drove the car. Modesty sat beside him. In the back, Dinah huddled against her husband. She had stopped crying now but he could still feel her small body shaking.

'Oh, my God,' he said tiredly. 'Oh, sweet Jesus. Those pearls.'

'No good fretting.' Willie said philosophically. 'We've lifted a bit of loot in our time, the Princess an' me. So we can't squawk when it works out the other way round.'

'I was wearing them,' Dinah said in a muffled voice. 'If I hadn't worn them—'

'I practically made you,' Modesty said. 'If I'd worn them myself it would have been just the same. And if we'd started trouble there'd have been a massacre with those shotguns. You haven't a shred of responsibility for what happened, Dinah. And Willie's right, I'm in no position to complain.'

'I know,' Dinah's voice was weary, defeated. 'But everyone who's nice to me gets hurt. I'm a Jonah. I'm bad luck.'

Collier had never felt so sad or helpless. He lifted his wife's face and kissed her. He could think of nothing to say.

During the next two days Collier came slowly to realize that Modesty and Willie were not putting on an act for Dinah's sake, that they genuinely felt the way they had spoken. But Dinah was inconsolable.

A very subdued Caspar telephoned to apologize and declare his distress. His arm was healing well, he said. It was only a flesh wound.

On the third day, in the afternoon, Collier drove into Cannes with Dinah to do some shopping at the market. They returned early, Collier driving fast, and ran down to the boat house where Modesty sat watching Willie as he finished servicing the engines.

Collier's rather lean face was alight, and Dinah looked a different girl.

Willie laid down a spanner and stared. 'What's the excitement. Somebody at the market understand your French?'

'We ran into McReedy,' Collier said. 'Just for a minute or two.' He looked at Dinah. 'You tell them, sweetheart.'

'I'd never been close to McReedy before,' she said tensely, 'but it's *him*! I mean, the man with a hood who went round with the waiter and the tray —he was standing close when Willie took the necklace off and put it on the tray. That was McReedy!'

Modesty and Willie looked at each other. Modesty said, 'You're sure, Dinah?'

'I *know*! Oh lord, I can't prove it. But I'm never wrong about a scent, you know that. McReedy smells like . . .' She screwed up her sightless eyes. 'Like a half-inflated balloon feels. I *know* he was the man in the hood.'

They were not surprised by her simile. For her, the sensory impressions of sound and touch, taste and smell, were a unity. They knew that in Dinah's dark world Modesty's scent was as the taste of brandy, and Willie's as the sound of a muted trumpet.

'McReedy,' said Willie. He sat down on the gunwale and began to smile, watching Modesty.

After a long silence she sighed and shook her head. 'I've been slow. It's a little tortuous, but it was all there. Now Dinah's come up with the one piece that makes all the rest fall into place.'

'What rest?' Collier asked, perplexed.

'Little things. The Costa Smeralda. Best bibs and tuckers. The terrace room. A playboy yacht with no girlie guests. McReedy getting beaten up. Caspar spinning the gun on his finger. Casper getting a scratch from a .45.'

'She's gone potty,' Collier said to his wife. 'I'll hold her nose while you pour castor oil down her throat. It's a sovereign remedy.'

'Shut up, idiot.' Dinah shook his arm impatiently. 'What are we going to do, Modesty?'

'I'm going to fix lunch.' Modesty got up. 'Come and give me a hand, Dinah. And we may need you when we pay a visit to Caspar's yacht tonight.' She paused. 'We'd better keep an eye on it. Will you and Steve take turns, Willie love?'

It was half an hour after sunset that day when Collier rang from the harbour. His voice was very controlled. 'They've just up-anchored,' he said tautly. 'They've bloody well up-anchored and they're pulling out.'

Modesty said, 'Check their direction if you can, Steve, then come straight back here.'

Twenty-five minutes later Collier reached the villa. Willie was waiting in the drive, wearing a warm waterproof jacket. 'They turned east,' Collier said, 'or a bit south of east. Should be passing here.' His face was a little drawn with anxiety.

'Where are the others?'

'Boat house,' said Willie. 'Come on.' He led the way with long strides. As they came round the corner of the villa he pointed seaward. It was dark now. A yacht was passing a mile off-shore, brilliantly lit. Caspar's yacht.

'They could be going anywhere,' Collier panted as they ran down the narrow path.

'I know. That's why we can't afford to lose 'em now.'

The powerboat waited by the jetty, showing no lights. Modesty was wearing a wet-suit and hood of black neoprene. There was a small winch in the stern. Dinah was bulky in sweaters and a waterproof jacket. As Modesty started the engines Willie opened a locker and brought out more clothes.

'Get into these,' he said to Collier. 'It's going to be a long wet night.'

Collier obeyed. The powerboat was picking up speed, hugging the coast. He realized that Modesty intended to tail the *Delphine* at long range, probably waiting until the dark early hours before she closed on it. But he could not imagine what came next.

'She cruises at twenty knots,' he said, bewildered. 'We can catch her, but we can never run alongside and board her. You'd have to be a grasshopper to make it. Besides, they'll see us or hear us, or both. And they've got guns.'

'We're not going to get close enough for them to see or hear us,' Modesty said. 'There's very little moon, these engines are pretty quiet, and I'm using the black kite.'

Kite? Collier sat very still. His eyes had grown used to the darkness now, and he could see the slender lengths of duralumin lashed along the side of the powerboat— the framework for a kite.

'You're mad!'he said. 'You'll never make it!'

'It won't be too bad.' Modesty had given the wheel to Willie and moved to the stern, checking the winch. 'The sea's reasonably smooth for take-off, and there's a good steady wind, which means I can fly at low speed. I'll be on a long tow, and that will let Willie stay well clear of the *Delphine*.'

'Long? How long?'

Dinah said unhappily, 'She says seven or eight hundred feet.'

'*What*?'

Modesty turned from the winch. 'Stop jittering, Steve. There are some Australian kiters who've flown a thousand feet up on a two-thousand-foot tow-rope. That was by day, but we need darkness anyway and it's a perfect night for the job.'

'It's a perfect night to break your neck! The boat's going to need *slide-rule* handling, and Willie won't be able to see you !'

'I'm wearing a throat-mike, Willie has a receiver and headset. I can control things from my end. In theory it ought to work all right.'

'Never mind the blasted theory!'

'Oh, don't nag, darling. You're always the same. It only makes me nervous.'

Collier gave a wild laugh. 'Nervous? You haven't the bloody sense to be nervous!'

Dinah said, 'Don't, Steve. You know it's no use.' She moved to sit close beside him, groped for his hand and held it tightly. He let out a long breath and slumped in his seat. Their faces grew wet with fine spray as the boat surged steadily on through the night.

By two hours past midnight the sea was dark under a thin moon. The yacht lay almost three miles astern. Only her navigation lights showed now. Willie Garvin killed the twin engines and began to assemble the kite framework, securing the long alloy spars with interlocking joints. Modesty pulled goggles over her eyes and slipped over the side. At a word from Willie, Collier began to unfold the terylene sail. Five minutes later the kite floated astern, with Modesty holding the bar beneath the slanting sail.

Collier felt very cold. She would wear the harness until she was airborne and in position, and she would make a few practice manoeuvres well away from the *Delphine*, to test the handling of the kite and communication with Willie. Then she would free herself from the harness. She would hang by her hands from the trapeze bar with no other support while Willie made the approach. He would cross the wake of the yacht at least a hundred yards astern, at an angle of thirty or forty degrees to the *Delphine's* course, heading straight into the favourable wind. It was unlikely that the boat would be heard or seen. Apart from the navigation lights and a faint glow from the wheelhouse the yacht was in darkness now. There would be one or perhaps two men in the wheelhouse, but they would not look aft except by remote chance.

The floating kite was forty feet astern of the boat now,

almost lost against the darkness of the sea. Willie had the receiver headset on, listening. He opened the throttle. Collier could just make out Modesty's dark figure rising up out of the water on her slalom ski, the kite a great gash of blackness above her. She skimmed the surface for a few seconds then lifted into the air.

Willie called, 'Pay out.' Collier gripped the winch control, letting the line run out slowly but steadily, watching Willie for any signal. Dinah sat very still, enclosed in her own world of permanent darkness. Wishing they would tell her what was happening from moment to moment, but biting back the questions for fear of causing any distraction.

A full two hundred yards astern, her face cold, her body warm in the wet-suit, Modesty sailed a hundred and fifty feet above the sea. The tow-rope angled down ahead of her, vanishing into the darkness. Beyond she could just see the wake of the boat. The rounded surface of the throat-mike rested against her larynx. She said, 'I'm going to try a few left-hand slaloms, Willie. Here we go.'

She shifted her weight on the bar, and the kite planed smoothly down to her left. Down, down, far wide of the boat with this enormous length of tow-rope. The wind plucked at her and whistled through the framework. Just before her ski touched the water she moved again and said, 'Up!' The kite soared, carrying her up and to the right in a two hundred yard traverse. Three times she slalomed, then settled at a hundred and fifty feet again and said, 'All right. Make the run, Willie.'

During the fifteen minutes of practice manoeuvres they had operated far out to port of the yacht, and it had passed them by. She had lost sight of it, but as Willie brought her round slowly, carefully, in a great circle, she picked up the navigation lights a mile or more ahead now, and to her right.

She kicked off the ski, dropped the gloves she had

been wearing, freed herself from the harness, and hung by her hands from the bar. Willie was closing on the *Delphine* from out on the port quarter. She would have to time her long slalom to begin well before he crossed astern, slanting down so that she would reach the afterdeck at the exact moment when the tow-rope brought her in line with it.

She began to speak. 'Slower, Willie. Slower still. There's a good headwind up here and you can go down to ten knots. Good. Now starboard a little. Hold her like that. Hold her . . .' She moved her weight. The kite began to drop smoothly, as if sliding sideways down an invisible slope, moving obliquely down towards the stern of the yacht.

Fifty feet up now. The length of the *Delphine* showed clearly ahead and to her left. She was going to undershoot. 'Throttle, Willie. Just a touch. Right . . . ease off. Steady. Steady . . .'

The afterdeck, which had looked impossibly small, grew suddenly larger. She swept down, twisting her body to face forward along the deck. Her feet passed over the stern rail. Too high. She would hit the windows of the saloon, or the speed of the tow might even whisk her over the starboard rail. Too late to compensate. She shifted her weight to tilt the sail, snapped '*Up!*' and dropped to the deck ten feet below as the kite flashed up and away over the stern.

Her body was limp, already curling as her feet hit the deck, and she plunged forward, rolling in a loose somersault and then slithering to a halt against the saloon.

She lay there for a full minute, conscious now of the ache in her shoulders, alert for any sound, any movement. Then she mouthed softly, pressing the mike against her throat, 'Tell Steve he can stop biting his nails. And stand by, Willie. I might be a little while.'

She unzipped her wet-suit jacket and switched off the

pencil-sized transmitter clipped inside. Her movements were deliberately slow, for her hands were still a little unsteady from the long minutes of physical strain and total concentration. One side of her face was sore, and she knew she had picked up a graze slithering along the deck.

A small flat packet, neoprene-wrapped, was tied to her thigh. She loosened the nylon cord and stripped off the sealing tape. Inside was a Colt .32 revolver, a box with a hypodermic, a roll of surgical plaster, and an aerosol spray containing ether.

She got to her feet and eased silently round the corner of the saloon.

Half a mile off, the powerboat held a parallel course.

Dinah said, 'How long before we can move in, Willie?'

'When she gives me a call. Allow 'alf an hour, love. She's got to get the crew buttoned up, an' there's eight of 'em.'

'Will it be tricky?'

'No. The tricky bit's over. They sleep in the lower cabins. Caspar and McReedy 'ave got a deck cabin apiece. Caspar showed us over the yacht a couple of weeks ago, so Modesty knows the layout. And she's got a box of tricks with 'er. A squirt of ether and a yard of plaster each. That'll keep 'em quiet.'

Willie stretched, arching his back, and exhaled. His hands on the wheel were relaxed.

Collier said accusingly, 'You were worried. You sound different now.'

'I didn't like it too much,' Willie agreed. 'If she misjudged that long slalom she could've come down right into the screws.'

'Then why the hell didn't you help me talk her out of it?'

Willie smiled. Dinah said, 'Don't be a dope, honey.'

Collier sniffed. He felt a lot better now. 'All right,' he said sourly. 'But if it had to be done, why didn't that

Cockney layabout do the tricky bit? Where are his manners? You don't say "After you" to a lady when it's a matter of being chewed up by propellers.'

'But I'm chicken,' Willie explained.

Dinah giggled. 'He's more than half as heavy again as Modesty. With the same sail, that means a lot more speed to keep him up. A landing at that speed just wasn't on.'

Collier knew that perfectly well. He said scornfully, 'Excuses, excuses.'

Caspar came drowsily awake. A hand was shaking him by the shoulder. He grunted, 'What the hell is it?' The bedside light in his cabin clicked on. He blinked at the Colt held in front of his eyes, then looked past it to the black-clad figure bending over him.

He felt suddenly cold, and his thoughts were in fragments. Modesty Blaise . . . in a wet-suit with the hood thrown back . . .

One smooth cheek marred by a raw graze . . . holding a gun in his face. He lay stiffly, looking up at her with dazed eyes. Her own eyes were like two cold, dark-blue stones. He tried to work out what had happened, to frame the lies that were needed.

She said softly, 'Apart from the man at the wheel, everyone else is asleep. And I've made sure they'll stay asleep. Don't fidget, Caspar, or I'll put a bullet through your arm. A real one, not a blank like McReedy used the other night. You won't have to break a sachet of pig's blood to pretend you're wounded.'

She saw that he was wide awake now. The first shock had passed. He was watching her narrowly and did not seem to be afraid. 'You are in trouble,' he said coolly. 'Bad trouble, my old. Assault, piracy, God knows what else.'

She said, 'We won't waste time. I'll tell you what I know. McReedy's the boss, not you. He chartered this yacht, I've checked that. He organized the raids. You're the playboy front. The actor. You made a lot of jet-set friends and got them all together at a party on the Costa Smeralda. Best bibs and tuckers. All competing with their most glittering rocks. And then you took them. The bullet-wound your bouncer got then was as phoney as the wound you got the other night. But it stopped any other heroics.'

She stepped back and sat down on a locker, the gun held steady. 'Then you pulled one or two other raids. Outside jobs. I'm guessing the next bit, but it's a good guess. McReedy wanted to try the same idea again, to get a big haul. You got scared. Another raid at a Caspar party and somebody just might begin to wonder. You begged McReedy to lay off, but he wouldn't listen, and you're too frightened of him just to walk out. So you got a little desperate, Caspar. Now I've stopped guessing. You tried to put him out of action, maybe for good. You laid on those two thugs for the job, but Steve Collier stopped them before they really got going.'

Sweat was gathering on Caspar's forehead, and there was panic in his eyes now.

She said, 'Yes, McReedy's a rough man, isn't he, Caspar? You were afraid the French police might make those thugs talk, and that meant McReedy finding out what you'd done. So you played the clown, let them grab the gun and escape. I never really believed your act, I just thought it was harmless. But that escape bit was too much. So was the party, held at a place with a sea getaway, as before. So was the bullet that grazed you but didn't hit anyone behind you.'

Caspar said, dry-mouthed, 'Try to prove any of it.'

'I'm not going to.' She studied him thoughtfully. 'You and McReedy aren't buddies. He's your boss, and you're very, *very* scared of him. Now, what do you think he'll do to you if I tell him that it was you who had him beaten up? I wouldn't have to prove it, Caspar, just give him the thought. He'll figure it for himself.'

Caspar seemed to have shrunk. His young wrinkled face looked like an old wrinkled face. He said hoarsely, 'If you've got a deal I'll play along. What do you want?'

She said, 'A little cooperation, Caspar, that's all. And the loot, of course.'

The yacht lay rolling gently in the swell, her engines stopped. The man in the wheelhouse slept, his wrists bound with surgical tape, his feet with nylon cord. Willie Garvin brought the powerboat alongside. The gangway had been lowered. He made fast and went up on to the deck. Dinah followed, Collier guiding her.

As Collier reached the deck he saw Modesty with Caspar beside her. She was saying to Willie, 'Thank God we brought Dinah along, or we'd have wasted the whole damn trip.'

The deck lights were on now. Willie put a hand out and turned her head a little to peer at the graze on her cheek. He made no comment but said, 'The loot's aboard?'

'Yes. But I've boobed.' She was frowning, annoyed with herself.

'Foolish woman,' Collier said reproachfully. 'What have you done wrong?' He felt wonderful now.

She looked at him. 'McReedy's the top man and he doesn't seem to trust his colleagues very much. He's the only one who knows where the loot's stashed away. Because he's the danger man I gave him a shot that will keep him out for hours.' She shrugged. 'I doubt if we could have made him talk, anyway. We're not the thumb-screw types.'

She put a hand on Dinah's arm. 'That lays the whole thing on you, Dinah. Searching a ship is murder, even one this size. We'd need about a week, and we've only got hours. If you can't find the loot for us . . . well, we've lost.'

Dinah smiled and wiped her spray-wet face. In the

light from the deck lamps Collier saw that she was bubbling with an eager happiness that he had not seen in her for a long time now. 'I wore those pearls for several hours,' she said, 'so I have a sense of what I'm looking for. And anyway, there was quite a bit of gold with the loot. I can't miss. Let's have the locaters, Willie.'

Two minutes later she was walking slowly along the deck, near the starboard rail, her hands held in front of her. In each hand she gripped a short length of copper tubing. A piece of galvanized wire, bent in a right-angle with one arm longer than the other, rested in each piece of tubing. The longer arms of the two wires pointed forward.

Collier moved behind her, guiding her with a gentle touch. The strange gift never ceased to fascinate him, even though he was deeply familiar with all forms of psychic phenomena. Until a year ago, this had been Dinah's occupation. She had worked for construction companies in North America, locating pipes, cables, sewers. She had worked for mining companies, locating copper, silver and gold. It was this gift which had put her into appalling danger and had led to those grim days in the Sahara which Collier would never forget, the days when Dinah had been forced to seek a vast treasure buried when the Romans held Numidia. There she had searched a small city; here there was only the deck area of the yacht to cover.

As they turned and moved aft to cover another strip of deck he saw that Willie Garvin was in the wheelhouse now. Caspar stared with a strange, bewildered look as Dinah passed. Modesty was watching Caspar sharply.

It was twenty minutes later, in the saloon, that the two wires resting loosely in the tubing Dinah held in each hand swung smoothly towards each other and crossed. Dinah stopped, her eyes closed, a frown of concentration on her face. She edged a little to the left and stamped a foot.

'Below here, Steve. About ten feet down, maybe less.'

'Hold on, I'll get Modesty.'

It took several minutes to ascertain that Dinah stood directly over a between-decks bulkhead and that this divided the air-conditioning unit from a combined workshop and paint store. Willie stayed on deck while the others went below. Dinah moved slowly about the little workshop with her locaters. The wires swung together again.

'Here,' she said, standing facing the bulkhead. 'About deck level.'

'There's a ventilator grid in the bulkhead, down by your feet,' Modesty said. 'Steve, get a screwdriver.'

The four screws came out easily. In the shaft beyond the grid lay a leather satchel. Collier drew it out. The mass of jewellery and gold within was carefully wrapped in cottonwool and oilskin.

'You've done it, sweetheart,' he breathed. Dinah's face puckered. Her eyes brimmed suddenly. Collier hugged her with his free arm and laughed exultantly.

Caspar said, looking at Modesty strangely, 'That's a good trick. Now what?'

'Back to your cabin.' She motioned with the gun. 'We're leaving. If you want, we'll give you a barbiturate shot, the same as I gave McReedy. Let one of the others be the first to come round and wriggle free. It shouldn't take more than an hour now, and it might be safer for you.'

'It would,' Caspar said bleakly, and turned towards the door.

Fifteen minutes later the silhouette of the *Delphine* faded into the darkness as Willie sent the powerboat planing over the long smooth swells, heading north-west. He had put up the rain hood and it was cosy in the little boat now. Collier lit cigarettes and passed them round.

Willie produced a half-bottle of brandy.

Collier said, 'I feel in a dream. A very pleasant one. When are you going to hand over that bag of beads to the police?'

'I'm not.' Modesty took a few sips from the bottle and passed it to Dinah. 'I'm no fan of the McReedy-Caspar bunch, but if I send them down it will be a bit like dog eating dog. So this story can't be told. And if I turn up with the loot and say I found it hidden in a cave on one of the Iles de Lérins, I'll be suspect. My dossier may be dusty, but the French police won't have thrown it away.'

She yawned suddenly, then put out her cigarette with care, lowered the back of the seat, and curled up with her head on a cushion. 'You and Dinah will have to turn the loot in, Steve,' she said. 'But not just yet. For one thing I want you to find it in front of witnesses, and for another I want to wait until the insurance companies have got together and published an offer of reward.'

Collier blinked. 'Reward? I hadn't thought about that.'

Willie gave a chuckle. 'It won't be less than ten per cent. Dinah, my old darling, you can reckon on twenty thousand quid in your pocket, tax-free.'

There was a silence. Then Dinah said in a startled voice. '*My* pocket? Don't talk crazy, Willie.'

'I'm not. You fingered McReedy. You found the loot. Without you, we'd never 'ave found it. And with no proof against Caspar we could've been in dead trouble for tonight's effort. Right, Princess?'

There was no answer from Modesty. Collier leaned forward to peer down at her. 'Good God,' he said indignantly, 'she's asleep'. There was no pretence. He had seen her in sleep before. She always looked very young and curiously defenceless. Tonight, with her hair tousled, her face grazed and dirty, she looked like a tired urchin. He knew now that she had the reward in mind ever since Dinah had pinpointed McReedy, and a sudden wave of measureless affection for her stirred within him. He gave a disgruntled snort and said, 'Asleep, and with guests present. She's got no bloody manners, that's her trouble.'

He found Dinah's hand and looked at Willie. 'All right. Dinah found the loot. But Modesty put us on the yacht. Modesty risked her neck with that damn kite.'

Willie shrugged. His face was serious. Somehow he was holding down a huge admiring grin. 'If you've got the nerve to offer 'er half, go ahead,' he said doubtfully. 'But she'll be 'opping mad, I can tell you.'

It was on a morning two days later that Stephen Collier and his wife made a trip to Ile Ste Marguerite with a number of tourists on an excursion arranged by a travel agency. At eleven o'clock, sitting on one of the rocky beaches while photographs were taken, Dinah felt a piece of tarry rope beneath her. She pulled on it. The rope ran down some two feet into a crevice filled with loose stones. Attached to the end of the rope was a leather satchel. The contents of the satchel set the whole excursion buzzing with excitement, and the mystery of why the gang responsible for the recent jewel robbery had chosen to hide their haul in such a place caused endless speculation.

While Collier and Dinah were at the police station handing over their find, Willie Garvin lay extended on a lounging chair on the terrace of the villa, enjoying the sun and thinking. He heard the click of Modesty's sandals as she came from the big lounge.

She was wearing a bright yellow swimsuit, her hair was loose, tied at the nape of the neck. She perched on the end of his chair, facing him. There was a slight uncertainty in her manner, as if she wanted to say something but found it difficult. Willie sat up, moved his feet to make more room for her, and said, 'Well, twenty thousand quid ought to see Steve and Dinah in the clear. And with a bit to spare.'

She nodded absently. After a few moments he went on, 'Mind if I ask you something, Princess?'

A quick smile. 'When did I ever mind?'

'Well . . . I've been wondering why you didn't say anything to me about it. I mean, about knowing the hold-up was coming off, and that McReedy and Caspar were be'ind it.'

She stared. 'You guessed?'

'Not till after Dinah smelled McReedy out. I suddenly knew it wasn't news to you. Then I figured that maybe you 'ad them tagged all along.'

She was looking at him oddly, and with an air of relief. 'Not really tagged. But after that night at the Boule d'Or I had a pretty strong hunch. There were all those things that didn't add up unless you added them up a particular way. If I was guessing right, then there was bound to be a hold-up at Caspar's party. Afterwards, I was going to wait for the reward offer to be published and then come up with the bright idea that Caspar and McReedy were the villains. A hunch, but with enough substance to carry it. When Dinah smelled McReedy out, that was a bonus. It made her the one who got us going.'

'You were going to 'ave us clobber 'em and make the search in harbour one night?'

'Yes. When the yacht sailed without warning, it meant improvising a little.'

Willie smiled. 'And Caspar knew where the loot was?'

She made a wry grimace. 'So you figured that, too?'

'You put McReedy out for hours. That didn't make sense unless you were setting up a situation for Dinah.'

'I was. Caspar knew where the loot was hidden, if you could call it hidden. It was in a locker in McReedy's cabin. Caspar didn't hold back when I leaned on him —

anything rather than have me tell McReedy exactly who hired that muscle to beat him up. But just picking up the stuff the easy way wasn't any good. It left Dinah out. So I hid the satchel in that ventilator shaft for her to find, and told Caspar to keep his mouth buttoned.' She frowned suddenly. 'For God's sake, Willie, why didn't you tell me you knew? I've been feeling guilty as hell all this time.'

He stared at her in surprise. 'What for? Only reason I didn't say anything was because *you* didn't, Princess. I couldn't figure why, but you always know what you're doing. Then . . . well, you seemed a bit troubled these past couple of days, so I thought I'd ask.'

She looked at him wonderingly. 'The pearls, Willie love. I couldn't be sure what the hold-up would yield and I wanted to boost it for the reward.'

'So you made Dinah wear the pearls. Sure. Marvellous idea.' He looked at her, still baffled.

'Willie, I *gambled* them. It worked out, but I gambled the pearls you sweated to give me. It was an impulse. And I've felt like the world's biggest heel ever since.'

Understanding dawned on him. The pearls. He began to laugh. He had fished them up from the sea bed and made a necklace for her. It had taken seven years and given him infinite pleasure. That would always remain. Nobody could steal the sweat. He saw that she was smiling back at him now, more than smiling, laughing at herself with him, and he knew that she understood.

'They're only pearls,' he said, 'and it was a good cause'. He got up. 'I'll go and put some champagne on ice so we can celebrate when Steve and Dinah get back.'

THE long twilight came at three in the afternoon, laying its soft purple mantle over pine and spruce forests which the first snows of winter had already dressed in a thin white undershift.

The house stood in a wide clearing between a narrow dirt road and a small lake dotted with tiny green and white skerries. Beside the house stood a sauna bath-house, set closer to the lake for the ritual icy plunge of the steam-broiled body.

The timber-built house was on one level, most of the space within was taken up by one very large room. It was warm in the room. An open log-fire in a big stone fireplace at one end supplemented the central heating. In the cellar below the thick pine floor, a small diesel generator supplied power for the boiler-pump and for the well-planned fluorescent lighting which produced a daylight effect over the solid bench where a man stood working.

He held a mallet and a half-inch gouge of shallow sweep, but he had not set blade to wood for thirty minutes now. He was working only with his rather deep-set eyes, looking from the clay model on his right to the mahogany statue in front of him, twenty-four inches high, and then to the living original from which the preliminary clay sketch had been modelled three weeks earlier.

Modesty Blaise said, 'Can we take a break, Alex? Coffee and a cigarette?'

The man did not answer, seemed unaware that she had spoken. He was of medium build, dark, with big clumsy-looking hands. Usually his manner was slow and patient. Now he was a little tense, chewing his lower lip as he stared at the statue, assessing the values of the planes and hollows in the rich dark wood, feeling in his mind the sweep of the grain, the curve of limb and breast, the soft subtle column of the neck.

Modesty Blaise sat on a round, blanket-covered table with a revolving top. Her legs and feet were drawn up together on one side, a hand resting loosely just below the knee. She was leaning sideways, a little, supporting herself on one straight arm. Highlights gleamed on her naked body. Her hair was drawn back and tied at the nape of her neck. It was an easy, natural pose. Alex Hemmer had caught it exactly in the clay model; and now, after three weeks of work, the pose had been captured in wood. But both on the model and on the carving, the face was still undefined.

Modesty closed her mind to the ache that had crept into her supporting arm, and watched as Alex Hemmer put down his tools neatly beside the long row of chisels and gouges, moved to the clay model and began once again to work on the face. He had modelled and destroyed a dozen faces in the clay during the past two days, but this was nothing compared with the agonies and frustrations she had watched him suffer in the beginning.

She wondered if John Dall would be pleased with the final result — if Alex ever made it.

The thing had all begun with John Dall. As one of the richest men in America he could afford to indulge an expensive whim. And so, on a day three months ago now, one of his minions had escorted Alex Hemmer from his remote house in northern Finland to Dall's ranch near Amarillo, Texas, where Modesty Blaise was ending a six-week visit.

Hemmer was not a world-famous sculptor, though he might yet become one. But he was a first-class representational sculptor whose technique was admired even by the abstract school.

'I don't want a Moore or a Hepworth,' Dall said. He was a lean, fit man nearing forty, with thick black hair cropped short and a face that betrayed a touch of Redskin ancestry. 'I want a statue that looks like her, Mr Hemmer. Not life-size. About this high.' He held a hand at about table height. 'And I'd like this sort of pose, it's the way she often sits.' He sat down on the great Persian carpet and leaned sideways on one arm.

Modesty laughed and said, 'You look cute, Johnnie.'

Dall got to his feet, grinning a little. 'That's more than you ever will, honey. If the statue looks cute, our friend here will have failed pretty badly.' He turned to the sculptor. 'How about it, Mr Hemmer?'

Alex Hemmer put down his untouched drink and stared at Modesty. She sat at one end of a big couch, looking back at him without embarrassment. The silence went on, and Alex Hemmer's patient gaze was so concentrated that it was as if he had fallen into a trance. Once Dall started to speak, but Modesty stopped him with a little movement of her hand.

At last Hemmer said, 'Marble or bronze?' He spoke good English and with care.

'Neither,' Dall said tersely. 'Wood. I know wood tends to hide itself, but good lighting can fix that. My choice would be mahogany — I'll listen to argument about that, but not about wood. It's warmer than marble or stone or bronze, and it's a living thing.' He looked at Modesty. 'It's right for you.'

Hemmer nodded slowly. 'Thank you. If you had said marble or bronze, I would go away. The material must be in harmony with the subject. As you say, wood is warm and alive. Also, with wood a sculptor can be more adventurous. It is the only material for a statue of this lady.'

'You have a pretty good instinct,' Dall said, and smiled. 'Mahogany?'

'Yes. The colour grows better with time. But it must be unpolished.'

'Fine. When can you start?'

Hemmer would work only in his own workshop, and before all else there was the matter of finding the right block of wood. It must not be green wood; kiln-dried might do, but best of all would be seasoned wood.

Dall could arrange that. He owned a number of mills and two hundred thousand acres of timber, including forests in Central America where mahogany was cut.

Next day Dall flew with Hemmer down into the timber country. Modesty went home. Some weeks later she received a polite cable from Hemmer, in Finland, saying that the selected block of mahogany had arrived and he was ready to begin.

For the first week she stayed in a small hotel near Tepasto. Daily she drove her hired Volvo 144S fifteen miles out into the pine forest where Hemmer's lonely house stood. He began the clay model with quiet enthusiasm, but by the third day she saw that he was close to despair. There were no dramatics about it. He began to pull chunks of clay off the armature on which it was built and said, 'I am very sorry. I think I am not able to do this. It will not come right.'

She had little creative ability herself, but deep intuition, and this allowed her to sense how shattering it must be for the artist who strikes a creative block. She made him stop work, then got dressed and busied herself making fresh coffee and a good meal.

For the next three days she would not let him work. They talked, took long walks in the forest, sawed logs for the fire with a big double-handed saw, and when dusk came they played bezique until it was time for her to go.

She had to teach him the game, and he had no card sense, but though he played badly he seemed to enjoy it.

There was a telephone in the house, because by good fortune the cable between Muonio and Ivalo ran close by. She had never heard it ring, and had seen him use it only once to order supplies, but he always called the hotel an hour after she left him, to make sure she had got home safely.

During this time she came to know him well, and developed a gentle affection for him. To her surprise she learned that he was not Finnish, but Hungarian. As a young man he had taken part in the abortive revolution of '56. In those days he had seen horrors which had destroyed all the romantic fires of youth in him. The girl he was to marry had been crushed under a tank, and in the dying hours of the fighting he had fled across the Austrian border.

He had settled in Finland, partly because there was a strange similarity of language but mainly because it was remote, a land of quietness. Alex Hemmer had opted out. He would never again allow himself to be involved in the clash of nations or ideologies or commerce or even personalities. He did the work he loved and had learned to do well, and he was content.

But now his contentment was undermined and she knew he was beginning to feel afraid. She believed she knew the cause of his creative power drying up. After three full days of idle leisure they agreed that he should start work again the following morning.

That day she checked out of the hotel and arrived at his house with her luggage in the boot of the car. He was waiting nervously, gazing at the shapeless mass of clay on the armature, bracing himself, his face a little drawn. But when she had undressed and put on the wrap she wore between sessions, she did not take up her pose on the table. She went to him and took his anxious face between her hands and kissed him long and hard on the lips. She knew it was only then he realized that desire for her had been sleeping within him.

Throughout that day they made love. He was not deeply versed in the art, but neither was he completely without experience, and it was made joyful for her by his total absorption in her, an absorption that sprang from the feeling of a sculptor for his material. When they lay together in the small warm bedroom he would feed upon her with the senses of sight and touch, dwelling upon every plane and muscle and subtly differing texture of her body.

He was slow and gentle, sometimes lost in wonderment at the sight or touch of some quality in a curve of flesh, sometimes studying her face with an intent, slightly baffled smile. Then would come the warm joining and the long smooth ascent, growing swifter to the final happening and the great sigh.

That day, as the early twilight came, they broiled themselves in the steam of the sauna bath-house and afterwards broke the mushy skin of ice at the lake's edge for the breathless plunge. They dried, glowing, in front of the fire, and she made a meal.

At last, when they had eaten, she posed for him once again. He began to shape the clay on the armature, working with easy confidence. By midnight the model was finished—all but the face, which he intended to leave until after the carving of the body in wood had been completed.

That night he had taken her into his arms and fallen instantly into a deep sleep of utter contentment. Now, three weeks later, the mahogany sculpture was almost finished. He was having difficulty with the face, but there was no return of anxiety. He was enjoying the challenge, as a man might enjoy the challenge of a high mountain.

He put down the wooden spatula he had been using and said, 'Yes, of course.'

'Of course what, Alex?'

'You said you would like coffee and a cigarette.'

'That was fifteen minutes ago.'

He stared. 'Truly?'

'Truly. But that's not a record.' She picked up the wrap that lay behind her and drew it on as she got down from the table. 'Last night I asked you to stop working and come to bed. Forty minutes later you said, "Yes, by God!"'

He rubbed a hand ruefully across his brow, leaving an oily smear. 'It is your own fault, Modesty. You have a maddening face.'

'Thank you.' She lifted the coffee pot which stood on a hob by the fire, and poured coffee into two big china mugs. He gave her a cigarette and lit it for her, then took her chin in one hand and turned her head first one way and then the other.

'At one moment it is a very young face, the face of a rather wicked child. The next moment it is older than the face of Eve.'

She smiled. 'You'd better capture the old one, Alex. I missed out on being a child.'

'No. You are sometimes that now.' He looked at the sculpture. 'I must capture both in the wood. And many other things also. I know I can do it.'

'Good.' She sat down, sipping the hot, sweet coffee. There was a comfortable silence. Alex Hemmer gazed absently at the statue. After a while he said, 'You have no vanity. You do not particularly want to have this sculpture made. Why did you agree?'

'John Dall asked me, and I owe him a debt.'

'What kind of debt?'

'He once came halfway across the world to help me when I needed it.'

Alex Hemmer nodded thoughtfully. 'He told me a little about you. I know that you have known much danger.

And that you saved Dall's life, you and a strange man called Willie Garvin.'

'There's nothing strange about Willie. Rare, perhaps. Not strange. And preventing John Dall being murdered was just a spin-off that came about because he helped us.'

'Will you tell me the story?'

'No, Alex. It's past. And anyway, it would offend your principles. You don't believe in people getting involved.'

'That is only for me. I do not try to persuade anybody else.'

She smiled. 'Good. But you haven't much chance, living like a hermit.'

After a moment or two, still gazing at the statue, he said, 'Will you tell John Dall that we made love?'

'I'd tell him if he asked me, Alex, but he'll never ask.'

'He will know, though,' Alex Hemmer said quietly. 'When he sees that statue, he will know.'

She looked at the carving, then at Hemmer, and grinned suddenly. It was a sparkling grin, full of wicked humour, that lit up her face as if by a bright light from within. 'I expect he will,' she said.

'And so?'

'So it doesn't matter. He's not under the impression that he owns me or has any exclusive rights.'

Hemmer said, a little wryly, 'I do not think any man would have that impression.' He paused. 'I am curious about Willie Garvin. Tell me something of him.'

'No. You'll only get confused, Alex. Everybody does. But I expect you'll be seeing him.'

Hemmer looked surprised. 'He is coming to Finland?'

'He's already here. We travelled over together. He's spending a month working in a lumber camp near Rytinki.'

'Working? I understood he was a rich man.'

'He is. But he likes a change and he likes logging.'

'Logging is a very tough change.'

'That's probably the point. You see? You're getting confused already. Anyway, I expect he's finished his stint by now and moved up to that little hotel where I was staying. I left a message there to tell him I'd moved in with you. I expect he'll call, if he doesn't get too tangled up with that lovely Finnish girl who runs the bakery.'

Hemmer pushed a hand slowly through his hair and shook his head. Vaguely he could think of a number of questions he wanted to ask, but he had a suspicion that they would only lead to still more questions and that in the end his curiosity would remain unsatisfied.

As he put down his empty mug there came a faint sound from the heavy door between the big main room and the outer porch. It was an odd sound, as if someone were slapping at the timber with an open hand.

Modesty said, 'A visitor?' She threw her cigarette in the fire and belted the wrap more firmly about her.

Alex Hemmer said, 'I did not hear a car, and who would come on foot?' He moved to the door and opened it. A man who had been kneeling slumped against the door fell across the threshold. He wore heavy cord trousers tucked into stout boots, and a windcheater that had once been white but was now wet and caked with dirt. The hood had fallen back from his head. His ungloved hands and his face were very white with cold.

Modesty came past Hemmer, bent down and put her hands under the man's shoulders. She said, 'Take his feet and help me get him in front of the fire, Alex. Then close the door, bring some brandy, and put hot-water-bottles in the bed,'

Hemmer opened his mouth to voice a useless question, then closed it again. Together they lifted the unconscious man on to the rug in front of the fire. Hemmer brought a bottle of brandy and a glass from the cupboard, then went into the kitchen to fill hot-water-bottles.

When he returned he saw that Modesty had dragged off the man's boots and icy wet trousers. She had also partly taken off the windcheater, but his right arm was still in the stained and blackened sleeve.

The man had thinning brown hair and was perhaps in his middle forties, not a big man, but wiry. He had a lean face with a long jaw that bore a day's stubble of beard. His eyes were closed and he was muttering in a foreign language.

Hemmer said, 'It sounds like German.'

'Yes.' Modesty looked up. 'Pass me the scissors, Alex.'

He gave them to her wonderingly, and watched as she began to cut away the sleeve of the windcheater and the thick sweater beneath. Then he realized that the black stains were dried blood.

'He is hurt?'

'Yes. Will you get your first-aid box from the bedroom, Alex? And a bowl of hot water, please.'

He brought them for her, knelt down and began to massage one of the frozen hands, watching Modesty. She worked quickly and competently, as if no stranger to this kind of thing. The man still muttered occasionally, a rather desperate note in his voice.

'What is he saying?' Hemmer asked.

'He's saying, *"Don't let them find me, please. They're not far behind."* '

She had soaked the clothing away from the wound and was washing the long deep gouge torn in the flesh of his upper arm. It was an ugly wound, raw and oozing. Hemmer had seen far worse during the bad days in Budapest, but even so he had to swallow a wave of nausea as he said, 'What do you think he means, Modesty?'

'I think he means that the men who shot him are close behind.'

'*Shot* him?'

'It's a bullet wound. You can see the two holes in the arm of his windcheater. In and out. It missed the bone, but it's taken a lot of flesh.' She laid a strip of lint over the wound, spread a pad of cottonwool on top and began to bandage the arm. 'We'll make a better dressing of it later. And we'll save the brandy for then, too. The main thing now is to get him out of sight in the bedroom before his friends arrive.'

Hemmer stood up, his big hands opening and shutting nervously. 'If we hide him, we are involved,' he said.

She finished the bandage before she answered. Her face was quiet and without anger. She said, 'All right. I know how you feel. But he's a hurt man. Just help me get him to the bedroom.'

'I will not help to hide him,' Hemmer said stubbornly. 'For God's sake, he may be a criminal! The people he fears may be the police. We do not know *anything* yet.'

'That's right, Alex. We don't know yet. So let's find out before we throw him to the wolves.'

He paced away across the room, pounding one fist gently into the palm of the other hand, dismayed and uncertain. As he swung round he saw that she had managed to lift the limp figure into a hunched kneeling position. Suddenly, with astonishing strength, she heaved the man upright, ducked so that he folded forward across her shoulder, then straightened up slowly.

Hemmer swore in Hungarian and started towards her. 'All right! I'll carry him!'

She looked at him, slightly bent under her burden. The wrap had fallen open and he could see the flat plane of her taut stomach-muscles. She said, 'Alex, we were involved from the moment he fell into this room, whether you like it or not. Leaving him on the floor here for his enemies to find, whoever they are, is just as much an act of involvement as hiding him from them. I'm not asking you to make a choice, I'm just telling you that I've made my own for the moment. Either I hide him now or I take him to the car and start driving. I'm not pressing you one way or the other, but just say which.'

Hemmer swore again and said, 'The bedroom! Don't just stand there with that weight on your back!'

She turned and moved slowly through the doorway. Hemmer followed, and helped her lower him to the bed. She stripped off his damp underclothes, put the hot-water-bottle around him, and piled on blankets and eiderdown.

The man stopped muttering. It seemed that the warmth had induced a sleep of exhaustion. Hemmer stood looking down at him, feeling a muddled blend of compassion and anger. Modesty was bending over her open suitcase. She straightened up, went to the door, beckoned Hemmer out and switched off the light.

'Get his clothes and all that first-aid stuff out of sight, Alex,' she said softly, closing the door. Hemmer obeyed with dull resignation. He had to admit to himself that she had not used any wiles to secure his help. Her alternative of driving the wounded man away in her car had not been a threat, simply a statement of intent.

She had brought out a mop and was drying the floor, working with her head cocked slightly, listening. 'Soon now,' she said, and put the mop away. Hemmer held his breath to listen, and after a moment could just make out the faint drone of a car moving in low gear down the slight slope of the dirt road.

Modesty ran her eye over the area in front of the fire where the wounded man had lain. Satisfied, she sat on the edge of the big round table, swung her legs up to take the familiar pose, then slipped the wrap off and let it fall behind her. She said, 'Start modelling, Alex. And don't answer when they knock. I've left the door on the latch so they can walk in.'

'But you *can't*—' he began incredulously.

'It couldn't be better,' she said with a touch of impatience. 'Could anything look less likely than that we have something to hide? Oh, come *on*, Alex. Forget about our new guest and just be yourself. If you can go into one of your creative trances, so much the better.'

With sudden angry energy he snatched up the mallet and a fishtail gouge, swivelled the table an inch or two, then moved to the statue and began to carve the line of the brow, ignoring the clay model, carving direct. His lips were tight and he was breathing hard through his nose.

Three minutes later, when a hand knocked sharply on the door, he merely glanced at her briefly from under lowered brows and went on with his work. The knock was repeated. After a long pause there came the sound of the heavy iron latch lifting. The door opened tentatively. A voice said, 'Excuse me, please.'

Modesty did not move. Her back was half turned to the door and she could see it only from the corner of her eye. Hemmer put down the mallet and began to use the palm of his hand on the handle of the gouge, tapping delicately.

Three men moved uncertainly over the threshold, then stopped short, staring. One said, 'Please. I am sorry we intrude but it is urgent.' He did not speak in Finnish, but in the widely understood Swedish tongue, and with an accent. An icy wind stirred in the room, and one of the men closed the door.

The first man spoke again. 'I am sorry. It seems very bad to intrude, but—'

Modesty said without moving, very coldly, 'Alex, there are people here.' She spoke in Swedish. Hemmer might not have heard. His face was feverishly intent as he changed to a skew chisel and picked up the mallet again.

The men shuffled uneasily, perplexed. Modesty lifted her voice and said, 'Do you know whose house this is?'

'No. I regret, *Fröken*. A friend of ours is lost. He was hurt in an accident. We thought he might have found his way here.'

Modesty said, 'This is the house of Alex Hemmer, the most famous sculptor of this country. He is engaged in important work. It is bad enough that you enter unasked and stare when I am posing in this way. But to disturb Herr Hemmer at work is an outrage. Have you understood me?' On the last words she turned her head suddenly to glare with angry indignation.

Three men. Well dressed in expensive winter clothing and boots, with fur hats. Different faces but the same eyes. No, the same gaze. The familiar cold flat gaze, usually empty and incurious but now hazed by confusion and unease.

She had barely turned her head and sighted them when Hemmer let out an explosive oath. 'Keep still!' he cried. 'Dear God, you sit still for weeks and at this moment you move! *This* moment!' He flung down the chisel and pressed his hands to his eyes as if trying to retain an inner vision.

Modesty said in a low, furious voice, 'Get out, you fools — see what you have done!'

'But . . . our friend,' the spokesman persisted doggedly.

'You think Herr Hemmer entertains lost strangers tonight?' she said with fierce contempt. 'Get *out*!'

She turned her head back into position. There came a muttered apology, a scuffling of feet. The door opened and closed. She listened for the sound of the car starting up, then for the fading sound as it moved away.

Hemmer dropped his hands from his eyes and drew in a deep breath. 'Do not move again!' he said urgently. 'What the devil got into you? Now hold it just like that. Hold it!' He picked up the chisel.

Dumbfounded, trying to keep her eyes from widening in astonishment, trying to suppress a sudden huge urge to laugh, Modesty Blaise said dazedly to herself, 'My God! . . .' And held it.

Half an hour later Hemmer put down a spoon gouge, stepped back from the bench and eased his cramped fingers. 'I have got you,' he said with quiet but intense triumph. 'Not finished. Barely sketched in. But it is there, Modesty. I can see it there in the wood.'

'I'm very glad for you.' She got down from the table and put on the wrap. He was rubbing his eyes, but suddenly he snatched his hands away, stared at the bedroom door and then at Modesty. 'That man!' he exclaimed.

'Yes.' She tied the belt. 'I don't think you noticed much about his friends when they came for him. They weren't policemen. And they weren't at all nice.'

He sank down on a heavy teak chair and gestured vaguely towards the statue. 'I suddenly found what I wanted . . .'

She smiled. 'So I gathered. And very convincing it made you.'

He drew in a long breath, frowning, reaching back into memory. 'Yes. I remember now. But suppose they had searched? Suppose the man had called out in his sleep?'

She took a small automatic from the pocket of her wrap, drew the magazine out and worked the slide to eject the cartridge in the breech. 'Then there would have been an argument, Alex. We might well have disturbed even your concentration.'

'A gun,' he said with weary distaste. 'I hate guns.'

'Guns are neutral. It's more logical to hate me.' She looked at the big clock on the mantelpiece. 'Time we had something to eat. Do you mind if I make a phone-call first? I want to see if Willie Garvin's at the hotel.'

He gripped his big hands between his knees and said slowly, 'I will not be involved any further, Modesty.'

'I know.'

He got up. 'I will start preparing the meal while you make the call.' He went into the kitchen and closed the door.

It was ten minutes later when she joined him. He saw that she had dressed now, in a shirt and dark slacks, with calf-length leather boots. She said, 'Thanks, Alex. I got through. Willie arrived this morning. And our guest is still sleeping. I sat him up and got a little brandy down him. He said, "*Danke*," and went to sleep again without even opening his eyes. But I'll have to rouse him later. I've got to find out what it's all about.'

Hemmer looked at the automatic which now rested in a little holster on her belt. He said, 'Why are you wearing that?'

'Those men may come back. We convinced them just now, but they could have second thoughts. I'd rather be safe than sorry.'

The meal was a silent one. Hemmer brooded, a little sulky. Modesty was not unfriendly but seemed busy with her own thoughts. When they had cleared away she carried a big bowl of hot water into the bedroom. The man in the bed had thawed out now, and there was colour in his face and hands.

Hemmer sat watching as she gave him a blanket bath, washing the sweat and grime from his body. When she had dried him she drew the covers over him again and took the rough dressing from his arm. She examined the wound closely, nodded her satisfaction, then brought a little bottle of clear liquid from her suitcase. It was after she had swabbed the wound and was re-bandaging the arm that the man's breathing changed.

He stirred, opened his eyes, went rigid for a moment, then slowly relaxed. The eyes were blue and wary. They focused on Modesty as she bent over him. He gave a feeble laugh of disbelief and murmured, '*Lieber Gott* . . .' A pause, and the next words were in English, the voice stronger. 'You have changed very little, Mam'selle . . . except that your hair was up when I last saw you.'

One of Modesty's eyebrows lifted sharply. 'You know me?'

'We have not met. But I saw you in Vienna, five years ago. You are Modesty Blaise. Your people called you Mam'selle, I remember. You were there on business . . . and I was on the same business.' Humour touched the intelligent blue eyes. 'To your cost, I now regret. I am Waldo.'

Modesty said, 'My God.' She sat down on the edge of the bed and began to laugh. 'Fifty thousand you cost me, wasn't it?'

'A little more, I am sorry to say.'

'Thank you for the flowers you sent afterwards. I'd have liked to meet you at the time.'

'I have always been a very retiring man.'

'Yours is that kind of business, Waldo.'

'It was. And perhaps even a gentlemanly business. But no longer.' He looked down at his bandaged arm. 'The game has changed, Mam'selle. You did well to retire. I am taking the same road myself.'

Alex Hemmer stood up and moved to the bedside. Modesty said, 'Waldo, this is Alex Hemmer, your host.'

'I am in your debt, Herr Hemmer.'

'Not mine.' Hemmer looked at Modesty. 'Will you explain to me what you have been speaking of?'

She nodded and took out a packet of cigarettes. Hemmer shook his head. She lit two, and placed one between Waldo's lips.

'For the last fifteen years,' she said, 'Waldo has been the top industrial spy in the business. The top solo man, anyway, and a founder-member of the profession. Quite a lot of what he does is legal. Some of it isn't. And the whole business works only because some of the biggest corporations in the world are ready to hand out a lot of money for details of new procésses and inventions their rivals are developing.'

'This I know,' Hemmer said with a shade of impatience. 'I have read of it.'

'No doubt,' Modesty said. 'But you won't have read of Waldo. He's known only in special circles. Quite a big section of my own organization was devoted to industrial espionage, and very rewarding it was. In Vienna, five years ago, Waldo and I were both after something the Farbstein Corporation had come up with, and he snatched it from under my nose.' She smiled. 'Afterwards Waldo sent me a beautiful bouquet with a very witty and charming note of apology.'

'I hoped you would know it was an act of courtesy and not of vanity,' Waldo said.

'I knew.' She studied his tired, ageing face. 'It showed style, Waldo. I've always liked style.'

Somehow Waldo contrived to bow while lying in bed. 'Your own great quality, Mam'selle. But a dying thing. The game has changed.'

'So you said. Your three friends called and went away satisfied, but I don't know whether they'll remain so. Who are they?'

'Salamander Four.'

She stared. Hemmer said, 'What is Salamander Four?'

Still looking at Waldo she answered, 'International group based in Amsterdam. The big boys of industrial espionage. Very businesslike. Very high-powered men at the top. There are names in Salamander Four that you can read in the city and society and even political columns of newspapers in a dozen different countries. But they've always worked clean. I've never known them to hire killers.'

Waldo gave a little shrug, and winced. 'That also has changed. Mam'selle. I did not believe it myself until now.'

'What happened?'

'The Kellgren Laboratories in Sweden have developed a new colour film. Salamander Four were after the process. So was I, for a client of my own in West Germany. Well . . . I won, and Salamander Four lost. That should be the end of it. But they do not have your appreciation of style, Mam'selle. They want me dead, and I have been running hard for two weeks now.'

He stubbed out the cigarette in the ashtray she held for him, and smiled resignedly. 'But Europe has become too small. They caught up with me about seven kilometres from here, I think. They rammed my car. I went into a ditch, but was able to get out and run into the forest. They followed, shooting at me. I was hit in the arm, but in the end I lost them.' He grimaced. 'I lost myself, also. I don't remember very well how I came to this house.'

Modesty got up and paced the little room, holding her elbows. After a while she said, 'What were your plans, Waldo?'

'Australia.' His gaze was rueful. 'I can afford to retire, and the work has no pleasure for me now. Salamander Four will not reach out to Australia for me. It will be enough for them that I have been driven from the scene.'

'What route?'

'By air. Each night for the next three nights there will be a private aircraft waiting at Ivalo to fly me across the border and down to Leningrad.'

'Will you be safe in transit across Russia?'

'By air, yes. I have industrial contacts, there. They are very different from the politicians. All arrangements have been expensively made. It is only the journey between here and Ivalo that is dangerous for me.' He hesitated, then went on apologetically. 'Is it possible to borrow or to hire a car, Mam'selle?'

Hemmer grunted. Modesty said, 'You can't drive with that arm. I'll take you to Ivalo myself.' She looked at Hemmer. 'Tomorrow morning, if that's all right with you, Alex. Otherwise we'll leave tonight.'

Hemmer got to his feet. 'You must do what you think best,' he said, and went out of the room.

After a moment Waldo said, 'I have caused trouble. I am sorry.'

'It's nothing. Artists are difficult people. They dream up a nice world to live in, and it makes the real world very hard for them to cope with.' She smiled at him. 'I've got some hot soup ready. You're going to eat, Waldo, then sleep until I wake you tomorrow.'

He sighed. 'I wish I had the words to thank you. In a way I am like your friend. All these years I have evaded physical conflict, and now that it comes upon me I am lost. I have never swum in these waters.' He thought for a moment. 'It is possible Salamander Four will keep watch on this house, I think.'

'They may do. I'll wake you early, so you can be tucked down out of sight in the back of the car before first light. An hour later they can watch me come out and drive off on my own, if they're interested.'

He nodded, and looked about him. 'This is the only bed. Where will you sleep?'

'Alex can sleep in the other room, on the rug in front of the fire.'

'And you?'

She touched the gun at her wrist. 'I'll be sitting up, Waldo. Just in case our Salamander Four friends come back tonight. You can sleep soundly. I've swum in these waters quite a lot.'

An hour before dawn, heavy smoke began to belch from the chimney, rolling and billowing around the house. Under cover of the smoke and the darkness, Modesty took Waldo out to the Volvo. He lay down on the back seat with a thick rug over him and three hot water bottles. He wore a sweater and a warm jacket provided by Hemmer. The rest of his clothes had been dried overnight. He had eaten and slept well, and his hurt arm was strapped comfortably in a sling under the jacket.

Modesty went back into the house and raked aside the oily rags she had put on the fire to make smoke. Hemmer stood gazing absently at the statue, running a hand over the chiselled curves of the close-grained wood.

She said, 'Will you be able to finish it without me, Alex? You said you could see what you wanted in the wood now.'

He shook his head. 'I can see it. But I cannot carve it without also being able to see your face.'

'Would you like me to fix breakfast for you? I've got an hour, and it won't take me long to pack.'

'Thank you.'

There was little conversation, but she seemed to feel no sense of strain, and her manner was amiably relaxed. Hemmer felt confused. Once he said, 'Do you think I am a coward because I will not let myself be involved?'

She said, 'No, I don't think that, Alex. I've no criticism at all. Will you have some more coffee?'

Later, after the sun had risen, she came out of the bedroom wearing a tartan lumberjacket and black slacks tucked into her boots, a little white fur cap on her head, suitcase in her hand. She put a hand to his cheek, kissed him lightly on the lips and said, 'Goodbye, Alex. Take care of yourself.'

He took the case and walked with her to the car to put it in the boot. The cold made her tanned cheeks glow, and he found her heart-achingly lovely.

He said, 'Will you come back?'

'What do *you* think, Alex?'

'I don't know.' He managed to smile. 'I just hope that if you come back it will not be simply for Dall's sake.'

She said nothing, and he could read nothing in her eyes. After a moment she turned and got into the car. He closed the door and stepped back. The engine fired and revved. She waved, and eased the car smoothly away over the rutted snow, its studded tyres biting firmly.

The dirt road curved gently up through the forest to join a road which led on to Highway Four, the arctic highway running north to Ivalo. But she had decided to branch off and take the lesser road, through Pokka and Inari, since it was more direct. With winter only just begun, the road would still be clear of heavy snow.

She said, 'Are you comfortable, Waldo?'

His voice behind her answered. 'So comfortable I could sleep, Mam'selle. It was beginning to grow cold, but now the car-heater has taken effect.'

'Sleep if you can. There's a long drive ahead. And there may be a lot of hanging around at Ivalo if the weather isn't clear for take-off. We could wait all night.'

'But there is no need for you to wait with me, Mam'selle.'

'Don't argue. With Salamander Four in the field, I'm going to see you off. You can thank the flowers for that.'

She heard his soft, pleasant laugh, and said, 'Whether you sleep or not, stay tucked down. If Salamander Four didn't take careful note of this car last night, they're not the men they ought to be. And if they know you were heading north, they'll be watching out. I hope they'll watch Highway Four, but I won't bank on it. If they see me alone at the wheel it's one thing, but seeing me with a passenger is something else.'

It was an hour later, after they had passed a small village north of Hanhimaa, that the grey Mercedes came on their tail. Here the road wound round a long low hill, with tall spruce on one side and a shallow drop on the other. All along the edge of the drop were set big stones to mark the limit of the road. A thin layer of unfrozen snow covered the surface.

Modesty roused Waldo, who was dozing. 'I think they picked us up going through the last village,' she said. 'Don't quite know what they'll try, but nothing drastic to begin with, I imagine. They're only working on suspicion so far.'

'Can you leave them behind?' Waldo asked quietly.

'I don't fancy trying to run away from a Merc, and I don't want to drive rally-style for the next few hours.' She studied the mirror. 'Only one man in the car, I think. We'll aim at settling things as soon as he shows his hand.'

She took the automatic, a MAB .25, from her pocket and passed it back to him between the bucket seats. 'I don't want any shooting, Waldo, but if things go wrong you can look after yourself with this. Stay down when we stop, and don't show yourself. If anyone opens the back door to look in, you can take it something's gone wrong and I'm out of action. Then it's up to you.'

He hesitated, and she knew he wanted to protest, but after a moment he said, 'Understood.' She allowed herself a brief smile. Waldo was a professional, not the man to jog your arm when you were calling the shots.

Behind her the Mercedes drew closer, flashed its lights and peeped its horn. She slowed a little, turned and looked over her shoulder. There was only one man in the car. Evidently he was intending to make a soft approach . . .

anxiety about a slight rear-wheel wobble on the Volvo, or a suspect tyre. Any excuse to stop her and take a look in the car.

She had switched the heater to 'screen' two minutes ago. Already the side windows were heavily misted, and only the electrically heated section of the rear window was clear.

Flash of headlights from behind, and a more urgent peep of the horn. Ahead the road swelled to form a short lay-by. Here, by some freak of trapped warmth from the sun, the thin snow had melted. The surface was smooth dry tarmac, in contrast to the dirt and gravel surface of the road.

She drew into the lay-by and halted. The Mercedes cut in ahead and stopped sharply. The man who emerged was the spokesman of the night before. She was out in the road, had closed the door and was moving to meet him as he came towards her. He smiled, but his eyes remained very cold.

'Excuse me, Fröken. There is something hanging loose under your car—' He stopped short with assumed surprise. 'Surely it is the lady we met last night?'

'Did you find your friend?' Modesty said. His right hand was in the pocket of the thick thigh-length jacket he wore. He stopped three paces from her.

'No, we did not find him, Fröken,' he said, watching her. 'Did *you*?' The smile had vanished. She knew that her quick exit from the car and the closing of the door had sharpened his suspicions. When she made no reply he said, 'I wish to look in your car, please.'

She said, 'No. Go back to Salamander Four and tell them—'

That was as far as she got. The use of the name was calculated to freeze him for an instant, long enough for her to take one stride and strike with the kongo, the little double mushroom of hard, polished sandalwood that was gripped in her right hand, the two knobs protruding from her fist as it rested in the slanting pocket of her lumberjacket.

But her calculation was wrong. Almost as the words 'Salamander Four' left her lips, he jerked a revolver from his pocket and fired at her head.

It was her own speed of reaction, far faster than thought, which saved her; and perhaps also the long experience which had taught her that to duck or dodge away from a gun at short range is foolish. A bullet kills as readily at ten feet as at two feet, and moving back allows a gunman more shots.

She had ducked sideways and was lunging towards the gun. The bullet cracked past her head, missing by a finger's width. Then her left hand closed over the cylinder and breech, squeezing with all her strength, holding the hammer back and forcing a pinch of her flesh between hammer and cartridge.

She made no attempt to force the gun sideways or to wrench it from him, but went with the movement of his arm as he jerked back hard, and in the same moment struck with the kongo in her right hand, aiming for the temple.

As he staggered back across the front of the Volvo the gun came free of his grasp and was left reversed in her hand. The blow with the kongo had been awkwardly struck and was slightly off target. He did not fall, but recovered his balance and thrust towards her again, his face twisted with shock and fury. She went to meet him, and took him with a drop-kick, her booted feet smashing home just over the heart.

As she landed in a crouch he went back three tottering paces and fell. She heard the soft thump as his head struck one of the big stones bordering the edge of the road. His legs twitched, and he lay still.

Carefully she detached the gun from her left hand. It was a Smith & Wesson Chief's Special .38. She eased the hammer down, grimly thankful that it had not been the Centennial Model with the enclosed hammer, and sucked her hand where the pinched flesh oozed a bead of blood. As she put on the safety she walked to the Volvo and called, 'Relax on that trigger, Waldo. It's me.' Her voice was taut with fury.

When she opened the rear door his pale face stared up at her and she saw the MAB in his hand. He sat up slowly and said, 'When I heard the shot, I thought . . . .'

'You very nearly thought right.' He saw her lips compress in a thin hard line, saw that her blue-black eyes were stormy. She was breathing hard, not from exertion but from anger.

'The bastard!' she said, seething. 'If he'd *known* who I was, if he'd even *known* you were in the car, I wouldn't mind. But he didn't know a damn thing. As far as he knew I was just a girl who stood here and said "Salamander Four". So he tried to blow my brains out.' She reached over to put the Special on the front seat, and picked up her gloves. 'No questions. Just out with the gun, and bang!'

Waldo made a sympathetic noise, then watched as she walked to the unconscious man and knelt over him. He felt an inward chill, knowing that if he had been in her place he would have been dead by now. He saw her take off a glove and rest her fingers on the man's neck. Ten seconds later she stood up and walked back to the car.

'How is he?' Waldo asked.

She shrugged, frowning a little with annoyance. 'He hit his head on that stone, and he's what might best be described as dead.'

Waldo laughed shortly. 'I shall try to remember him as he was when he was alive. It will help to ease my sorrow.' He looked past her at the body. 'But it makes a bad situation. Will you arrange a car accident?'

'No.' She looked up and down the empty road, pulling on her glove. 'It would take too long to make it convincing. Better to keep things simple and just bend the truth a little. Stay there.'

She walked to the Mercedes, backed it to within a few feet of the body, then switched off and got out. He saw her unlock the boot, take out the jack, toolbox and spare wheel. She spread them around on the ground, returned to the Volvo, and took a quart can of oil from the boot.

Unscrewing the cap of the can, she poured a little oil on the dry tarmac close to the dead man's feet, then smeared some on the soles of his boots. She scraped her foot through the puddle of oil once or twice, put the cap on, but did not screw it up tightly. When she laid the can down on its side, oil dripped from it very slowly.

Crouching by the offside rear wheel, she took a thin screw-driver from the toolbox and jabbed it between the treads of the tyre, pressing hard. The tyre deflated. She returned the screw-driver and used her gloved hands to brush a little dirt from the breast of the man's jacket, where her drop-kick had landed.

After a final study of the scene she walked back to the Volvo and got in behind the wheel.

Waldo said, 'He was preparing to change the wheel. The oil leaked a little from the can. He stepped on the oil-patch and his feet went from under him. His head hit the stone when he fell. A matter of simple deduction.'

'It's better than anything fancy,' Modesty said, and started the engine. 'Next village or garage we come to I'll report it, to account for our tracks. I'll be very upset and rather shaky, not quite sure that he's dead, but I think so, and anyway, I was too scared to move him. You stay under the rug, Waldo.'

As she drove out of the lay-by Waldo leaned back in his seat. 'I wonder where his two colleagues are?' he said thoughtfully.

Modesty changed up and the car gathered speed. 'I think we could both make a good guess,' she said.

They came on foot, two hours after sunrise. When the door opened and they walked in, Alex Hemmer was sitting staring into the fire, as he had been sitting ever since Modesty Blaise drove away.

He recognized them from the night before, though he had not been consciously aware of them then. One had a gingery growth of beard. The other, a little taller, had a pasty face and a thin nose. Hemmer got to his feet, feeling sudden unease as the door closed behind them.

The thin-nosed one walked forward and said, 'You lied last night. He was here. There is a trail in the snow, and spots of blood. Impossible to see in the dark, but clear enough now.'

He hit Hemmer across the face with sudden ferocity. It was a back-handed blow, and the shock of it seemed to scramble Hemmer's brains. He reeled back and toppled over a chair. The man with the beard kicked him and said, 'Where is he?'

'Gone . . .' Hemmer wheezed, fighting down the sickness that threatened to overwhelm him. Through the sound of his own harsh breathing he heard footsteps move across the room, heard the bedroom door thrown open, then the kitchen door.

'The woman took him when she left in the car?' said a voice. Hemmer's vision cleared a little. The two men were standing over him. He shook his head.

'Gone where?' said the thin-nosed man.

'I . . . don't know.' Hemmer felt completely helpless before the casual ruthlessness of these two men, but fear had not touched him yet, only a slow and impotent anger. Stolidly he began to get to his feet. A knee hit him under the chin and he sprawled again.

Vaguely he was aware of being hauled to a kneeling position, of rough hands doing something to his right arm, forcing it into a gap with smooth wood on each side. When his head cleared a little he found that he was crouched against the back of the heavy fireside chair. His arm had been thrust between the vertical wooden rails and his hand rested on the broad seat.

The thin-nosed man stood on one side of the chair, bending a little to grip the imprisoned forearm. The man with the beard had picked up the beechwood mallet that lay on the table by the statue.

'Where did they go?' the thin-nosed man said with cold anger.

Hemmer shook his head again. 'I don't know.'

The man nodded to his companion. 'All right. Break his hand.'

It was then that fear struck into Hemmer, piercing and incredulous fear. He tried to rise, but his legs had lost their strength. The bearded man moved forward and lifted the mallet high. Staring up at him through the wooden rails, Hemmer screamed soundlessly within himself.

He felt a gust of cold air on his back, and saw something glitter as it flashed three feet over his head from behind. The bearded man jumped as if stung. The mallet jerked in his grasp. In the moment before it fell, Hemmer saw that the five-inch blade of a small throwing-knife with a dimpled bone haft had driven through the handle of the mallet just above the point of grip, so that the edge of the blade had nicked the bearded man's fingers. Spots of blood fell as the mallet clattered to the floor.

The thin-nosed man jerked upright, a hand streaking to the pocket of his fur jacket.

A voice said, 'Garvin.' It was a deep, relaxed voice, and its effect was astonishing. As if the single word held some potent magic, both men froze instantly in mid-action, their postures slightly grotesque. Into Hemmer's dazed mind flickered the memory of the ancient Nordic legend which held that a troll overtaken by sunrise is turned instantly to stone.

He twisted his head round slowly. A man stood in the open doorway, a man in his middle thirties perhaps, with thick fair hair and a brown face that was pleasantly unhandsome and a little rough-hewn. He was hatless, and wore a lumberjacket of dull green and brown, with dark trousers tucked into leather boots. In his left hand was a knife, a twin of the other, held by the blade between two fingers and a thumb.

Hemmer's first impression was one of hugeness. Then he realized that though the man was big, well over six feet, it was the impact of his personality that made the room seem to shrink. It extended beyond his physical body like an aura. In it there was an immense vitality combined with a quiet, vast assurance that contained no element of conceit.

'Willie Garvin,' said the man, though clearly the knife and the single word had been sufficient introduction for the two intruders. Then, as Hemmer drew his arm free and made to rise — 'Stay down a minute, Mr 'Emmer. You might get in the way.'

Hemmer stayed down. The two men were still frozen and there was a glaze of fear in their eyes. Willie Garvin pushed the door shut behind him and moved forward unhurriedly, the knife-hilt resting lightly on his shoulder now.

'Better get to know each other,' he said as he passed the thin-nosed man. 'Who're you?' On the last word his right arm lifted and swung in a backward jab, so fast that to Hemmer it was a blur. The elbow struck just under the man's ear. His knees folded and he melted to the floor without a sound.

Now Hemmer saw that the knife had been reversed and was held by the hilt. Willie Garvin made a quick jab towards the stomach of the bearded man. It was a feint that compelled instinctive reaction. The man's hands dropped to ward off the thrust, and as they did so Willie Garvin took another half-pace forward and struck upwards under the side of the jaw, hitting with the inside edge of his empty right hand.

The bearded man seemed to grow taller for a moment, then crumpled in a heap.

'I wonder if you could find me a bit of cord, Mr 'Emmer?' Willie Garvin said politely. 'We'll get 'em tied up, and then p'raps we could 'ave a nice cup of coffee.'

Hemmer got slowly to his feet. He tried to frame a question, but his mind was too confused. 'Cord,' he repeated at last, and nodded. 'Yes.' He went through into the kitchen.

When he returned with a length of picture cord, Willie Garvin's knives had disappeared and the mallet with the split handle lay on the table. 'Sorry about the damage,' said Willie. 'The Princess told me not to play rougher than I 'ad to, so I figured a nice fancy throw might keep 'em quiet.'

'And your name, also, I think.'

'It rings a bell with some people,' Willie acknowledged.

Hemmer rubbed his brow. 'You said . . . the Princess?'

'Modesty.' Willie took the cord from Hemmer and knelt over the thin-nosed man. 'She rang me again last night, after you'd gone to sleep. I left the Land-Rover the other side of the lake an' came the rest of the way on foot. Been waiting in the bath-'ouse since a couple of hours before dawn.'

'But . . . that was before she left!'

'Well, we 'ad to overlap, and she didn't want me on show. These two might 'ave been watching, and she reckoned you might get upset and start a lot of argument. Any chance of that coffee, Mr 'Emmer?'

Hemmer went into the kitchen and began to make coffee. He found that his hands were shaking with the reaction from that moment of piercing terror. When he returned five minutes later the two men had come to their senses. They lay with their hands bound behind them, and their faces were pallid with fear. Willie Garvin was smoking a cigarette, studying the statue with great concentration.

'You've really got something 'ere,' he said slowly. 'John Dall's going to love it. The body's perfect. It lives. You can pretty well see the 'eart beating. Only got the face to finish now, eh?'

Hemmer put down the coffee pot and the mugs. He said, 'She brought you here to guard me. How did she know what would happen?'

'It stuck out a mile that Waldo must've left quite a trail,' Willie said gently. 'And it was an odds-on chance that Salamander Four would double-check and pick it up in daylight. This is the only 'ouse for miles. So Modesty fixed for me to cover you.'

'I did not realize they would come back,' Hemmer said simply. 'It just did not occur to me.'

'She said it wouldn't.' Willie took the mug of coffee offered him, and stirred in several spoonfuls of sugar. 'She told me about you not liking to get involved, and all that. It's a nice idea, but it makes things rough when you run up against a couple of villains like we got 'ere.'

Hemmer gave a little start and put down his coffee. 'There were three of them,' he said. 'There is another!'

'That's right. We figured they'd split, so that one or two could cover the road while the other one or two checked this 'ouse.'

'Then . . . the third one will be waiting for Modesty on the road.' Hemmer's big hands worked anxiously.

Willie nodded. 'That's 'is bad luck,' he said cheerfully, and drained the mug. 'I'll go an' fetch the Land-Rover. Be back in about twenty minutes.' He went out, whistling a Chopin mazurka with remarkable accuracy.

In the time of waiting, Alex Hemmer found much to occupy his thoughts. The two men made no move, and spoke only once, when the thin-nosed one lifted his head and said listlessly, 'The woman, she is Modesty Blaise?' Hemmer nodded, and the man slumped down again, dull-eyed.

When Willie Garvin returned Hemmer said, 'What will you do with them?'

'I was thinking about that, Mr 'Emmer. Just dropping 'em in the lake would suit me all right, but the Princess wouldn't like it. She'd say it was the lazy way out. So I'm taking 'em down to that lumber camp where I've been working. I can make it in six hours.'

'The lumber camp?'

'That's right.' Willie looked at Hemmer. 'I like working with Finns. You got the most literate country in the world 'ere. Even the jacks, now, they're 'ard as nails but they've got a bit of culture. So they're quite proud of people like you, Mr 'Emmer. And when I tell 'em these two were going to smash your 'ands with a mallet, they won't like it much.'

Willie turned and squatted in front of the bound men, staring at them with frosty blue eyes. 'It's going to be the longest winter you ever lived through,' he said slowly. 'Those jacks'll keep you 'auling on ropes and 'eaving on saws till you feel like one big raw blister.'

The bearded man said with a flash of defiance, 'Salamander Four will get you.'

Willie Garvin smiled. Not a warm smile. 'It'll be a long time before you can tell them anything.' He held up a hand with the finger and thumb half an inch apart.

'There's a dossier that thick, a blue-print of Salamander Four, pretty well the whole structure, with names an' facts an' figures. Especially names. It's a souvenir from when Modesty Blaise ran The Network. We spent three years compiling it.'

He stood up. 'In a couple of days that dossier will be with a man called Tarrant. He'll open it if anything nasty 'appens to Modesty Blaise or me. Then the roof falls in on Salamander Four. So when you get back, tell 'em that. I don't know who your immediate boss is, but at a guess I'd say it's Walburn or Geiss or Sarmiento. Maybe de Chardin, going further up the scale. Whoever it is, just tell 'im.'

For a moment the two men were startled out of their apathy by the list of names. They exchanged a shaken look. Willie Garvin turned and said, 'Excuse me while I get 'em in the truck, Mr 'Emmer.'

He herded the bound men out of the house and spent several minutes securing them in the back of the Land-Rover to his satisfaction. Hemmer watched from the doorway. Everything had happened so quickly that his mind seemed to have seized up. He felt drained.

Willie Garvin came back into the house. 'Just wanted another look at that statue before I go, if it's all right with you.'

For long minutes he studied the work, absorbed, moving round to gaze from all sides. 'It's great,' he said at last, very softly, and touched a big hand to the column of the neck. 'That's what always gets me, Mr 'Emmer. I could look at 'er throat for hours.'

Hemmer stared. That this rough, dangerous man with the strange Cockney accent should have reflected Hemmer's own inmost visual pleasure so exactly was astounding.

'That is my feeling also, Mr Garvin,' he said. 'Yet the throat, the neck, came easily. It is the face that is difficult.'

Willie Garvin laughed. 'I can imagine. You 'ave to choose one look, and you want 'em all.'

'I can get them,' Hemmer said. 'I can do it, if she comes back. But I think she despises me now, Mr Garvin, because I would not be involved. Or tried not to be.'

'That's your privilege,' Willie Garvin said simply. 'She wouldn't think any less of you for it.'

'You think she may come back, then?'

Willie Garvin shrugged, and when he spoke his face was as neutral as Modesty's had been when she spoke the same words. 'What do *you* think?' He did not wait for a reply, but held out his hand. 'Well, so long, Mr 'Emmer. Been nice meeting you.'

It was not until five minutes after the Land-Rover had moved off that Hemmer realized he had not spoken a word of thanks to the man who had saved him from a maimed hand.

Five days passed before he finally gave up hope that she would return. It was only then that he went to the clay model and began patiently, stubbornly, to seek the face that he wanted.

Throughout the day he worked without success. At nightfall he took up his chisel and turned to the wood, deciding that he must take the final gamble. By working direct on the carving, some miracle of imagination might guide his hands to find what he wanted.

It was then that he heard a car turn off the dirt road and stop outside the house. He stood watching the door, telling himself it was foolish to hope. If she had intended to return she would have done so days ago.

He had left the door on the latch. It opened and she came in, taking off her gloves, saying, 'Hallo, Alex.' She looked at the statue, then sat down in the chair by the fire and pulled off her boots and socks.

Hemmer said, 'I thought you would not come back.'

'I've been over to London.' She stood up and took off her jacket and sweater. 'I had to see about some papers there.'

'A dossier? For a man called Tarrant?'

'That's right.' She walked across the room and kissed him. 'How have you been, Alex?'

'I have been thinking a lot.' He gave a little sigh. 'It has not changed what I believe, Modesty.'

She smiled, and said gently, 'Alex, I don't care a damn about what you believe.'

He put down the chisel and rubbed his brow. 'Tell me something. You did not just hide Waldo from the men who wanted to kill him. You went to much trouble to help him, to get him safely out of danger. It seemed that you liked him, *wanted* to help him. Why was that?'

She took off her shirt and slacks, and stood up, reaching behind to unclip her bra. 'I haven't thought about it. But . . . I suppose because Waldo has style. Yes. Maybe I'll start a society for the Preservation of Style.'

He nodded soberly. 'It is something hard to define. How does a man acquire style, Modesty?'

Naked now, she sat on the edge of the table and swung her legs up on to it. 'God knows, Alex. You could start by learning to laugh a little. At yourself, at me if you like, or at a situation. Waldo laughed when he first opened his eyes and saw me, remember?'

'Do you think you can teach me to laugh a little?'

'I can try. A good time to start is when we're making love.' She took up the familiar pose. Her eyes held a smile, natural and unforced, a smile both young and old, innocent and experienced, candid yet concealing.

Hemmer gazed for a full two minutes before he said, 'Making love is something to laugh about?'

'It ought to be all things, Alex. Even hilarious sometimes. How long have I got for teaching you? I mean, how long before you finish the statue?'

'I could finish it in a day and a half.' A little glint of amusement came into his eyes, and he gave a slow smile. 'But I am a slow learner, so I will make it last at least two weeks.'

Her face lit up. 'There! That had a touch of style.'

He was still smiling as he turned to the statue and took up his chisel and mallet. He could see the contours of the face clearly beneath the surface of the wood now. The image filled his mind, and his hands almost stung with the sudden tingling of blood in them.

The grain . . . so. The curve . . . so. A small slanting plane here, and the imperceptible rounding to give the highlight there . . .

With a long inhalation of pleasure he set the blade to the wood and began to tap.

THE SOO GIRL CHARITY

~

EVEN at eighty yards, the legs were worth looking at. Willie Garvin looked at them with pleasure, and found it refreshing on this hot summer day as he sat at the wheel of the Jensen waiting for the London traffic to bestir itself.

The owner of the legs wore a navy and white polka-dot dress that moulded itself to her figure in the slight breeze. Her hair was black, shoulder length, and drawn back at the nape of the neck. She carried a collecting box in one hand, and although her back was towards Willie he could see that she carried a tray hung about her neck.

He had noticed one or two other flag-sellers as he drove. What the charity was he did not know, but decided he would stop and cross the road to buy a flag from this girl. She had chosen a good pitch, on the wide pavement outside the huge new concrete ant-hill which housed Leybourn Enterprises.

As he lit a cigarette, still watching her, she moved a few paces, and Willie Garvin's eyes widened in surprise. Though her back was still towards him he recognized her beyond all doubt by the way she moved.

His pleasure increased, and he wondered what in the world had persuaded Modesty Blaise to volunteer as a flag-seller. She was not, he knew, uncharitable; but this was outside her usual line of charity.

When the traffic moved he cruised on past the Leybourn building, pulled into a parking space, bought half an hour on the meter, then sat behind the wheel again, moving the mirror slightly so that he could watch her. She was busy with two or three customers, all male, and had not noticed his Jensen.

A cautious man, Willie Garvin did not yet know for sure whether she would want him to recognize her openly. The flag-selling might be a cover. Her hair was down instead of being piled in a chignon, and the dress she wore was off-the-peg, but that hardly rated as a disguise. He could see her face now, and it was the face of Modesty Blaise, unaltered by pads in the cheeks or special make-up.

It seemed likely that she was just selling flags. The different hair-style and the simple dress made sense for that. Too much sophistication would have been wrong for the part.

He saw her turn. Her gaze moved idly past the car, then jerked back. Willie put his hand out of the window and flicked ash from his cigarette. In the mirror he saw her wave. Satisfied, he got out of the car and went across the road.

''Allo, Princess.'

'Hallo, Willie love.' She nodded down at the tray. 'It's all right. This is for real.'

'I'd better buy one then.'

He reached for his wallet, vaguely puzzled. Though her smile of greeting was warm, he sensed a thread of underlying tautness in her, a thread that probably he alone knew her well enough to detect. He said, 'Tell you what. Make me a price for what you've got left, then come and 'ave some lunch.'

'I can't, Willie. I'd buy the lot myself, but I promised Madge I wouldn't.'

'Madge Baker?'

Modesty pulled a face. 'Who else?'

Madge Baker was a woman a few years older than Modesty and of infinite energy, most of which she devoted to good works of various kinds. The rest she devoted to men, a subject in which her immense enthusiasm and cheerful inventiveness had made her highly qualified. Willie had once spent a stimulating month with her in

Greece, an experience he recalled with pleasure as he folded a pound note and put it in the collecting box.

'She burst in on me with this yesterday,' Modesty said. 'And you know what Madge is like when she's made up her mind.

You can't refuse her.'

'I never tried,' Willie said reminiscently. Modesty laughed, and pinned a flag to the lapel of his jacket. He noticed that it was in aid of Mental Health, and that there were only about twenty flags left on her tray.

'Won't take you long to sell out, Princess. What about lunch then?'

'I've asked Tarrant to lunch at the penthouse. You come back with me, and we can have ten minutes in the pool first.'

'Lovely. I'll wait in the car.'

A man had stopped, fumbling in his pocket. Willie turned away. As he waited for a break in the traffic he heard Modesty say with wintry politeness: 'For twopence, you stick it in your lapel yourself, sir.'

She was stroppy, Willie thought, very stroppy. Something must have happened to cause that. Odd for her not to say anything. Perhaps it was just that selling flags turned out to be quite an eye-opener when a girl came to try it.

As he stepped off the kerb he heard her voice again: 'Thank you. Now, for sixpence you keep your chin up while I pin it on. Looking down my dress comes out at half-a-crown minimum.'

Willie grinned to himself. No, he decided, this definitely wasn't her line of country for charity.

Sir Gerald Tarrant sat at a table by the residents' pool below the luxury block of flats overlooking Hyde Park, a Campari soda at his elbow. He felt relaxed and content. The Foreign Office Intelligence section he controlled had several grim and intractable problems on its plate, but for ninety minutes these would cease to exist for him.

At the moment there was nothing that even looked like becoming the off-beat, specialized sort of job which might arouse the interest of Modesty Blaise. This, for Tarrant, was a very pleasant thought. He had been responsible for sending more than a few people out to die in his time. It was an inevitable part of his work, and those who died were paid agents. Modesty Blaise was not.

Even so, he had used her, and Willie Garvin of course, several times. They both carried scars to remind them of those occasions. Tarrant had promised himself that he would not be responsible for any more scars, and hoped that he would keep that promise.

It was some minutes since Modesty and Willie had swum past him along the length of the pool. He leaned forward, and saw that the surface was clear. They were lying face down on the bottom at the deep end, a few feet apart and perfectly still.

To keep down like that they must have exhaled all possible air from their lungs, Tarrant thought. He wondered what the object was. It would probably be obscure, and seemingly pointless to other people. But then, these two pursued their own curious interests and amusements without worrying about how anyone else might regard them.

A minute passed. At last they came up together and swam to the side of the pool where Tarrant sat.

'I bet it's proportionate,' said Willie, panting a little.

'Yes.' Modesty shook the water from her face. 'Up to a point, anyway. The more you oxygenate the blood by deep breathing before you go down, the longer you can stay down with only residual air in your lungs. And you don't need weights.'

'Might come in 'andy sometime. I reckon with ten minutes deep breathing you could stay down three or four minutes ex'aled, with a bit of practice.'

Willie drew himself out, reached a hand down to Modesty and lifted her on to the side of the pool. As she pulled off her cap Tarrant said, 'Have you two been having one of those murderous work-outs in Willie's combat room?'

Modesty shook her head. 'Not for about a month now. Why?'

'Your—ah—upper leg is bruised.' Tarrant pointed. On her thigh, towards the back and just below the line of her swimsuit, the firm flesh was discoloured by an ugly purple bruise. She twisted to look down, and Willie stared.

'Blimey, I didn't do that, did I, Princess?'

'Not that one, Willie love.' She slipped her arm into the robe he held for her. 'I got that this morning, flag-selling. Come on, let's go up to the penthouse. Weng should just about be ready to serve lunch.'

As she moved away, Tarrant looked at Willie with raised eyebrows. 'Pinching bottoms is one thing. But that looked rather severe, surely?'

Willie nodded, his eyes following Modesty speculatively. 'I wonder what she did to 'im?' he said.

An hour later, over coffee served on the penthouse terrace by her houseboy, Weng, Modesty Blaise said, 'It was this man Charles Leybourn.'

Willie said, 'Well that's one for the book.'

Tarrant looked puzzled, and said. 'I'm sorry, You have to fill in the gaps for me, my dear. I'm not Willie. What was this man Charles Leybourn?'

'The bottom-pincher.' Modesty gazed out over the park, frowning. 'I've had it pinched in Paris, Rome and Lisbon. It's just part of the atmosphere there, a friendly gesture. In London it's usually furtive and a bit pathetic. But this was different.'

'Charles Leybourn?' Tarrant said incredulously. 'Leybourn Enterprises?'

'He got out of his Rolls,' said Modesty. 'I stood in front of him, smiled, and shook the collecting box. He took a flag, and put in a penny. So I asked him if he wanted any change. He didn't answer, but just walked past into that big bay entrance of the office block. He's about forty, with a thin, good-looking face and nasty eyes, and he walks as if he's smearing insects with every step.'

Tarrant nodded. 'I know what you mean. I've met him a couple of times.'

'Then he called to me,' said Modesty. 'He was just outside the swing doors with his wallet in his hand. I went up to him. He put the wallet away and threw another penny on the tray. I turned my back on him. And then he pinched me. He's strong. I thought his finger and thumb were going to meet.'

'He must be out of his mind,' Tarrant said wonderingly. 'Good God, it's an assault.'

'He took a risk.' Modesty inhaled on her cigarette and looked at Tarrant. 'But I don't think he could help himself. And he built up Leybourn Enterprises on taking risks, didn't he?'

'There's a difference.'

'Not that much difference. The way we were placed, what he did couldn't be seen. One in three women might bring a charge, maybe. The odds were with him.'

Willie said with interest, 'What did you do to 'im, Princess?'

'Nothing.' She smiled briefly. It was hard not to react. I think the collecting box helped. I damn near crushed it when he pinched. I was all set mentally to break his arm, but I didn't. I just froze, and took it. Then it was all over and he was through the swing doors.'

Willie Garvin looked unhappy. Then his face cleared and a sparkle touched his blue eyes. 'A contribution?' he said.

'Yes.' Modesty stubbed out her cigarette. 'That's what I had in mind. Twopence isn't much. I think a man like Charles Leybourn can afford at least five thousand for the—what is it?'

Willie looked at the flag on his lapel. 'Mental Health.'

'Very suitable. He could do with a little of that himself.'

'I knew you were mad about something.' Willie leaned back in his chair. 'How we going to work it, Princess?'

'I don't know about we. It's my bottom, Willie.'

'Oh, sure.' He looked a little hurt. 'But I'm entitled to declare an interest.'

She smiled. 'All right. I just didn't want to push you. We'll need a few days to size things up. Will you take the house and domestic side while I take the business background?'

'Fine.'

Tarrant's cigar had gone out. He relit it, trying to absorb the fact that Modesty Blaise was serious. 'You really intend to get five thousand pounds from Leybourn?' he said.

'Yes.' Her tone was absent. 'Have some more coffee. Sir Gerald.'

'Thank you, no. How do you imagine you might be able to put the screws on him?'

'No screws. It won't be blackmail, even if we find a lever.' She shrugged. 'We'll just have to see. Maybe he gambles. Maybe he keeps a lot of cash at home—tightrope walkers like Leybourn usually do. I hope we won't have to build a con situation. It's interesting but it takes a long time. What I'd prefer would be a straight steal.'

Willie said, 'What d'you know about Leybourn, Sir G?'

'Are you inviting me to subscribe to the commission of a theft.'

'Why not? If you wanted us to do a safe in some Foreign Trade Mission you wouldn't think twice, you bloody old hyena,' Willie said amiably.

And that was true, Tarrant reflected. When he considered the matter it was self-evident that Modesty's bottom was of far greater intrinsic importance than a packet of secret papers. And there was also the benefit that would accrue to the Mental Health organization, of course. He saw the amusement in Modesty's gaze as she watched him, and made up his mind.

'I don't know a great deal,' he said regretfully. 'Leybourn doesn't socialize much. His one passion outside business is playing bridge. He plays at Crockfords most nights, but for small stakes only. And he's extremely good. He lives in Surrey, somewhere in the stockbroker belt. His wife comes from Java, a girl of Chinese stock and very beautiful, so I'm told. He's made a lot of money in comparatively few years. His methods of finance are legal but chancy, they're certainly not liked in the City. His social personality is pretty colourless, but that must be misleading. He's tough, wary, and a difficult man to steal from, I would think. As for his prospects, I can't imagine he'll stand still; either he'll grow a lot richer and stabilize his empire, or the whole thing will crash.'

'Thank you.' Modesty stretched her legs and rubbed her thigh. 'We'd better get his contribution while the going's good, Willie. I'm sure we can make it a straight steal.'

'That'd be nice.' Willie gazed out over the balcony musingly. 'It's a long time since we stole anything.'

Three days later a man from the Electricity Board called at Charles Leybourn's house in Surrey. The house was Georgian and stood on five acres of ground. The man from the Electricity Board had made an appointment by phone earlier that day, explaining that the meter reading for the last quarter was abnormally high and the Board therefore wished to fit a check meter.

He arrived in his small van promptly at the appointed time and spent an hour in the large cupboard under the stairs, where the meter and switches were housed. He was a big man with rather shaggy brown hair and rough-hewn features, his accent pure Birmingham. Bridget, the Irish maid, found him attractive and rejoiced that it was the housekeeper's afternoon off.

She gave him tea and showed him from room to room so that he could test the various power-points for earth leaks. He did not see Mrs Leybourn, who was resting in the sun-room beside the pool.

He made a date with Bridget for that evening in the village. Since she was rather plain and distinctly plump, Bridget had often been stood up on dates, despite her warm nature, so it was to her surprise and pleasure that the man from the Electricity Board met her as arranged.

What happened later, in his big old car after a fish-and-chip supper, came as an even greater surprise and pleasure to her.

'I didn't 'ave to pump her,' Willie said the following night as he stood with Modesty in the darkness of the trees, watching the house. 'She kept on talking all the time. Well, nearly all the time.' He pondered, then added with vague surprise, 'First time I've tumbled a girl wearing a wig.'

'You may have done without knowing,' Modesty said. 'It's hard to spot them these days.'

'No, I mean *me* wearing a wig. The brown shaggy one.'

She smothered her laughter and punched his arm gently. This was a good caper they were on tonight. Not the kind Tarrant usually pitched them into, a bloody dog-fight against professional killers, but a nice stimulating exercise in ingenuity.

She carried no gun. Willie had left his own throwing-knives at home. They were dressed alike, in black slacks and long-sleeved shirts, plimsolls and nylon gloves. The car they had travelled in was parked two miles away in a wood. They had made the last lap of the journey on foot and across country.

Willie took her arm and drew her down a little, pointing away to the left of the house through a gap in the foliage. 'That's the lodge, Princess.'

She nodded, and straightened up. Willie had done remarkably well. This was not a fact that surprised her, but it was one that she never failed to appreciate. Having Willie Garvin on your right was something too far beyond price to be taken for granted.

Leybourn's domestic set-up was clear now. A married couple, cook-housekeeper and chauffeur-handyman, lived in the lodge which stood eighty yards from the house. Bridget had a room in the lodge. She was always clear of the house by nine, unless the master and his wife were entertaining, which was a regular once-monthly affair. They did not entertain casually.

The Leybourns had been married two years. She was Leybourn's second wife. He had met and married her in Java, where he had rubber interests. Nobody seemed to know anything about her background. Charles Leybourn called her Soo. She was, in Bridget's opinion, almost young enough to be his daughter. Nobody saw much of her, except when the master entertained and she was on show. She did not run the house or give any orders. This was done by the housekeeper, assisted by Bridget, whose proud task it was to supervise the daily help from the village.

Charles Leybourn was frequently home late from Crockfords. He would be home late tonight, about twelve-thirty. It was now ten minutes to midnight. Willie had been given a guided tour of the house. He knew that it was fully protected by burglar alarms and that there was a small modern safe built into the wall of what Bridget called the study. He did not know, but thought it highly likely, that Leybourn kept a substantial amount of cash in the safe. Modesty thought so, too. The lines of inquiry she had pursued suggested it. Leybourn was precisely the sort of man to have a lot of folding money instantly available.

'This Soo girl, his wife,' Modesty said. 'She doesn't seem to have any real function, Willie. Did Bridget manage to give you anything on her between rounds?'

Willie shook his head. 'The way Bridget put it, she's quite nice-looking for a Chink. You got to be dumb as a tombstone to talk like that. I couldn't get a picture of 'er at all. Bridget rolled 'er eyes a bit and kept oohing and ahhing as if there was lots she could tell. Maybe there is, but if she'd known it she'd 'ave told.'

'A mystery girl. Leybourn seems to keep her tucked well away.'

'Bridget said he was like a feller with a big doll that he kept in a box but took out and wound up sometimes. I don't know for what.' Willie paused, then added, 'My little Irish 'eart-throb tags Leybourn for a right bastard, but she didn't 'ave any special reason, so I don't reckon he's tried any bottom-pinching in that direction.'

'Maybe he specializes in flag-sellers.'

'It's a thought. I expect the 'ead-shrinkers have got a word for it.'

There was silence for five minutes. It was not a tense or restless silence. They had infinite patience and could wait with relaxed vigilance, untouched by time or discomfort or weariness.

They were going in by an upper window, because the security locks on the ground-floor windows were key-operated. The front door was too tricky to offer a quick way in. Two keys were needed for it once the alarms had been switched on for the night. One key cut out the system briefly while the other turned a heavy mortice deadlock. The alarm would be no problem now, but the deadlock was a time-waster.

There was light in one upper room of the house, the Leybourns' bedroom. Presumably Soo Leybourn was still awake. Willie Garvin had seen the bedroom suite. It was furnished in oriental style, with silk drapes, rich carpets, and a huge low divan.

Modesty looked at her watch again. It was a minute after midnight. With Charles Leybourn due home at twelve-thirty or soon after, time was running out.

'It doesn't look as if she's going to sleep, Willie. We can't wait any longer.'

He nodded agreement. 'Shouldn't make any difference. She's at the other end of the 'ouse.' Crouching over a black rucksack he took out something that looked like a transistor radio, about the size of a cigar box. Two switches were mounted on the thin metal chassis. He tested the battery connections at the side, then flicked the first switch and drew out a thin collapsible antenna. Moving away from under the trees, he threw the second switch.

Inside the house, in the big cupboard where the fuses and switch-boxes were mounted, a relay clicked open, operated by the radio beam from the transmitter in Willie's hand. The opening of the relay disconnected the burglar-alarm system at its source. If the system had been tested since Willie fixed the relay in the circuit, it would have worked perfectly—until this moment.

He switched off the transmitter, put it away and picked up the rucksack. Together they moved soundlessly over the grass to the east side of the house.

No word was spoken. When they halted Modesty took a drawstring pouch from the rucksack and looped it over her shoulder. Willie handed her a short alloy tube, tapered slightly and with a double-pronged steel hook at the tip. She clipped it on her belt. They gripped hands, Willie crouched, she stepped on his bent knee and then swung round and up on to his shoulders. Facing the wall of the house, she stepped on to the palms of his hands. He straightened his arms. Now she was thirteen feet tall, leaning in and turning slightly so that one shoulder rested against the wall.

She drew out the sliding sections of the alloy tube, extending it to its full eight feet in length, then reached up. The sharp tines of the hook caught on the stone sill above. She climbed, using her arms only so that the pull on the hook was directly downwards. Five seconds later she was sitting side-ways on the sill.

It was a leaded window with diamond panes. From the pouch she took a broad paint-scraper and eased up the flange of lead round one of the panes. Carefully she removed the diamond of glass, reached through the hole and unfastened the security lock.

Before climbing into the room she brushed the soles of her plimsolls and pulled on two over-slippers made from dusters, with elastic tops to grip the ankles.

Willie saw her vanish into the dark room. A few moments later a black nylon rope-ladder dropped down the wall. With the rucksack on his back, he went up the ladder, paused on the sill to pull on over-slippers, then went through the window and closed it after him. This was a spare bedroom used as a sewing-room. He had seen several superb pieces of embroidery on frames during his tour as the man from the Electricity Board.

Modesty stood waiting for him to lead the way. He switched on a pencil torch with a filter lens, and eased the door open. Together they moved along the passage and down a broad staircase to the hall below. Leybourn's study lay beyond one of the doors opening from the square hall.

Inside, the heavy curtains were drawn. Willie closed the door, switched on a table lamp, and nodded towards the safe set in the wall beneath shelves of box-files. Modesty moved across the room to examine it.

The safe was a 1967 Eschenbach with a combination lock, a magnificent piece of skilled engineering. It would not yield to gelignite unless the area round the lock could be drilled, and the toughened steel would resist this for many long, noisy hours.

It could be cut open with a thermic lance, but the apparatus was cumbersome and the heat would destroy all non-fireproof contents. There remained the lock. This was a six-figure combination which could be broken, given enough time, skill, patience, and a miniature computer.

Willie put his rucksack down on the floor and said quietly, 'I'll only be a couple of minutes 'ere, Princess. But I'll need about ten in the dining-room for the main job.'

'All right. I'll go and keep an eye open for the Soo girl.'

In a set-up like this, with somebody in the house, it was better to keep tabs on them than to risk being surprised by a sudden appearance. Modesty paused at the top of the stairs and pulled a stocking with eye-holes over her head, then went on down the long passage to the main bedroom.

When she pressed her ear to the door she could hear a faint sound of movement from within; a chair being pushed back, perhaps, and the slight clatter of something being put down on a glass-topped dressing-table.

Light shone through a transom over the door. Modesty brought a chair from an adjoining room, stood on it, and inched her head up cautiously until she could look down into the bedroom. It was as Willie had described it, with a door leading off to a dressing-room and bathroom.

The Soo girl was beautiful. Young, ivory-skinned, and with great dark eyes set above the symmetry of her high cheekbones, she sat at the dressing-table in a vivid silk dressing-gown of golden dragons sporting against a crimson ground. Modesty could see her face obliquely in the mirror, and at this moment it was a face of quiet and utter tragedy.

All the tragedy lay in the eyes as she looked blindly through her own image. The features were calm, smooth, expressionless, but the eyes were wells of sorrow.

Slowly, as if sleep-walking, the girl rose to her feet and crossed the room. She took a cushion from one of the chairs and set it on the green-carpeted floor at the foot of the bed. For a moment she moved out of Modesty's line of sight, then she returned, her hands hidden in the wide sleeves of the dressing-gown, and sat down cross-legged on the cushion.

Modesty felt a sudden touch of unease. The girl's back was angled towards her and she was sitting with head bowed, perfectly still. Then she extended her arms and lifted them.

The sleeves fell back. Gripped in both hands was an oriental knife with an ornate hilt and a golden cross-guard. The blade was pointed at the girl's chest. She began to sway back and forth, lowering the dagger slightly but still keeping the point aimed at her heart. Through the glass transom Modesty could hear a soft, sad wailing in a language strange to her.

She got down from the chair. Soo Leybourn was about to kill herself, and she was doing it in Oriental fashion. The swaying would increase, then suddenly she would topple forward over her crossed legs and fall on the knife, driving it into her heart.

Modesty pressed the kongo from the squeeze-pocket on her thigh. Her fingers gripped the stem joining the two rounded knobs of polished sandalwood which protruded from the sides of her fist. As she opened the door the wordless, keeping chant of sorrow sounded more clearly. The girl was rocking back and forth in a wider arc now, and the hilt of the knife as she held it was almost touching the floor, the blade angled up towards her.

The lament ceased on a thin haunting note. The red and gold figure swayed back. Before it could swing forward for the death-stroke, Modesty Blaise had crossed the room in three long strides and struck with the kongo, a sharp tapping blow to the nerve centre below the base of the skull. The knife fell to the carpet in front of the girl's crossed legs, and Modesty knelt with the unconscious form slumped back against her.

She pursed her lips and gave a curious two-note whistle in a minor key, like a bird-call, soft yet penetrating. Thirty seconds later Willie Garvin appeared in the open doorway, a stocking pulled over his head. When he saw that Modesty had taken her own mask off he followed suit, then moved forward, looking with narrowed eyes from the slumped figure of the girl to the knife on the floor.

'She was just going to kill herself,' Modesty said quietly. 'We picked a bad night.' She looked down at the girl. 'Or a good one. Put her on the bed, Willie.'

He lifted her easily and moved round the bed. As he laid her down on her side, the loose dressing gown fell away from her shoulder. He moved a hand to straighten it, then stopped and drew in a sharp breath. Gently he pulled the gold and crimson silk lower.

Modesty was beside him, staring. There were small scars on Soo Leybourn's back, many of them. Some were thin lines, some were small round spots; some were old, and had healed to white lines or dots, others were new and angry. There were fresh dark bruises, and old yellowing ones.

Modesty pulled the gown down and away. From some inches below the shoulders, the scars and bruises on the beautifully moulded body spread down the back and over the buttocks.

Willie Garvin whispered, 'Jesus!'

Modesty eased the girl over on to her back. The front of her body was similarly marked, from beneath the fine breasts to the top of the thighs.

'He doesn't stop at pinching bottoms,' Modesty said, thin-lipped. 'The small ones are cigarette burns I suppose. And the weals—well, we'd probably find a little whip here if we looked.'

There was sick anger in Willie's eyes. 'So Leybourn's a full-blown kink,' he said. 'And that's his kick. Poor little bitch.' He bent and drew the robe up over her again. 'What d'you want to do, Princess?' Modesty did not answer at once. When at last she spoke her eyes were still on the girl's smooth, empty face. Now that the eyes were closed there was no expression. The wells of sadness were hidden.

'Short of breaking Leybourn's neck there's nothing we can do for her,' she said slowly. 'We stopped her killing herself tonight, but there's always another night.'

'I don't mind breaking 'is neck,' Willie said simply. 'It's either her or him by the look of it.'

'She has to work it out her own way,' Modesty said a little wearily. 'She could leave him. But she's an Oriental, and maybe it involves too much loss of face. Anyway, you can't go around killing women's husbands for them.' She looked at her watch. 'Have you nearly finished downstairs?'

'I'll need another few minutes.' Willie looked at her. 'We go ahead, then?'

'Why not? It'll give Leybourn something else to think about for a few days.' Modesty took out a small phial of anaesthetic nose-plugs and shook one on to the palm of her hand. 'I'll give her a whiff to keep her under, then put the light out and join you downstairs.'

Willie nodded and went out of the room. He knew that for Modesty, as for himself, the exploit had gone cold now. They would finish it because there was no reason not to, but all pleasure in the caper had vanished with the knowledge that a girl in a strange land was being driven to die by her own hand, and there was nothing they could do about it.

Charles Leybourn put his car in the garage and let himself in by the front door, using two keys. He stopped, frowning, as he saw that the study door was slightly ajar and that a light had been left on.

His lips compressed. Soo was not supposed to go into his study. Also, he had warned her several times about being careful to test the alarms, put out all lights and close all doors before going to bed. His face relaxed in a curious smile. She would have to be punished for this.

He went into the study to switch off the table lamp, and shock hit him. A rug was rucked up where an armchair near the safe had been moved aside. On the floor in front of the safe stood a square black box about a foot high.

Warily he moved to look at it more closely. There were three dials on the machine and two vernier controls. Earphones were plugged into one side. From the other side, thin insulated wires ran up to three small suction discs which were stuck to the steel door of the safe round the dial of the combination lock.

Sweat gathered on Leybourn's brow. The safe door was closed, but . . .

He turned and snatched up the phone on his desk. His hand shook as he dialled. The bloody operator would be asleep of course.

She answered even before he heard the ringing tone.

'Emergency switchboard. Which service do you require?'

'Get me the police!' snapped Leybourn.

'Your name, please? And the number you're ringing from?'

He gave them impatiently.

'One moment, sir. I'm connecting you to County Headquarters.'

In the dining-room, sitting on the floor in darkness, Modesty Blaise pressed down the cradle of the telephone hand-set as she stopped speaking. The hand-set was connected to the GPO junction box mounted under the window-ledge, where the exchange line came in. Leybourn was cut off from the exchange. He was connected only to Modesty's telephone hand-set, two rooms away from where he stood.

She passed the phone to Willie, then released the cradle. Willie spoke in a brisk voice, with no trace of his usual Cockney accent. 'County Headquarters Information Room.'

Leybourn's voice was almost a snarl. 'My name is Charles Leybourn. I'm speaking from The Old Spinney. That's off the London Road between Faring and Limpton Green, about a mile from Faring. My house has been broken into. I want somebody here right away.'

Willie said, 'One moment, sir.' He pressed the cradle down, allowed ten seconds, then relaxed it and spoke again. 'We're sending out a radio call to the patrol car nearest you, sir. Would you hold, please? The Inspector would like a word with you.' Willie clicked the cradle twice. When he spoke again his voice was pitched lower and held a slight West Country accent.

'Inspector Tregarth here, sir. I'm sorry about this business. Do you happen to have a safe in the house?'

'I bloody well do, and it's supposed to be burglar-proof,' Leybourn said viciously. 'So's the house for that matter. But they got in. And there's some kind of gadget here—'

'A gadget?' The calm voice took on a tinge of regret. 'I was afraid of that. A control box with wires running up to the combination lock?'

'Yes. Do you know what it is?'

'Well, it's something pretty new, sir. A stethostrobic pulse detector. This is the third case we've had in a month. It's the first time they've left one behind, though.'

Leybourn wiped his brow. 'The safe's still shut. I may have scared them off when I arrived.'

'Let's hope so, sir.' The voice sounded doubtful. 'Leaving the SPD behind doesn't signify much. They're dirt cheap to make if you know how to do it. Only the diaphragms are expensive, and they're burnt out after one operation. Would you mind checking the safe, Mr Leybourn?'

'You mean open it? What about fingerprints?'

'I'm afraid these people are professionals, sir. They don't leave any prints. But wait till our men arrive if you like, and they can check with you.'

'No. I'll do it now. Hang on.'

Leybourn laid down the phone and moved to the safe, suddenly glad that the Inspector had suggested checking. Much better to open it now, before the police arrived. If the thieves had failed, there would be an embarrassing amount of money stacked inside; illegal dollars, which, as a citizen of the United Kingdom, he was not supposed to hold.

Touching the dial very gingerly he turned it through the six-figure sequence. He had left the study door open, and he did not hear Willie Garvin enter behind him. The combination completed, he gripped the handle of the three-inch steel door and pulled. As it swung open, Willie Garvin chopped Leybourn down with a hand like a spade.

'There was a touch of temper about that,' Modesty said from the doorway. She moved forward, put down the rucksack, turned Leybourn on his back and slipped an anaesthetic plug up one nostril.

Willie said reasonably, 'I thought a really solid stiff neck might keep 'is mind off whips and cigarettes for a couple of weeks.'

The safe was divided in two compartments. One held bundles of paper money in five-, ten-, and twenty-dollar bills.

'It's the way we figured,' Modesty said, and began to flick through each bundle before dropping it into the rucksack. 'But now we've met his wife we'll raise the ante. Let's say thirty thousand dollars. That still leaves him about half of what's here.'

Willie detached the stethostrobic pulse detector, folded it flat and slid it into the rucksack. It was no more than a mock-up of dials and knobs, with no components inside the chassis, but it had served very effectively in getting the safe open. The idea had been Modesty's. Willie thought it was a rave. He felt rather sad that circumstances had taken all sparkle out of the caper. With an inward sigh he went through to the dining-room to disconnect the telephone hand-set and restore the exchange line to the junction box.

Modesty finished packing the money, then went upstairs to replace the pane from the leaded window and fasten the security lock. When she had finished they would make a final check on their tidying up, then leave by the front door, using Leybourn's keys and taking him with them. He would wake up to find himself sitting at the wheel of his car in the garage, the keys in his pocket as usual, and he would be driven to wonder if he had suffered a seizure combined with a bad dream. The confusion and misunderstandings when he finally called the police promised to be of epic proportions.

Modesty had almost finished replacing the window pane when Willie came upstairs. He looked at her a little uneasily and said with a casual air, 'About that radio relay I fixed in the cupboard, Princess. D'you want me to take it out or leave it? I reckon it could stay there for years without anyone spotting it.'

She said gently, not looking up from her work. 'Look. If that girl kills herself, we're not going to come sneaking back here one night to string Leybourn up or something. I'm sorry for her too, Willie love. But we're not The Four Just Men.'

'No.' He rubbed his chin. 'OK, I'll whip it out. Won't take five minutes.'

The thin flange of lead was folded back into place now. She closed the window and locked it. Together they went out into the passage and down the stairs. It was as they reached the hall that there came from the study the sound of a soft impact, a small and curious thud. They froze. There came another sound, a chair-leg scraping momentarily on the polished strip of flooring of the study.

They moved forward, pulling their masks into position. At a nod from Modesty, Willie kicked the door wide and they went in very fast. Three paces into the room they stopped dead. Soo Leybourn sat on an upright chair by the wall, her hands resting limply on her lap. She wore the gold and crimson dressing-gown. Her feet were bare. The smooth, beautiful face held no emotion. The dark eyes were unfocused, staring blankly ahead of her.

Leybourn lay on his back on the floor beneath the still open safe, as they had left him. There was only one difference. The oriental knife from Soo Leybourn's bedroom was driven deep into his chest. There was hardly any blood, just an irregular stain on his white shirt around the cross-guard of the knife. With the blade through his heart he had died instantly.

Willie Garvin dragged his gaze from the dead man to stare again at the unmoving girl. She was a thousand miles away and had no awareness of them

'Christ,' he said hoarsely. 'It's all 'appening tonight!' He saw that Modesty had pulled her mask off, and thankfully pulled off his own, then wiped the sleeve of his shirt across a damp brow. 'I wonder what she does for an encore?'

'I suppose this is the encore,' Modesty said slowly, looking at Leybourn. It was a full two minutes before she spoke again. Willie waited without impatience, glad to leave all decisions to her. There was plenty for her to think about.

He did not regret that Leybourn was dead, or blame Soo Leybourn for killing him. But he wished she had chosen another night to be impulsive. It complicated matters enormously.

Modesty Blaise said, 'Let's keep this simple. I'm damned if I'm going to let her be put away for years if I can help it. And they'll put her away all right, even with all the scars to show. If a husband does that to you, leave him. You don't kill him.'

'She's an Oriental, Princess.'

'I know. But she killed him *here*.' Modesty stepped forward and slapped the girl's face hard. Soo Leybourn barely flinched, but a vague awareness crept into her dark eyes.

Modesty said, 'Look at me,' and hit her again. The girl shook her head as if to clear it, then a sudden kaleidoscope of emotions flickered in her face; fear and horror, bewilderment and sorrow, and finally a weary fatalism.

Modesty said, 'You know you've killed your husband?'

'Yes.' The voice was a submissive whisper.

'You know the police will come and put you in prison?'

The dark head nodded.

'Do you want to get away? To escape?'

A tired, hopeless shrug. 'I have nowhere to go.' The whispered words were carefully enunciated.

'You have no family?'

Tears welled suddenly from eyes that stared without hope across an immeasurable distance. 'My family is too far. They are in Kalimbua.

'Is that a big town?'

'No. Small. A village.' The beautiful hands moved in a gesture and fell limp again. 'By walking and the bus, three days from Surabaja.'

'Are you in touch with your family? Do you write letters?'

'Charles did not let me write. He said I did not belong to my family now, because he had paid my father much money to buy me. More than a hundred dollars.'

Modesty looked at Willie, then back at the girl. 'Do you ever get any letters from your family?'

'Twice there was a letter from my father that someone had written for him. Charles showed them to me, but not to read. Then he burnt them.' She spoke without bitterness.

Modesty drew in a long breath and let it out slowly. The essentials of the picture were clear now. Soo Leybourn was from a peasant family which by chance had thrown up a child of rare beauty. How Charles Leybourn had met her was unimportant. He had rubber interests in Java, and could have met the girl in a dozen different ways during one of his trips to the Far East.

Something in her had seized his twisted imagination with compelling force. Her submissiveness, perhaps. He had bought her, married her, brought her to England. She was the ideal creature to serve his peculiar pleasures.

'Would you like to go back to your family?' Modesty asked.

The flash of hope in Soo Leybourn's eyes was swallowed instantly by passive fatalism. 'They are too far. It is not permitted. Charles has told me.'

'Charles was wrong. You can go back. Will your family take you? And do you want to go?'

The girl lifted her head and stared wonderingly for long seconds. Then she tried to speak, began to sob, and nodded her head again and again as if unable to stop.

Modesty held her by the shoulders until she was quiet, then said, 'Can you write in English?'

'A little. Yes.'

'Then write what I tell you. Find some paper, Willie.'

Five minutes later a note written in a laboured, childish hand lay under a paperweight on the desk: *I have gone away. I cannot be happy here because I am afraid to be hurt so much. Please do not try to find me.*

Modesty took a thin metal box from the pocket of her shirt. Inside lay a small hypodermic and three ampoules. 'She must have snorted that nose-plug out, Willie. It's a pity I didn't do this to begin with.' She pulled the girl's dressing-gown down from one shoulder to bare her arm, saw again the fine network of scars, and added bleakly, 'Or maybe not.'

Willie looked at the dead man and said, 'What about Charles?'

'He'll have to go.' Modesty made the injection, settled Soo Leybourn back in the armchair, and straightened up. 'We'll take the rest of the dollars and make everything tidy. I'll pack a bag for the Soo girl. While I'm doing that, you get Leybourn's car out of the garage and put him in the passenger seat. Don't use lights or engine, we'll push the car down the drive. And leave the knife in him for now, there won't be any mess as long as he's corked.'

She moved to the safe and took out the remaining bundles of money. There were little crow's-feet of concentration at the corners of her eyes as she went on: 'When you've dropped us by the hired car, head back this way with Charles. After a quarter-mile there's that tight bend in the secondary road. Wrap the car round a tree there, put Charles behind the wheel, take the knife out of him, and make sure the car really burns out.'

Willie nodded. 'Ashes to ashes.'

'As near as you can make it without benefit of a crematorium.'

'They're doing road repairs there, Princess. If I was to 'it a tar barrel first, bust it open and knock it in the ditch with the car perched on top, and then start the fire? . . .'

'Better still.' Modesty was sorting through a number of documents in the safe. She put them back and said, 'I was hoping she might have a passport here, but she's probably on Charles' passport. Never mind. You join us again when you've seen Charles off. We'll drop you at Dimple Haigh's place. Rake him out of bed and get him busy on a passport for her. Can he do an Indonesian one?'

'I'll be surprised if 'e can't.'

'All right. Pick a good enough photograph from his Oriental section, and use her maiden name. We'll find out what that is before we get there. I'll take her on to the cottage at Benildon. You come on down with the passport when it's ready. She can sleep the night at Benildon, and by morning I'll have Dave Craythorpe laid on for a quick hop across to Dublin in his Beagle.'

Willie rubbed his chin doubtfully. 'That's still a long way from Java.'

'It's only thirteen hours to Panama City. I'll go with her to Dublin myself and see her on the plane there. Miguel Sagasta can meet her at the airport and fix the rest of the journey. I'll ring him tonight.' Sagasta was a police captain in Panama City and a trusted friend.

'You think she'll be OK on 'er own?' Willie said, and looked at the sleeping girl. 'She's not all that bright, I reckon.'

Modesty shut the safe door and spun the dial. 'She's going home, Willie. She'll keep going till she gets there. All she needs is plenty of money to smooth her way and she can't go wrong.'

Willie Garvin held open the rucksack while Modesty

wedged in the remaining bundles of currency. He said hopefully, 'We let the Soo girl 'ave this, then?'

'We must. It's all she'll get. If we leave her to face a murder rap she won't get any of the estate. They don't let you inherit from a husband you've murdered. Even a husband like Leybourn.'

'Ought to be a reward for it.' Willie knelt to buckle the straps. 'Still, she'll be well set up with this lot. I'm glad we've been able to 'elp the kid a little.'

'She'll be rich back home.' Modesty paused, frowned, and gave a little shrug of annoyance. 'Pity about Madge and her mental health thing, but that's out of the question now.'

Willie suppressed a snort of laughter. Her concern over that point, which he had entirely forgotten, struck him as slightly hilarious. 'You'll 'ave to go back to selling flags,' he said, then stood up, looked about him and shook his head wonderingly. 'It's been a funny old night, Princess.'

The girl slept. Charles Leybourn lay dead. The hilt of the knife jutted from his chest like some beautiful but evil growth. Modesty picked up the rucksack that now bulged with dollars. 'It's been a bit unusual, Willie love,' she agreed.

It took the police twenty-four hours to be reasonably certain that the charred and crumbling bones in the burnt-out car were the remains of Charles Leybourn. The announcement caused a considerable flurry on the Stock Exchange.

The fact that Leybourn's wife had run away on the night of his death roused a natural suspicion which did not last very long. Inquiries soon showed that the Oriental Mrs Leybourn would have been totally unable to cope with the technicalities of faking a car accident for her husband. She was not even able to drive, and she had certainly been in the house at the time her husband left Crockfords in his car to drive home.

That she had run away on this particular night was simply a puzzling coincidence. It remained a coincidence, but ceased to be puzzling, when the whips and canes, the shackles and other curious impedimenta, were found in Leybourn's exotic bedroom.

So the man was a kink, a vicious one, and she had run away. It was hardly to be wondered at. The police put out routine inquiries to trace her, and Leybourn's solicitors issued an appeal asking her to come forward in the urgent matter of her husband's estate. Their appeal remained unanswered.

But long before this, even before the police decided that the crash victim must be Leybourn, Modesty Blaise stood in the lounge at Dublin Airport as the first call went out for the night flight to New York.

'You're on your way home, Soo,' she said. 'Don't worry about anything. Just remember you have your old name again now. And when you need money, there's plenty in your bag.' She tapped the little overnight case. 'Hang on to that all the time.'

Soo Leybourn nodded obediently. She wore a blue off-the-peg coat and a grey headscarf. In the past twenty-four hours she had asked no questions, expressed no surprise, shown no apprehension, and offered no thanks. Her eyes were faraway, fixed on the goal ahead.

'This is as far as I can go with you,' Modesty said. 'Just follow the stewardess and the rest of the passengers to the aircraft. Tomorrow you'll be in Panama, and soon after that you'll be home with your family.'

Soo Leybourn gazed distantly past Modesty's shoulder and said, 'When I am with my family again I will be happy.'

'I'm sure you will. But don't speak to anybody about what happened last night. Forget you ever knew Charles Leybourn.'

The girl closed her splendid dark eyes for a moment,

then opened them again. 'I cannot forget. But I will never speak.'

She paused, her eyes focused, and for the first time she looked at Modesty Blaise as if aware of her as a person rather than as a voice which guided and directed her. She said in a low, sad whisper, 'The thing I did was very bad, very wicked.'

Modesty shrugged. Her own word for it would have been stupid. But Soo Leybourn came from a different world, and there was no point now in arguing that you didn't have to kill a sadistic husband to be free of him. 'Try not to feel guilty about it,' she said. 'He used to hurt you badly. I saw.'

A slow, puzzled lift of the long eyebrows. 'Excuse me?'

Modesty felt a flash of irritation. She had felt the same thing many times in the past twelve hours or so with Soo Leybourn. 'I saw your body,' she said patiently. 'I saw the things he'd done to you. So I can understand what you did.'

'Oh.' The girl nodded gravely but still without comprehension. Then understanding dawned in her face, followed by surprise. Slowly she shook her head.

'It was not for that. Not because Charles hurt me.' There was a hint of shock in her placid voice.

'*Not?*' Modesty stared, shaken.

'No.' A shadow of pride came into Soo Leybourn's face. 'Charles was my husband. It was for me to make him happy, and I did.' The pride was engulfed by grief, and she closed her eyes. 'But then he found another girl to make him happy. He told me four days ago, and he told me all the things he had done to her. He was very pleased with her.' The eyes opened, brimming. 'I could not bear such hurt.'

The final call for the flight sounded on the Tannoy. Soo Leybourn collected herself, tried to smile, and said,

'You have been very kind.' She turned away, joining the handful of other passengers moving through the door, walking with quiet grace and holding the little case packed with dollar currency tightly in her hand.

Modesty Blaise sat down on a bench seat and stared blankly out through the dark, rain-specked window. She found that she had taken out a cigarette and lit it, but did not recall going through the motions.

For five minutes she sat smoking quietly, alone in the lounge now, looking at her blurred reflection in the big window and trying to decide what she was feeling. Deflated certainly, angry perhaps. And she knew that mentally her mouth was hanging open. But above all there was a rising indignation which she knew to be quite ludicrous.

She thought of Willie Garvin, imagined the look on his face when she told him, tried to imagine what he would say. And it was then that she choked on her cigarette as all other emotion was swept away in a wave of helpless laughter.